Praise for Am̲.̲.̲.̲.̲.̲

5 Angels! "Readers hold on to your seats because *Hunted* by **Amelia Elias** is a thrilling, action-packed novel that will blow you away. From the start I was caught up in the dynamics of this wonderful story. Whether it was the suspenseful plot, the non-stop battle of the wills, the mind-boggling sexual encounters or the comical moments – I was hooked! ...I enjoyed this story immensely and eagerly look forward to **Ms. Elias'** next exciting installment in the *Guardians' League* saga." ~ *Contessa, Fallen Angels*

"The first book in *The Guardians' League* series is action-packed, fast-paced, and totally hot! ...Both Sian and Diego are complex characters with hidden depths and burdens they carry around. From the moment I first met Diego and Sian, I was hooked. They made me laugh, wince, sigh, get hot under the collar, and smile before the book ended. ...Amelia Elias has written a wonderful beginning to what I believe will be a very intriguing and engrossing series that you won't want to miss. Head over to Samhain and order your copy of HUNTED today." ~ *Sinclair Reid, Romance Reviews* Today

5 Cups! "Ms Elias has written the ultimate page-turner. The excitement in this book makes it virtually impossible to put down. The humor will have you laughing aloud while the sex will have you boiling...Hunted is the start of a wonderful series. I cannot wait for the next book." ~ *Sherry, Coffee Time Romance*

"I loved reading **Hunted**; it was quite simply a beautiful story with amazing characters...There are several interesting secondary characters introduced in **Hunted** and I will be anxiously waiting to see if their stories are told in the future. This was my first book by Amelia Elias, but it won't be my last!!" ~ *Shannon, Joyfully Reviewed*

Hunted

Amelia Elias

A SAMHAIN PUBLISHING, LTD. publication.

Samhain Publishing, Ltd.
2932 Ross Clark Circle, #384
Dothan, AL 36301
www.samhainpublishing.com

Hunted
Copyright © 2006 by Amelia Elias
Print ISBN: 1-59998-261-7
Digital ISBN: 1-59998-034-7
Cover by Scott Carpenter

First Samhain Publishing, Ltd. electronic publication: June 2006
First Samhain Publishing, Ltd. print publication: September 2006

Dedication

To Kim, who loved Diego at first sight and never let me give up on him.

Prologue

The blue sedan looked almost black in the golden light of the sunset, but Sian was certain it was the same car that had been tailing her for the last half hour.

It was a nightmare she'd become all too familiar with over the last three years.

Sian shifted gears and accelerated around the corner, darting into an almost nonexistent space between a semi and a tour bus and hoping to disappear before the sedan caught up with her. After this her pursuer would know she'd spotted him, but there was no help for it. There was no way in hell she'd lead him any closer to her home.

"Come on, Baby," she murmured to the engine. "Give me a little more!"

Baby was up for the challenge. Sian blessed the ever-present California traffic for the cover it provided and ignored the blasting horns as she wove recklessly through tiny gaps between cars, flooring it and racing up the first onramp she found. Not for the first time, Sian was grateful she hadn't resisted the urge to buy the Mini Cooper. Baby had cost more than she could reasonably afford to spend but it had been love at first sight. She hadn't regretted it. The little car's insane acceleration and maneuverability more than made up for the cost.

Sian stayed on the highway only until the next exit. After whipping through the turn-around, she sped back the way she'd come from before turning off the access road. She kept a wary eye on the rearview mirror as she tried to lose the sedan in the maze of downtown San Francisco. Her little trick would have fooled most drivers but she didn't dare relax. These people were professionals.

Professional hunters, professional trackers. Professional killers.

The sun slipped below the horizon as the light bled from the sky. The fading daylight made it difficult to be certain, but after fifteen more minutes of aimless driving passed without sign of the sedan, Sian breathed a sigh of relief. Her intuition told her she'd lost them. She wished she'd been able to get the license plate but hadn't dared let the car get close enough to her for it to be visible.

No matter. She shivered. She was certain it would be back.

Her heart sank even as her mind raced, cataloging all the things she had to do to get ready to run again. She always kept a getaway bag packed under the bed so she didn't need to worry about clothes. Her only personal keepsakes, a photograph of her parents and her mother's wedding rings, were right on the bedside table—no problem there, she'd just stuff them into her purse on the way out.

Her gun was always on her.

Nothing else in her little apartment meant anything to her but Sian still seethed with impotent rage at being forced to leave it. She'd been in San Francisco six months, long enough to get to know her neighbors as more than potential allies or threats, long enough to befriend the homeless cat always hanging around her door, long enough to fall in love with her little flat, which cost more than a three thousand square foot house would have back home in Savannah. Those six months had felt like a lifetime, an eternity of safety after the hell of the two and a half years before it.

She couldn't even remember how many times the Witness Protection Program had moved her around before she'd struck out on her own. No matter where they sent her, she'd always been found. It hadn't taken her long to suspect someone was leaking her whereabouts but she'd never been able to get the agents in charge of her case to take her suspicions seriously.

"You must've told someone," they'd said. "You must have slipped up, Ms. Lazuro." It was always Ms., never Officer, and it never failed to make her grind her teeth. "It happens. You need to be more careful." According to them, the Witness Protection Program was infallible. It had to have been Sian, who had the most to lose, who'd screwed up.

Apparently this time she had. The Witness Protection Program was a thing of the past and she'd come to San Francisco on her own, telling no one where she was headed and changing everything she could on the way—her hair, her clothes, her car and her name. She'd thought she'd lost them at last.

Clearly, she'd been wrong.

Her enemy had found her yet again. Deep inside she'd been expecting it for a while now, the slightest sense of something wrong growing closer day by day. She'd learned to trust her instincts from the cradle and they'd never let her down during her years as a cop.

And right now those instincts were screaming at her that danger was here. The life she'd created was dead and if she didn't want to join it in the grave she'd better hurry. It was a warning Sian had every intention of obeying.

She'd just switched lanes to cut through an alley, intending to take a shortcut home, when someone sprinted out of the shadows right in front of her. A massive figure was in hot pursuit and as the first man disappeared between the buildings, his pursuer whirled around to freeze in the beam of her headlights.

Sian screamed and jerked the wheel out of reflex, catching only the briefest impression of a man with demonic cat-like eyes and teeth too sharp and long to possibly be human before Baby collided with him. The sickening thud of the impact filled her ears as she lost control. When the little car spun out, Sian's head whipped to the side and shattered her window.

And the world vanished into blackness.

Chapter One

Some nights, being one of the good guys just sucked.

Diego groaned as he picked himself up off the pavement, one arm wrapped around his screaming ribs. He flexed his jaw experimentally to see if it was broken. The instant explosion of pain confirmed that it was. He felt warmth on the side of his neck and traced it back to its source with his free hand. Blood oozed steadily from his ear and he bit back another groan as a fresh wave of pain crashed over him. Damn, that little car had flattened him but good.

If he'd been human, he was positive he'd still be lying on the pavement and not going anywhere soon. At least the Outcast had fled before he'd been run down or he'd be in a world of trouble right now.

The car had spun to a stop a few yards inside the little alley but gawkers already gathered. They couldn't see Diego—remaining unseen in a crowd during a crisis was an extremely useful trick he'd learned centuries ago—and were no doubt wondering what had caused the car to spin out of control. He watched for a moment, expecting the door to fly open and the driver to emerge, wild-eyed and shaken.

No one got out of the car.

"Look at the blood," one of the onlookers murmured with a sick sort of fascination. "Can you see in? Is she dead?"

He stepped gingerly over to the car, hissing in a sharp breath when the movement jarred his almost certainly fractured ribs. Blood was exactly what he needed, but even more importantly, he needed to see how badly injured the driver was. The last thing he'd intended was to cause a mortal pain tonight.

"Shoo," he grunted to the gathering crowd, infusing his voice with a compulsion they couldn't resist. "Go away and don't come back." They went and he opened the driver's side door, wincing again at the red smear that streaked the starred window.

The driver slumped over the steering wheel, blonde hair obscuring her face, a dark stain over her left temple. So much for his good intentions. He ignored the call of her blood and gathered his strength to heal her. He reached for her wrist and slipped her watch off to press his fingers to her pulse—present and steady. Good. Diego closed his eyes and sent his senses searching through her.

He swore when he found the skull fracture. Not good.

There would be no quick roadside healing. Diego reached across the woman's limp body and unfastened her seatbelt before lifting her carefully from the seat. The protests of his ribs rose into a symphony of agony. He clenched his jaw and bore it. Casting the cloak of darkness around her, too, Diego stepped back into the relative privacy of the alley before taking to the skies with the unfortunate woman nestled securely in his arms.

He sincerely hoped his Steward had restocked the emergency fridge recently because Diego was in no condition to hunt and the scent of blood rising from the woman's injury was more than tempting to a hungry vampire. His body ached for the life-giving liquid to heal his own wounds and he would be expending even more energy when he healed hers.

He could do nothing else. Hunting the Outcasts, vampires who killed their prey, was only part of his ancient vow to keep mortals safe. It didn't matter if this woman had been driving like a lunatic when he'd startled her. All that mattered was he'd caused this injury, however inadvertently, and now he would put it right.

By the time he landed on his lawn, Diego was in agony. "James!" he shouted, kicking the front door open and leaning against the wall, still holding the unconscious woman in his arms.

He heard the Steward pounding down the stairs a moment before he skidded to a stop in the entryway.

"God, Diego, what happened to you?" James demanded, recovering from his shock and rushing to him.

"Take her," Diego growled through his teeth, ignoring the question. He knew his fangs were showing but he hurt too much to care.

"You're in no condition to be bringing women home," James said as he took her from Diego's arms. Diego took a shallow breath and let it slowly out in relief when she was no longer pressing against his fractured ribs. One of the drawbacks of being a vampire was his heightened sensitivity. He felt everything much more intensely than a mortal, and these were wounds that would've rendered any mortal he knew unconscious from the pain.

But he couldn't give in to weakness yet. "Take her upstairs," he told James, pushing himself off the wall and squaring his shoulders. "She needs healing."

"You need healing," James countered, not moving. "What happened to you, Diego?"

Diego glared at him. James didn't seem to get the subservient part of his role at all sometimes. "It hasn't been the best night," he said, shrugging off his leather jacket with a groan and letting it drop to the floor. "Long story short, our guest here just ran me down with her car. Get her upstairs where I can take care of her and then you can fuss like an old woman, all right? After you go retrieve her car, that is."

"You really want me to bring home the instrument of your destruction?"

Diego barely managed not to growl. "No, but she might want it back when she leaves and I'm sure she'd rather it not be stripped to the frame when she gets it. Now will you please take her upstairs so I can heal her and get her out of here?"

James gave him a concerned look before turning to do as he asked. Diego kicked his boots off and left them lying beside the discarded jacket before following slowly.

James met him on the second floor landing. "I put her in your room," he said, still looking at Diego in concern. "You won't have to go far to collapse when you're done with her."

Diego nodded and started to move past him, but James stopped him. ""You need blood," he said bluntly, forcing Diego to look him in the eye. "And not the bagged crap you hate."

"The bagged crap will suffice."

James crossed his arms stubbornly. "You need the real thing, Diego."

Diego shook his head. "Either you're volunteering, which you know is against the rules, or you're offering to go drag some poor soul back here for me to feed on, which is also against the rules. Which is it?"

James rolled his eyes. "You and your rules," he growled. "You'd rather suffer than let me help, fine. Bagged crap coming right up." He turned and started down the stairs, grumbling under his breath about stubborn vampires.

Diego turned to his door and sighed. He really, truly didn't feel up to this right now, but there wasn't much choice. Dawn waited for no one and if he wanted James to have time to stitch him up before daybreak, he didn't have any time to waste.

The woman lay atop his comforter, unmoving but for the gentle rise and fall of her breath. James had wrapped a towel around her head and Diego was relieved to see no blood had soaked through it, indicating the bleeding had pretty much stopped on its own. He crossed the room and sat beside her on the mattress before taking her hand and sending his powers through her wounded body to heal her. He barely noticed James coming in with a large mug of warmed blood and drank it with hardly a thought. Her brain was bruised and swelling badly. He didn't dare ease his concentration for a second as he worked to stop it before she was damaged permanently.

An hour later, Diego breathed a sigh of relief and released her hand, certain she wouldn't have any lasting effects from their collision. His tired mind spun as he used a moist washcloth to bathe her face, revealing too-pale skin no longer darkened by bruises. She'd lost a lot of blood before he'd intervened, and although he had several bags of whole blood stored, he didn't dare try to replace it. He didn't know her blood type and, as a vampire, the only way he knew to discover it was less than scientific. He couldn't imagine she'd appreciate regaining consciousness to find a complete stranger sucking on her neck.

Besides, he was hungry enough that only taking a sip might be beyond even his iron control right now. He saw the spare blood bag James had left on the bedside table and reached for it, piercing it with his fangs and drinking it down despite the shudder that worked through him at the horrible, rubbery flavor. James was right. He hated bagged blood. The Steward's offer of his own tempted Diego for a moment before he rejected it. He'd rather choke down this nasty stuff than feed off someone under his protection.

Diego finished the bag and turned back to his patient, examining her face as he worked to wipe the last traces of her ordeal away. She wasn't exactly beautiful but something about her heart-shaped face and the delicate smattering of freckles across her nose and cheeks was absolutely charming. Blonde eyebrows, a shade darker than her golden hair, arched over her closed eyes. Her lashes lay thick and dark on her milky cheeks and he found himself wondering what color her eyes would be when she opened them again.

She was lovely, and it had been far too long since he'd seen a woman in his bed.

Diego shook his head. Those thoughts would get him exactly nowhere. He sighed again, looking down at her clothes in an effort to change the direction of his thoughts. Her dress was bloodstained, the vibrant coral fabric ruined. Any female he'd ever known would go into hysterics at the sight of blood covering her clothes, and the last thing he wanted to deal with was a hysterical woman. Much as he wanted to finish with her and allow James to tend his wounds, Diego had to get the bloody dress off her first.

He rose to grab one of his shirts before rolling her onto her side and easing down the zipper. Diego did his best not to look and stripped the dress off her in as an impersonal a way as he could, but he wasn't dead—despite the tales of folklore and legend—and there were some things beyond any red-blooded male's power to ignore.

Like her long, smooth throat, which drew his eyes inexorably down to what had to be two of the most gorgeous breasts lace had ever embraced. His palms itched to cup their fullness but he resisted, easing the dress down past her sweetly rounded hips. *Dios*, the woman had a body that could make a Victoria's Secret model green with envy. Sweat actually broke out on his forehead as he revealed a peach garter belt that perfectly matched her bra and panties.

His breath caught at the sight of it. He had always been a fool for a woman in garters.

And this was another line of thought he had no business pursuing. Diego forced his eyes away from temptation only to find himself staring at a pair of legs created to evoke only one thought in any man—how to get them wrapped around his waist, as soon and as often as possible. She was very tall and those luscious legs went on and on. He flung the dress aside and took a deep, fortifying breath before reaching for the clasp of her delicious garter belt. As lovely as it was on her, it would be far too uncomfortable to sleep in, and he was doing this for her comfort.

Honestly.

His fingers brushed skin soft as satin as he worked the stockings down her legs. He pulled them off one by one, trying not to notice her rounded calves or delicate feet. She had pretty little feet, elegant and vulnerable, her toenails painted the same peach as her lingerie.

Diego shook his head again but the haze of desire didn't fade. *Dios*, had it been so long since he'd last held a woman that even her *feet* were turning him on now? He ran a hand through his hair and dropped the garter belt to the floor as if burned, wishing he'd never had this crazy idea of making her more comfortable.

The bra he left alone. That was taking temptation too far.

Diego was still feeling a little desperate as he tugged his shirt onto her to cover up all that lovely skin and buttoned it as quickly as he could. It was huge on her, reaching almost to her knees and covering her completely, and he could almost have breathed a sigh of relief if not for one fact.

If there was anything he found sexier than a garter belt on a woman, it was one of his shirts.

He shook his head. What was wrong with him? He was almost too exhausted to move from the extensive healing she'd required and his own body ached viciously from both his battle with the Outcasts and the impact with her car. Blood-lust and sexual desire were almost synonymous to his people, but he was far too tired to feel much of either right now.

Diego rose from the bed, taking the bloody washcloth and dress with him and dumping both in the trash. He'd worry about what she could wear when she woke up. He'd find something somewhere.

But for now all he wanted was sleep. Healing was exhausting and she'd required a lot of it, and on top of his own injuries he felt ready to collapse.

Diego stared at the woman lying on his bed and sighed. He had more guest rooms than he knew what to do with but he just didn't feel up to carrying her down to one. Even summoning James to take care of his own wounds was too much trouble.

He shook his head. His bed was enormous, far larger than a normal king size, and it wasn't like this woman was in any shape to care if she was alone on it or not.

Diego pulled off his blood-splattered shirt but left on his jeans before stretching out on the bed as far from her as he could possibly get and closing his weary eyes. He'd rest just a minute before he called James.

It seemed like only a bare moment passed before Diego was awakened by a quiet "ahem."

He frowned, momentarily confused by the interruption of his rest and more than a little distracted by the soft woman nestled in his arms. The only other person in the house was James and he definitely knew better than to disturb Diego when he was sleeping. Rudely awakened vampires tended to be cranky, and much as James enjoyed needling him, he was smart enough to do it when Diego was awake.

Wait a second.

There was a woman in his arms!

Diego's breath froze in his lungs as he became fully aware of his position. The woman's back was snuggled against his chest, her head tucked beneath his chin, her legs entwined with his. Her cheek was cushioned on his right shoulder, the fingers of her left hand laced through his own. His other arm draped comfortably over her shoulders, snuggling her still closer. Her soft derriere pressed against his groin and the feel of her curves nestled intimately against him sent a wave of heat rushing to places he hadn't used in far too long. He scarcely dared to breathe, stunned at how very good she felt there in his arms. Sweet heaven, it had been far too long since he'd held a woman like this.

The intruder cleared his throat again and Diego pulled back at once. He looked up and found Eli standing at the foot of the bed, arms folded over his chest and dark eyes sparkling with the strange power that always emanated from him. He was the very last person Diego wanted to see.

Oh, this was not good at all.

It was Eli to whom Diego had given his vow all those years ago when he'd joined the Guardian's League, Eli who had brought him the shattering news of his brother's death a century ago, Eli who had slain his brother's killers and deprived Diego of the revenge he had so richly deserved. Seeing him made Diego's heart ache with the memory. It had also been Eli who had told him of the Governing Council's decree after Anton's death and robbed Diego of anything remotely resembling a normal life.

A visit from Eli was rarely good news.

Vampires were intrinsically sensual, their very nature seductive, always conscious of the chase and the thrill of victory whether in battle or in the bedroom. Diego had always reveled in both kinds of victories. As Patriarch of the Panther Clan, providing heirs had been his elder brother Anton's responsibility, a duty Anton hadn't delivered before his death.

The Governing Council had stepped in and commanded Diego to take his brother's place as Patriarch, despite Diego's protests that as the only surviving member of the Clan, having a Patriarch at all was pointless. It had been the wrong argument to use. Now not only was Diego the Patriarch of a Clan consisting only of himself, they'd decreed the next woman he bedded must become his mate and provide the heirs Anton had not. Diego had avoided the eternal bonding they'd insisted upon in the only way he could. He had been celibate ever since they'd issued the damn command.

A century added up to a lot of long, lonely nights.

Diego scooted away from the unconscious woman as fast as possible, wishing he'd remembered the damn decree before he'd collapsed there and well aware of what their current position implied. "Eli—"

Eli only smiled at him. "At last, Diego," he said, sounding pleased. "We were starting to think you'd never choose a mate."

Diego went cold. "No!" he protested. "I didn't—"

Eli held up a hand. "Congratulations," he interrupted, still smiling. "I'm here to formally recognize your mate on behalf of the Council."

Diego's jaw dropped. Eli looked disgustingly smug standing there as if he expected no resistance at all. Diego protested even though he had the sinking feeling it wouldn't do any good.

"This has nothing to do with the cursed decree!" he hissed, trying not to wake the subject of their argument. "I did not sleep with this woman!"

He might as well have saved his breath for all the good it did him.

"Diego, take a look around you," Eli said, utterly calm in contrast to Diego's fury. He raised one eyebrow as he glanced at the discarded garter belt on the floor beside the bed before giving the woman wearing Diego's shirt a pointed glance. "I find your story a little hard to believe. The evidence is certainly compelling, and when I got here you were wrapped around her like a second skin. Now you're honestly going to tell me you two haven't—"

"That's exactly what I'm telling you!" Diego knew this looked bad but he had to make Eli understand. "Look, I saved her life—"

"Oh, now it makes sense," Eli said with a nod, but those eyes still danced with what Diego could have sworn was amusement. "Healing is a very intimate process. It would be only natural to—"

"Don't even say it." Diego actually cringed. "It did not happen!"

Eli studied him for a long moment. Those eerie black eyes seemed to see all the way to Diego's soul and it was almost impossible not to squirm under the piercing gaze. Diego hated it when Eli used his penetrating stare on him, and he was pretty sure Eli knew it.

He was also pretty sure that was exactly why Eli did it.

After a moment, which seemed like an eternity, Eli shrugged. "In the end it doesn't matter, Diego," he said. "Despite what you seem to think, we didn't issue this decree on a whim. High-blood vampires are rare. It is far past time for you to take a mate and secure your line, and the omens all indicated the next female you took to bed would become your bondmate. I see you there in the bed with a woman. She is your mate. Why do you fight it?" He spoke with complete calm as though Diego's refusal to comply was completely unreasonable.

It made Diego's blood boil even as he still scrambled for a way out. How dare they interfere in his life based on some ridiculous omen? He didn't want a bondmate, damn it. He didn't need another person to protect, didn't want this woman made a target for the beasts he hunted simply because she wore a vampire's bondmark on her arm. Maybe someday he'd bond but was it too much to ask to let him choose his own mate, a vampire instead of a fragile mortal?

His thoughts stuttered to a stop. *A mortal!* Relief burst through him and Diego thanked the heavens. The perfect way out was there all along. "She's not even one of us, Eli," he said as the tight band around his chest loosened. Even Eli had to see the irrefutability of this argument. "She's mortal. She can't be my mate."

Eli shrugged. "I don't think you'll find her mortality a problem."

For a moment all Diego could do was gape. "Are you being deliberately obtuse, Eli? Of course it's a problem! I can't bond with her without Changing her, and you know as well as I do it's forbidden for a fledgling to bond with her own sire. Even you and your damn Council can't force me to take a mortal as my mate!"

Eli raised an eyebrow. This time his amusement was unmistakable. "I can't?"

Diego's heart sank and he regretted his outburst at once. He knew better than to issue any kind of challenge to Eli but something about the man made him act like a rash fledgling.

"Don't, Eli," Diego said, trying to sound stern instead of intimidated. He couldn't really force this, could he? Still, if half the things murmured about Eli were true... "Whatever you're thinking, don't."

"It's out of my hands. It's already done," Eli said, and Diego wanted to strangle him. "She's a pretty girl. I'm sure you'll make the best of it."

His smugness was the last straw. "Damn it, it's not only my life you're playing with now. What about hers? You don't even know she's not already married. What do you think gives you the right to force a mortal into this? Being Head of the Council doesn't give you the right to play God!"

The amusement left Eli's eyes but his tone didn't change. "I know everything about her I need to know. There's no husband, no family, no roommate waiting for her half of the rent. She needs you, Diego," Eli said. "As you said, it's her life now, too. Don't screw this up or you'll both regret it."

He turned and walked out before Diego could get out another word. The slam of the bedroom door behind him sounded like the crack of doom.

"I already regret it!" Diego shouted after him, knowing it was futile.

He sucked in a breath as the skin around his left wrist suddenly started to tingle. Horror filled him as a dark circle of twisted runes appeared there, a tattoo-like bracelet marking him mated. He grabbed the woman's hand and saw the same incomprehensible runes tracing their path over her pale skin.

"Oh no," Diego whispered, falling back on the pillows and groaning. There was no way out now. It was done, it was permanent, and it was completely impossible. Those marks shouldn't have appeared until after he'd thrice shared body, mind, and blood with this woman but Eli had apparently found a way to force them onto the unwilling. Diego felt as if he'd been plunged into a nightmare. Who knew the Council would be this…well, literal? "This can't be happening!"

It was no use denying it. Diego swore viciously in Spanish as his eyes fell again on the bondmarks now encircling their arms like shackles.

Impossible or not, he was bonded to a mortal woman and he didn't even know her name.

Chapter Two

Diego forced himself to take a deep breath and blew it out slowly. What was done was done and all the wishing in the world wouldn't undo it. Once the runes appeared not even the Council had the power to remove them—not that they would have been inclined to do so in his case. He rose up on his elbow and looked again at the woman who'd recently been nothing more than a stranger to him, wondering when she'd wake and wondering what the hell he was going to say to her when she did.

He didn't have long to wait. She groaned and rolled onto her back as he watched her, wishing she'd stayed unconscious just a little longer so he could figure out how to tell her they were, for all intents and purposes, married now.

Her lids fluttered open and she met his eyes, and every thought in his head scattered.

Wow.

She had stunning eyes, a clear, deep aquamarine that made him think of pristine waters. Not even the dark rings around them detracted from their beauty. He stared transfixed as those eyes traveled over his face and thought vaguely that these were eyes he wouldn't mind gazing into for the rest of eternity.

Her lips parted and Diego leaned closer, not wanting to miss a word and wondering if her voice would be as beautiful as those amazing eyes. However much his heart and his mind might protest, his body's reaction clearly stated it liked the idea of being mated to this woman just fine.

But she didn't speak. She hissed at him like a cat as her fist whipped out and connected solidly with his still-aching jaw in a punch that would have made Ali proud.

Diego barely had time to shake his head to clear the stars from his vision before she'd leapt from the bed and bolted for the door. He threw the blankets back and ran after her, thinking bitterly that this wasn't a very auspicious start to their life together. He caught her around the waist before she was able to wrench the door open.

"Hey, wait a second!"

She didn't. Instead, she elbowed him hard in his broken ribs. The burst of pain almost made him lose his grip on her. She followed up with a hard stomp to his instep, which would likely have broken something had she still had on her shoes. Diego's fangs tried to emerge with the vicious jolt of pain and adrenaline but he forced them ruthlessly back. Was this truly the same helpless-looking woman who had been limp in his arms only moments ago?

"Let go of me!" she yelled.

Diego didn't dare. She was inflicting quite enough pain on him restrained and he had no desire to see what she was capable of when free. "Will you take it easy and let me explain?"

His soothing words had the opposite effect than what he'd intended. Her nails sliced down his forearms as she continued to struggle and she reached back with one clawed hand, clearly searching for his face. He grabbed her wrists and spun her around before backing her up against the door, trapping her between the wood and his hard body.

"Calm down!" he demanded again, ignoring the protests from his wounds.

She glared up at him, her aquamarine eyes flashing in her pale face. Despite her blood loss and the aftermath of the head injury, she didn't stop struggling for her freedom and tried to bring a knee up into an area Diego would really rather not have her kick. He blocked her just in time and pressed hard against her to trap her legs. Mortal or not, this woman was a wildcat!

And she showed no signs of ceasing her struggles. "Waking up in bed with a stranger doesn't exactly inspire me to calmness," she pointed out in a voice quaking with fury. She glared pointedly at his hands pinning her wrists to the wall on either side of her head. "Neither does being manhandled."

"Look, lady, you hit me first!"

"Damn right I hit you—you were in *bed* with me! You took my *clothes* off! God knows what else you did to me while I was out—"

"Enough, enough!" Diego roared, cutting her off. Those diamond-hard eyes narrowed dangerously at the command but thankfully she kept her mouth shut. He found it a definite improvement. He couldn't believe this. Had he actually thought things couldn't get worse only a few minutes ago? Her body against his was taut, every muscle poised for action if she found the slightest opportunity to attack or escape. Diego didn't intend to give her one and didn't relax his hold one iota, but he gentled his tone. "Look, do you remember what happened to you tonight?"

"You think I won't press charges against you if I don't remember exactly what you did to me?"

He closed his eyes and prayed for patience. "*Before* I brought you here," he growled, looking back down at her. "You don't remember having a car accident downtown?" Her eyes wavered for the briefest instant. It was all the answer Diego needed. "You do remember!"

She lifted her chin defiantly. "What the hell does my car accident have to do with waking up in your bed?" she said. "Kidnapping is a serious crime, buster, and you can bet I'll be talking to the cops about you."

"Damn it, you stubborn woman, would you listen to me? I didn't kidnap you, and if I was going to hurt you, you've certainly provoked me enough for me to do it by now. I brought you here to save you, you vicious creature, and right now I'm regretting it!"

She blinked up at him. This was clearly not an answer she'd expected. "W—what?" she stammered. "You took me out of the wreck and brought me here?" She looked over his shoulder and around the room. "You mean, just you? Alone?"

"Is it that so hard to believe?" he asked, feeling slightly offended at her obvious doubt. Didn't he *look* capable of getting her from downtown to his house without help?

Of course, the journey with her weight pressing against his fractured ribs had been no picnic and by the time he'd gotten halfway home he'd been cursing himself for not calling James to come for them, and it *had* been James who'd carried her up the stairs, but there was no reason for Diego to admit any of that to her. "You were hurt," he added when she still looked at him suspiciously.

"Why did you bring me here instead of taking me to a hospital?"

Diego opened his mouth to tell her some soothing lie about being a doctor and wanting to save her a hospital bill and found his voice wouldn't work. Everything he'd ever believed protested at the thought of lying to his mate. He fought the urge to groan in frustration. She might not believe they were bound and he might wish it wasn't so, but honor dictated he treat his mate with respect at all times and that meant he would give her the truth.

Always.

No one ever said the truth was easy or comforting, though, and he hoped to whatever gods were watching he wouldn't scare the life out of her when she heard it. "You were pretty badly hurt," he said, choosing his words with care. "An ambulance would've taken time to get there and you didn't need to wait around in the ER. I brought you home and healed you here."

He realized his mistake at once when she snorted with disbelief. He'd forgotten that in this age, mortals sought healing at a hospital, not in a home.

"What in the world are you talking about?" She glanced around again as though looking for medical equipment and shot him a look when she didn't find any. "How?"

Oh, you know, magic. That's the usual way for vampires. It even sounded crazy in his head. There was no way in the world he could explain to her without making her think he was insane on top of being a kidnapper. A change of subject was definitely in order.

"Look, we got off on the wrong foot." The one she'd stomped was still throbbing. It was a night for understatements. "Let's start over. I'm Diego Leonides. What's your name?"

She frowned as if this was the strangest question he could have asked and he had the strong impression he hadn't fooled her at all with his misdirection.

"Sian," she finally answered, and he didn't miss the omission of her last name. "Wish I could say it's nice to meet you, but under the circumstances…" She looked pointedly back at his hands on her wrists. "Mind letting me go, Diego Leonides? That would go a long way toward convincing me you're on my side here."

He stifled a shudder. He had to gain her trust somehow, but she'd already caused him more pain than any mortal had in longer than he cared to remember. The thought of what she could do with both hands free definitely didn't appeal.

"Do you plan on punching me again?" he asked, buying time. "Because while I've never harmed a woman in my life, I have to tell you I am sorely tempted to turn you over my knee for that."

Sian glared at him again, her eyes flashing blue fire. "Try it, caveman," she growled. "You might get a surprise you won't like."

He'd already had several of those tonight. He released one wrist. "A compromise," he said, making sure his hand still covered the runes on her left wrist. Maybe it was cowardice but he didn't want to have to explain those one second sooner than necessary.

Sian planted her newly freed hand in the center of his chest and shoved hard. He didn't move for a moment, ignoring his wailing ribs and letting her know without words who was in charge, before taking a step back. "Better?" he asked quietly.

Sian pulled at the wrist he still held. "Let me go," she repeated. "I don't like being trapped."

Yeah, you and me both, Diego thought bitterly, wishing Eli was here to witness the chaos he'd created—or maybe just so Diego could throttle him. Yes, throttling him held a definite appeal. "Listen to me first," he said instead. "Sit down. You were hurt pretty bad and you're still weak from it. I don't want you passing out again."

"Don't get any ideas. I'm nowhere near passing out."

It was a blatant lie. Sian followed her captor back to the bed and perched on the edge, not that she had any choice. She hated admitting he was right, but her head was pounding and her vision kept going black around the edges. Right now, pure adrenaline was the only thing keeping her upright. It wouldn't last forever.

She needed to pick her battles carefully right now. This man, whoever he was, clearly outmatched her physically. Not only that, he seemed too stubborn to easily sway. This wasn't a situation she'd be able to muscle her way out of. She glanced around the room as subtly as she could, looking for her clothes and especially her purse.

Where was her gun?

She glared at Diego when he sat beside her and scooted back as far as his grip would allow. She didn't want to give him any reason to think she wanted to be on a bed with him.

"Okay, I'm listening," she said coldly, hoping he couldn't tell how muddled she felt. Had he drugged her? There was something she was forgetting, something important, she knew it, but the memories wouldn't focus. "Talk. Tell me how you saved me, all alone, without any medical equipment, when you say a hospital wouldn't have done me any good. I'm just dying to hear this."

He took a deep breath and ran a hand through his hair, hesitating. It gave her a moment to take in his features while he wasn't looking. Sian hated herself for it but she just couldn't help but notice how very gorgeous this man was. His hair was long and black as night and fell loose around his shoulders. His sensual mouth and glittering green eyes beneath dark eyebrows combined to create a face of pure male perfection. She'd never seen eyes like his before. They almost seemed to swirl and change in the dim light. Even with his dark goatee she saw his jaw was firm and stubborn, and those lips...*sinful* came to mind.

She already knew he was strong from his grip and the press of his body against hers, but the sight of his well-muscled bare chest made her mouth go dry. A black panther was tattooed on his right biceps and rippled temptingly with every move he made. And he was so tall. Although she was tall for a woman at five foot ten, this man towered over her. If they were in any situation other than this she would be seriously drooling at the thought of being in bed with someone this completely delicious.

But she didn't dare indulge in the luxury of fantasizing anymore, and especially not when it came to Diego. He reminded her of a wolf, beautiful and strong and deadly. She scooted further away from him on the bed. Something about this man made her want to run and hide and Sian wasn't the type of girl who scared easily.

"Well?" Sian prompted when Diego still didn't answer her.

Finally he looked back at her and she actually shivered at the intensity of those amazing eyes. "You won't believe me unless I prove it to you," he said softly, almost as if he were speaking to himself. She had to strain to hear him. "And if I prove it to you, I'm afraid I'll terrify you."

"You'll find me difficult to terrify," Sian said, lifting her chin and meeting those remarkable eyes head-on despite the little thrill of fear that shot through her at his words. Damn, he was good with intimidation.

"Come on, spill it," she added when he hesitated, knowing she wouldn't believe a single word he said. Never mind her innate ability to hear a lie and never mind those same instincts telling her he'd spoken nothing but the truth so far. She couldn't afford to trust him.

He sighed and closed his eyes. When he opened them again, Sian gasped.

Still just as green, still every bit as intense, his eyes were nonetheless completely different. The pupils had changed and were no longer round but now cat-like slits. His irises had expanded until only a hint of white remained around the edge. That impression of danger, of an untamed predator not quite concealed beneath the surface, intensified until she really did feel the first tickling of terror at the base of her spine. A sudden flashback to the terrifying vision that had made her lose control of her car streaked across her mind's eye and was gone before she could make sense of it.

She pushed the fear and confusion resolutely away. All right, he had strange contact lenses, and somehow he'd managed to slip them in so deftly she hadn't seen the movement, so what?

"Nice trick," Sian forced herself to say in a calm and unimpressed voice. "Are you ever going to get to your explanation?"

But when he opened his mouth to speak and Sian saw his teeth, she suddenly decided she didn't want an explanation anymore. She scrambled to her feet and tried to break for the door again, desperately attempting to pull her hand free, hardly listening to his words in her desperation to escape.

He had fangs. Long, gleaming, razor-sharp *fangs!*

Only three words registered before shock overtook her and the blackness closed over her vision, taking her down with the sight of those unnatural eyes and wicked fangs burning in her mind.

"I'm a vampire."

Diego caught her as she fainted and carried her back to the bed. "Well, I guess this means you believe me," he murmured to her unconscious face.

He sighed heavily. Damn, he hadn't meant to make her faint. He could have kicked himself. Impress her a little, maybe, especially since she'd shown such unflattering surprise when he'd told her he'd brought her here and healed her single-handedly, but not make her *faint.*

"Good first impression, Diego," he muttered as he tucked the blankets around her. "Oh, yes, all happily mated pairs start out this way—a good fist-fight followed by scaring each other to death." But then again, most happily mated pairs had actually chosen one another.

Right now he could happily stake every single member of the Council out for the dawn.

Well, there was nothing to be done for it now. He couldn't imagine any way this pairing could help but start badly. His job now was to make the best of it, as Eli had callously suggested, and soothe and protect his new bondmate the best he could.

When she regained consciousness, that was.

Diego sighed again. Sian was nothing if not a fighter. He'd best be prepared for another attack when she woke. Damn it all, he was hungry, he was hurting, and he was just too damn tired for this. He knew the sun was about to peek over the horizon by the lethargy that multiplied his fatigue almost beyond bearing. Thanks to Eli's interference there wasn't even time for James to come tend to his wounds before dawn.

Well, it wasn't the first time he'd slept injured. At least he could try to make sure Sian didn't injure him even more before he woke up again. He stretched out beside her and pulled her into his arms again, grasping her wrists and pinning her legs with his. There was nothing romantic in this embrace—it was purely self-defense. He had no desire to get socked in the jaw again, or worse, wake up to find himself staked through the heart in his own bed before he could figure out what to do with her. It wouldn't surprise him a bit for her to try it if she'd believed him after his ill-fated demonstration. He murmured a compulsion that would keep her asleep until sunset—

And ran into a mental block so strong his magic glanced right off.

Diego fought the urge to roar with frustration—it wouldn't help and his ribs hurt enough already. Apparently nothing was going to be easy in this. *Why* did he have to get stuck with a strong-willed woman resistant to mind control? There was only one option at this point.

"James!" he shouted. "Get your butt in here now!"

It only took a minute before his bedroom door flew opened and his Steward skidded into the room. "What's your prob—whoa, hey now, I don't need to see that!" James protested, clapping a hand over his eyes after one glance at Diego and Sian entwined on the bed. "I mean, I know modesty wasn't a big deal in the fourth century or whenever you were born, but you need to keep up with the times, man."

Diego ground his teeth. "It was the tenth century and forget modesty. I need you to get her out of here."

James cracked an eye open and looked at him disapprovingly. "That is way cold, man, even for you," he said. "Getting you out of the morning after isn't in my contract, Diego."

"Doing whatever I tell you *is* your contract, boy," Diego snapped. "And right now I'm telling you to take her out of here, without waking her up if at all possible. Get her something else to wear, too."

James rolled his eyes. "If I had a gorgeous woman in my bed I wouldn't be so hasty to get her dressed and out of—"

"Are you quite finished dissecting the biggest mistake I've ever made? Can we skip to the part where you help me now?"

James raised an eyebrow and gave Sian's curvaceous form outlined beneath the sheet a long, appreciative glance. "If you think she's a mistake, Diego, you need way more help than I'm qualified to give. I always said total celibacy was a sure-fire ticket to insanity."

"It's not what it looks like," Diego growled. "Now do you want to become my breakfast or are you going to get your rear in gear?"

James shrugged at the threat. "It not only looks like it, Diego, it sounded like it, too. I heard the shouting and wall thumping from across the house. Tone it down a little next time, okay? I don't want to deal with the neighbors complaining."

Diego bared his fangs. "You and Eli both have the wrong idea about this, but at least I can tell *you* to shut up!"

"I bet you told Eli to shut up just fine."

"James!"

James sighed and approached the bed. "Fine," he said, still annoyingly unintimidated. "Unwrap yourself from the gorgeous woman wearing your clothes who you did not make mad passionate whoopee with, and I'll take care of her."

"So glad you decided to see things my way." Diego released Sian from his hold and flopped back on the mattress in exhaustion as James slipped his arms beneath her carefully. "I don't have the energy to kill you right now, and training a new Steward is such a pain."

"Yeah, yeah," James said. He straightened with her in his arms and frowned down at her. "Where does she live, anyway?"

Diego closed his eyes and groaned. He had absolutely no clue where she lived and whatever ID she'd been carrying was still in the car James hadn't yet retrieved. This was going from bad to worse. "I have no idea," he admitted.

James shook his head, holding Sian carefully. "Too busy 'not making whoopee' to exchange addresses, I take it?"

Diego glared. "May I remind you that provoking a hungry, injured, and exhausted vampire is not covered by workman's compensation insurance?"

James shrugged again and shifted Sian in his arms. "Well, she's a luscious armful but I don't want to stand here with her all day," he replied, ignoring the threat as he ignored all the others Diego threw at him. "Direct your humble servant, lord and master. I can get her a change of clothes, but what do you want me to do with her? Chuck her out the back door? Install her in a motel? Dump her by the police station? What?"

"*Dios,* no," Diego said with a shudder, imagining losing his new mate and having to go find her again. Tempting as it was, he couldn't abandon her. Honor demanded he keep her safe and he could imagine all too easily what an Outcast would do to any mate of a Slayer.

Ice ran down his spine. The very thought was a nightmare. "Stick her in one of the guest rooms and keep her there until I wake up," he said at last. "I'll deal with her tonight."

James made a face. "Oh, I can hardly wait for round two. Just try to 'not make whoopee' a little more quietly next time, will you? I really don't want to hear all that again," he grumbled as he turned for the door. He ducked the pillow Diego threw at him and pushed the door closed behind him with a foot.

"You can be replaced!" Diego shouted through the closed door, already mentally composing the scathing email he was going to send to the Council as soon as he got the chance, and pretended not to hear James's derisive snort as his footsteps faded down the hall.

C* C* C*

Sian woke slowly, not wanting to relinquish the warmth and safety of her dreams. Something horrible waited for her in the waking world and she didn't particularly want to remember what it was.

She frowned, opening her eyes cautiously, trying to remember what had happened to her. Disjointed bits of an incredibly vivid dream flashed through her mind, flashes of sunset and city streets, shadows and a body colliding with her car, cat-like emerald eyes and gleaming white fangs. She shuddered in spite of the crimson late afternoon light streaming in through the windows. Where the heck had all that craziness come from?

Wait a second.

Her bedroom was always black as midnight. There shouldn't be any sunlight shining in her bedroom window—it looked out at a tall building right next door that blocked most of the daylight, and her heavy velvet drapes and mini-blinds did the rest.

This was not her bedroom.

She sat bolt upright and stared around at the strange bedroom, fighting down the urge to panic. This shirt wasn't hers, this room wasn't hers, and she had no idea where her purse—and therefore her gun—was.

Where the devil was she?

Sian pressed her fingertips to her temples and thought hard. Okay, take it one step at a time. She remembered dropping off her paintings at the gallery, remembered going out to Baby and driving away. She remembered catching sight of a blue sedan tailing her and driving like a crazy woman until she'd lost it. She remembered—

Nothing else.

It had been sunset when she'd evaded the sedan, but the light outside looked more like late afternoon than dawn. She squeezed her eyes shut, trying hard to remember and having no success. How long had she been here, anyway?

Sian opened her eyes and pushed up the too-long sleeve to check her watch and stopped dead. Her watch was apparently out playing hooky with her purse and gun, but she barely registered its loss. She was too busy trying to figure out where this strange *whatever* wrapped around her wrist had come from.

It was almost like a tribal-style tattoo, fine black lines twisted into strange symbols and runes weaving together in a band all the way around her wrist. It was unusual, it was gorgeous, and it was nothing she would ever have gotten for herself. Obvious and distinctive tattoos were necessarily discouraged for anyone hiding out with a price on her head. The strange letters in the design looked almost familiar, but she couldn't make anything of them. She licked her finger and tried without much hope to rub it off.

"Sian, girlfriend, what did you *do* last night?" she asked herself softly, staring at the dark band.

Another brief flash of memory teased her mind, the barest hint of a recollection of struggling with a man, a tall man with dark hair and goatee, olive skin, and determined green eyes.

Sian froze at the memory. She'd lost her badge, her home, her friends and everything she'd ever known by testifying against a tall dark Spaniard.

Her mind flew back to the blue sedan she'd been certain she'd shaken in traffic.

Had she been wrong about losing them?

No matter how hard she strained her mind she couldn't remember. Sian clenched her fists. Wondering would get her nowhere.

It was time for action. "Enough lying around," she told herself sternly, glancing back at the window. "Time to blow this joint." She had no idea what was outside this bedroom, but the window was a perfect, unguarded exit and she fully intended to use it.

She threw back the covers and strode to the window, but it resisted all her efforts to shove it open. She narrowed her eyes and tried once more, but no matter how hard she strained it didn't budge a millimeter. She crossed to the door and tried the handle, but it was locked. She would've been surprised to find it otherwise, and even if it hadn't been she still would've had to find her way through the house and sneak past anyone in it to get to freedom. There was no way out there.

No, it had to be the window.

Sian glared at the stubborn window for a moment, considering her next move. Her eye fell on the heavy, decorative curtain rod and she smiled. "All right, if that's the way you're going to be…"

A blaring alarm shattered the air as she punched out the first pane with the heavy iron rod but Sian didn't let it stop her from going to work on the others with grim enthusiasm. Undoubtedly someone would be in here any second and she didn't dare waste an instant.

The door flew open no sooner than she'd feared but quicker than she'd hoped. Sian spun, the curtain rod held in both hands, ready for whatever was coming. When a young man ran inside, she swung with all the strength in her arms.

He stopped so suddenly it looked like he'd hit an invisible wall and the sharp finial at the end of the rod missed him by an inch.

"Jesus!" he cried, stumbling back with his hands held out in front of him. "Back off!"

She sized him up warily. Six feet tall and broad shouldered, he looked more than capable of subduing her should she give him the slightest opportunity. She had no intention of doing so. Despite his sharp hazel eyes and imposing physical presence, her instincts assessed him as no threat, but for once she didn't dare trust them. Her instincts had also told her she'd lost the sedan.

Sian advanced on him with her makeshift weapon at the ready. ""Who are you? Where am I?" He gaped at her and she swiped at him again, deliberately missing but making her point. "What did you do with my purse? Where are my clothes?"

He held up his hands to ward her off. "Lady, I don't know anything about your purse or your clothes, and will you quit swinging that thing around?"

"Give me a reason to and I'll think about it," she growled. "Better yet, show me the door and we'll forget the whole thing."

He looked decidedly uncomfortable. "Sorry, lady, can't do that," he said, inching back. "Boss man wants you to stay, though it's clearly not for your sunny disposition."

She opened her mouth to demand answers again when he lunged without warning, grabbing the curtain rod, and she cursed her no-threat assessment for being dead wrong. Sian wrestled with him for a moment before giving up. Strong as she was, he was stronger, but she had a much better idea.

Letting go of the rod altogether, she hauled back and punched him in the jaw, following with an elbow to the back when he staggered.

He crumpled quite satisfactorily and Sian jerked the rod out of his hands. "Tell your boss man I have a prior engagement," she said sweetly to the back of his blond head, then stepped over him and walked out the door.

G G G

Diego woke with the sunset and leapt out of bed at the shrieking alarm. "James!" he shouted, running out of his room and tearing down the hall, every sense alert and winging through the dark house, searching for danger. "James, damn it, boy, answer me!"

He heard a groan and chased the sound. He found James sitting on the floor in one of the spare rooms, holding his head while rain blew in through a half-shattered window. "What happened? Are you hurt?"

James winced. "Is that in my head or is the alarm still going off?"

Diego shut it off with a thought and dropped to his knees beside James. "What happened?" he demanded again, grabbing his Steward's shoulders.

"Your freaky girlfriend happened!" James quit rubbing his head and met Diego's furious glare with one of his own. "You need to work on your taste in women, Diego, 'cause that chick is psycho. I come in here and she's busting out the window, and when I try to stop her, she tries to take off my head with a curtain rod!"

Diego's mind churned with a mixture of emotions too volatile to contain for long. "She attacked you?" he growled, his fangs coming out. James was his friend, the closest thing he had left to family. The Steward was under his protection and no one attacked him without Diego extracting a pound of their flesh in payment.

But damn it all, this was his *mate* who'd taken James down. A reluctant admiration tried to grow in his chest but Diego squashed it ruthlessly. She was supposed to be here, waiting for him, not running off in the rain wearing nothing but his shirt!

And with that thought, heart-freezing fear wiped every other emotion from his mind. His bondmate was gone, alone in the night with no concept at all of the beasts who would hone in on her now she was marked as his.

Diego swore viciously under his breath and pulled James to his feet. "How long ago did this happen?"

James shook his head and winced. "Maybe an hour," he said uncertainly, glancing at his watch. "It was a little before sunset, you'd know what time that was better than I do."

An hour. Diego swore again. In an hour she could've gone a long way. "Do you need a doctor or are you all right?" Diego scanned his Steward's face critically as he steadied him with a hand on his arm.

James shook Diego's hand off and ran his fingers through his hair. "Get off me, I'm fine," he snapped, his eyes flashing. "Just because a girl kicked my ass doesn't mean I need coddling."

"Can you drive?"

He shrugged, then winced as the motion jarred his bruised back. "Of course I can drive," he said irritably. "Didn't I say I'm fine?"

"Good. Get in the car and start looking for her. We've got to find her."

James looked at him like he was insane. "Diego, get real! She's obviously all healed up and I say good riddance. Give me one good reason why I'd want to help you bring that hellion back!"

Diego shoved his sleeve roughly out of the way and held up his arm, exposing his new bondmark. James stared at it in complete shock before closing his eyes, his expression one of utter horror.

"Oh, please tell me that's not what I think it is," he groaned. "Diego, I can't live with a woman who kicked my butt. You can't be serious!"

"It's exactly what you think it is, and I don't like it any more than you do," Diego snapped. "Thanks to Eli neither of us got a choice. Now I'll ask you again. Sian's running around the city right now with my mark on her arm and no idea what she's gotten into, and despite how neatly she tied you up in knots she's no match for an Outcast. Are you going to help me find my bondmate or not?"

James sighed heavily. "I'll get my keys."

Chapter Three

Sian ran through the huge house, wincing every time the alarm wailed, expecting to see big burly men bursting through every door she passed, ready to tackle her and prevent her escape. Her memories of the night before were horribly clear now. She reached the end of the corridor and raced down the stairs, pausing only a moment in the huge foyer at the bottom to try and guess the best way out. Finally she made a decision and ran. The iron curtain rod grew heavy in her hands and the drapes dragged behind her like a weird train, but she didn't dare to drop it. Awkward as it was, right now it was the only weapon she had.

Five minutes and two dead-ends later, she was growing desperate. So far she hadn't seen anyone, but the alarm still blared and she knew there had to be more than one person here. The young man she'd knocked out had mentioned someone else he called "boss man," and surely there were guards or something around here. The Santonyo family were nothing if not thorough.

Letting her live the first time was the only mistake they'd ever made. Surely after hunting her for three years they wouldn't let her get away unscathed now that they'd found her.

Sian threw open another door and found herself in a cavernous garage. She skidded to a stop, jaw dropping at the gleaming cars parked there—she wasn't a car fanatic, but she didn't need to be one to know there was an insane amount of money represented here. She started pulling on door handles, cursing under her breath to find them all locked—who locked a car in a garage, anyway? She looked around, hoping to see a key rack or something, but there was nothing. No chance of stealing one of these for her getaway.

Well, at least there was a door to the outside here. Sian hit the garage door opener and waited impatiently as the door slowly rose. When it was halfway up she had a sudden inspiration and, wrapping the long curtains around her hands, stabbed the box hard with her curtain rod. The sharp finial pierced the metal housing easily and drove deep into the circuitry beneath. She yelped and jumped back as electricity arced through the rod and burned her palms despite the curtain padding, but there was no time to waste trying to bandage them. She turned and ducked under the now-jammed garage door and ran down the drive as though the hounds of hell were at her heels.

If she couldn't drive off in one of those cars, at least she'd made darn sure no one else could, either.

She ignored the gravel biting into her bare feet and the pain in her burned hands, too glad to be out of captivity to care about her discomfort. Still, the ease of her escape bothered her. It made no sense. Enrique Santonyo had been hunting for her for three years, yet no one had come when the alarm went off. The huge house was definitely his style—big and lavish and filled with every creature comfort—but she hadn't seen one single personal portrait in her flight through the halls. Her feet slowed and she held the stitch in her side but she didn't stop.

There hadn't been a blue sedan in the garage.

She frowned, suddenly wondering if she'd jumped to the wrong conclusions. Last night was a blur, nightmares blending with strange images she thought were real, and she couldn't be sure which of her memories were dreams and which were real. She remembered a man telling her he'd brought her there and taken care of her when she'd been injured, but she also remembered fighting to get away from him. An image of a dark face with green cat-eyes and fangs tickled her memory but she pushed that image aside. That, at least, had to be a nightmare.

She groaned. Which memory was true? The dark man who'd held her captive, or the one who'd tried to help her?

Sian didn't dare believe the latter. She had only herself to depend on, and even if she'd escaped from a Good Samaritan it was for his own good. She didn't want to bring Santonyo's wrath down on anyone else.

The minutes stretched and still she hurried. The gravel drive seemed to have no end. Her feet ached and her hands throbbed. When it began to rain after sunset she shivered, utterly miserable, but didn't dare stop. There had to be an end to the driveway somewhere and a road she could follow afterward. She had to get out of this place and somehow find Baby so she could make her escape from San Francisco.

She was soaked to the skin by the time she made it to the end of the drive. A huge wrought-iron gate blocked her path and she swore in frustration. With her burned hands there was no chance of climbing the straight iron bars, and even if she had been able to do it, the spikes at the top looked anything but decorative. She looked for an easier escape route, but the thought of climbing the thick stone walls was just as daunting.

But she'd be damned if she gave up. Sian set her jaw and started walking again, following the stone wall. Surely it gave way to fencing somewhere—no one surrounded a place this big with a wall like that. Shivering, her hands aching, her feet protesting with every step, Sian walked the property line and hoped.

☪ ☪ ☪

Diego left James after being assured one more time that his Steward was all right. He ran for the front door, too worried about Sian to even think about taking a car to search for her. He could cover more ground faster without one anyway.

He threw open the front door and stood for a moment, closing his eyes and breathing deeply of the night air, sending all his heightened senses searching for her and wishing he'd taken her blood while she'd slept. It would've been dangerous—he'd been almost feral from hunger and pain—and it would have been against all his principles to take her blood without her consent, but the bond it created would've been extremely helpful now. As it was he had no link with her whatsoever, no way to track her down or know if she was hurt.

He was jolted from his concentration by the sound of James cursing. Diego frowned, turning toward the sound, and saw James scowling as he ducked under the half-open garage door. "Your psycho girlfriend fried our garage door opener," he complained, glaring at Diego as though it were his fault. "It's totally fubared, Diego. You're on your own, man. I can't get the damn thing open to get a car out!"

Diego narrowed his eyes at James. "Watch your mouth, boy," he growled. "She might not be your favorite person in the world right now, but she *is* my mate and you *will* show some respect. Understood?"

James jammed his hands in his pockets and made a visible effort to wipe the fury off his face. Jaw clenched, he nodded curtly. Diego turned and sent his senses out again, his anxiety tightening unbearably. She had to be on foot, which meant she was probably still on the property—his estate was huge and almost totally wild, but at least it was safe. Still, at this point he wouldn't put anything past Sian. His fists clenched at the nightmarish thought of her walking down the highway wearing little more than his shirt and his bondmark. *Dios.*

At last he felt her, a bright surge of life near the gate. His eyes flew open and he leapt into the air, shape-shifting into a large hawk and soaring toward her.

His heart stuttered with relief when he found her pushing through the overgrowth and cursing softly. He circled down before landing silently a few yards from her and shifting back to his normal form behind a stand of trees— after she'd fainted at the mere sight of his fangs, he didn't think she was ready to see any of his spookier tricks yet. He stayed still and let her approach him, and when she got within arm's reach he snagged her around the waist. She was trapped against his chest with her arms pinned at her sides before she could so much as gasp.

"Where the hell do you think you're going?" he demanded.

Sian didn't scream though Diego saw the sudden surge of panic in her clear eyes as she tried desperately to break away from him. She was strong but he was prepared this time and she didn't stand a chance.

That didn't mean she didn't fight. She kicked his shins with her bare feet and twisted in his arms. "Let me go!"

"Not a chance," he growled, hardly noticing her struggles. Relief at having her safe in his arms surged through him, that he'd found her before his enemies did, and his rioting emotions screamed for an outlet.

And he had the perfect one right here. He dipped his head and kissed her, needing this too much to allow her time to protest.

Sian saw his intention too late to turn away. She gasped as his hard mouth came down on hers, momentarily too stunned to fight, and a moment was all he needed to breach her defenses. His free hand came up and tangled in her hair, holding her captive, and her head reeled from the sheer heat of his skilled mouth taking hers. Sweet heaven, the man knew how to kiss!

He groaned against her lips and suddenly she came back to her senses. Sian tried to pull away but he didn't let her. Panic swamped her, killing the fire he'd started, and she bit his lower lip hard.

He growled and broke the kiss as his arms clenched around her. She shivered at the animalistic sound, but only when he pressed his open mouth to her ear did she realize his growl had been arousal, not aggression.

"*Querida,*" he whispered, his breath hot and his lips caressing her ear, "where I come from, that's foreplay. Shall I return the favor?" His teeth nipped at her earlobe.

Sian shoved hard at his shoulders, desperate to get away, and cried out at the sudden pain from the burns she'd forgotten.

Diego's tone changed at once. "You're hurt. Why didn't you tell me?" He moved back just enough to sweep his gaze over her. "Let me see, Sian. Where are you injured?"

She glared at him and closed her fists, hiding her palms. "Let go of me," she said through gritted teeth.

He sighed. "Why must you make this so difficult?" He reached up and captured her wrist while still holding her effortlessly against him with one arm. She tried to pull her hand away and couldn't. He gave her a quelling look. "Open your hand, *querida,*" he said. "It'll hurt you if I do it."

She refused to relax her fist. "That's not my name."

His green eyes glinted with a hint of amusement. "I know your name, Sian," he said dryly. "*Querida* is an endearment, woman, though why I use it on you is beyond me. Now quit stalling and let me see your hands."

She raised her chin stubbornly. "And if I don't?"

He leaned closer. "You're looking extremely kissable," he murmured, his warm breath caressing her lips. "And you can bite me again if you like, I certainly don't mind. Either show me your hands or pucker up, baby."

Sian hated the surge of heat that rushed through her at his words. "You're insufferable!"

"Then we're perfectly matched," he shot back. "Now what's it going to be?"

Sian glared at him for a moment longer before reluctantly opening her hand. Diego sighed. "Great. My mate thinks my kiss is a threat," he muttered under his breath, but she heard him.

"Your *what?*"

He gently turned her hand over in his, ignoring her question and swearing softly at the blisters on her palm. "What did you do to yourself?" he asked in exasperation. She tried to pull her hand away as he bent closer but he didn't allow it. "Be still."

She tugged at her hand again. "What are you going to do?"

"Shh."

Sian held her breath as he brought her throbbing palm to his lips and breathed gently over it. She winced in anticipation—the burns were incredibly sore and even the air hurt—but there was no pain. She watched in amazement as the blisters shrank and the redness faded before her eyes. A bare moment later, her palm was smooth and unmarked again, the burn only a memory. "How did you do that?" she whispered.

Diego dropped her hand and captured the other one. "Did you burn this one, too?" He didn't wait for an answer before gently teasing her fingers open. She stared in amazement as he repeated the process, and the wounds vanished almost at once. He looked up at her when he was done, his green eyes dark in the moonlight. "Anywhere else?"

Sian shook her head, momentarily robbed of her voice, so stunned she forgot to struggle to get away from him. How could anyone make burns disappear like that? She remembered him saying he'd brought her to his home to heal her after the accident. Suddenly his story didn't seem quite so far-fetched.

Diego set her gently back on her feet and held her at an arm's length, raking her with his electric green gaze. He sighed and shook his head at the scratches on her legs. "Am I to spend the rest of forever healing you?" he asked, a hint of amusement in his voice.

She danced back when he started to reach for her again, stopping only when he tugged her wrist again. There had been something inherently sensual about his breath softly kissing her palms. No way was she going to let a stranger put his mouth on her legs, no matter how much the scratches stung.

"What do you mean, the rest of forever?" she asked, her brain slowly starting to function again. "And why did you call me your mate?"

Diego ran his free hand through his hair and Sian wished she could stop noticing just how much the moonlight loved this man. He looked like some primitive beast bathed in silver, dark and sensual and devastating to a woman's senses. When he met her eyes again, it was almost impossible to breathe normally. Never before in her life had she had any man's undivided attention.

No. That wasn't true.

Enrique Santonyo had certainly given her his full and undivided attention.

That thought sobered her and Sian pulled at her wrist again in another futile effort to free herself. "Well?" she prompted when he still didn't answer.

Diego drew her to his side, ignoring her attempts to dig in her heels. "We'll talk about this inside."

Before she could protest, he swept her into his arms and strode up the gravel driveway. None of her protests or struggles made the least bit of difference and, after several frustrating minutes, Sian submitted to being carried with poor grace. She crossed her arms over her chest, stubbornly refusing to put them around his neck, purposefully making herself the most awkward burden possible.

Her effort was totally lost on him. He wasn't even out of breath when they reached the house ten minutes later.

James met them at the door and scowled at Sian. Diego shot him a warning glance and the Steward stepped aside without a word, but not before Sian asked, "How's your head?" in a smug tone that made James's fists clench.

The door slammed behind them and Sian jumped, positive no one had touched it, but before she could wonder about it, Diego dumped her unceremoniously on the couch. He threw himself into an armchair beside her and rubbed his temples silently as if he had the mother of all headaches.

She sincerely hoped he did. She hated to be manhandled. "So, are you going to get around to answering my questions now or are you going to drag me around somewhere else against my will?"

He shot her a look. "I'm trying to decide how to explain this," he said through his teeth. "Would it be too much to ask for you to give me a minute to gather my thoughts?"

"Yes," she said unsympathetically. "I want to go home, not listen to explanations. Spill it, caveman."

He rubbed his temples some more. "I knew you were going to say that," he muttered. Sian tapped her fingers on her elbows and waited impatiently.

Finally he sat back and pushed up his left sleeve, holding up his bare forearm. Her eyes widened in shock at the sight of the dark band around his arm. It was identical to the one on her arm. "Oh, no you did not," she breathed, staring. "How dare you tattoo me while I was unconscious?"

He shook his head. "No, I most certainly didn't, and I'm no happier about it than you are. This is a bondmark, Sian, and it means you and I are mated—like being married. Only this marriage is for eternity."

Sian gaped at him, momentarily too stunned to speak. The man was a lunatic, an absolute madman if he thought she was going to marry him based on some weird tattoo he'd put on her while she was unconscious.

Finally she managed to find her voice even though her throat felt much too tight. "You're in for a big disappointment if you expect me to happily play the little wifey for you. I think I'd rather go to one of those laser places, have the thing removed, and forget I ever saw you. How's that for a plan?"

The corner of his mouth twitched upward in the ghost of a grin. "Trust me, I had the same thought, but it wouldn't work."

"What, is it some special kind of super ink or something?"

"You could say that." He looked gloomily at his own mark. "Supernatural ink."

Sian stood slowly, ignoring the protests of her sore feet, and cautiously backed away. "Why did you do this if you're so unhappy about it?" she asked, trying to keep him talking while she edged closer to the door.

He was rubbing his temples again, not looking at her. "I told you, I didn't put them there. I had no more choice in the matter than you did. Want to be angry at someone? I'll give you Eli's number and you can yell at him. Let me know if it makes you feel better because it sure didn't work for me."

Sian wasn't going to ask who Eli was. She really didn't want to know how many men had been in that bedroom with her while she was unconscious, and she really, truly didn't want to know anything else about what they'd done to her. Her stomach clenched and she felt like vomiting as her imagination kicked into overdrive anyway.

She had to get out of here.

"Nothing happened to you, Sian," Diego murmured as she reached for the doorknob. Sian froze in place. He hadn't moved from his position, still rubbing his temples with his eyes closed. "No one touched you. I would never allow anyone to hurt you."

He did not just read my mind. Her hand hovered over the doorknob as she stared at him. *That's impossible. Don't even go there, Sian.* "Well, that's reassuring," she said, hoping her sarcasm didn't show too much. She didn't need a protector.

Well, maybe she *could* use a protector, or at the very least an ally, but she would rather have some say in choosing one. She couldn't see ever picking anyone as psycho as this guy. "How about you just keep an eye on me from a distance in the future?"

"Can't do it," he said resignedly. He finally looked up at her and she snatched her hand back from the doorknob, trying to look nonchalant. "Now that you know what this is," he touched the mark on his forearm, "I need to tell you what I am."

She crossed her arms over her chest and noticed for the first time how cold her wet shirt was. She glanced down and bit back a groan—it was plastered to her body, the material almost transparent. Her lacy bra and panties showed right through it. She snatched a throw off the back of the couch and wrapped it around herself furiously.

"Oh, wait, I remember this part," she snapped, outrage warring with sarcasm in her voice. "You're a vampire, right? Big bad bloodsucker? Is there something in undead etiquette that makes it okay for you not to tell me you can see straight through my shirt?"

Diego wished he could say he hadn't noticed, but he knew better than to try to lie to her. She looked far too delicious in his wet shirt and, after that smoldering kiss, he hadn't been able to stop himself from noticing. The memory of her lush body pressed against his last night was enough to make him want to howl.

Dios, it had been too long since he'd held a woman if he could want a woman who exasperated him as much as Sian did. He really wished Eli was here. He ached to inflict some serious pain on the interfering ancient. "I'm not undead," he told her instead, avoiding her question entirely.

"Oh, well that makes everything all better. Here I thought all vampires were undead, but hey, you learn something new every day."

"None of us are undead," Diego said with a patience he did not feel. "Will you try to calm down?"

"I've been kidnapped by a man who not only thinks we're married but also thinks he's a vampire, and you want me to calm down?"

Diego felt his fangs press against his lips and forced them away. One temper fit at a time was more than enough, and it was clearly Sian's turn. He rubbed his temples again, trying to find the right words, only to be brought up short by the sound of the door opening. He looked up to see Sian and James glaring daggers at each other and quickly got to his feet. "What is it, James?"

James tossed a set of keys to him and Diego caught them out of reflex. "Her car," he said shortly before ducking back out and slamming the door behind him.

Sian's jaw dropped when he tucked the keys into his pocket. "Give me those!"

Diego sighed again. "Not until you give me your word you won't try to leave."

Amazing how such cool blue eyes could burn with fury. "I will do no such thing," she ground out through gritted teeth. "That is my car and I've had just about enough of your nonsense. Give me my keys!"

Diego stood, making no move to retrieve the keys for her. "You're tired," he said, his voice very low. "You've had an ordeal and you need rest." It went against every principle he held dear to use compulsion on her, but until she was more rational he knew he didn't have a hope of reasoning with her.

"I'm not tired. I'm cold and wet and mad as hell, but I'm not tired."

He should've known it wouldn't work. If he hadn't been able to do it while she was sleeping, why should he be able to use compulsion on her while she was wide awake and wary?

"Fine," Diego said wearily, digging her keys back out of his pocket. "You need clothes anyway. Let's go."

She was clearly caught off-guard by his sudden change of heart but held out her hand for the keys anyway. He held them out to her but caught her wrist when she took them.

"Oh, I don't think so. I'm not taking you to my house and that's final," Sian said, clearly grasping his intent.

"Then you're not going." He felt absolutely no desire to be reasonable about this. "I'm not letting you out of my sight, Sian. Get used to it."

☾ ☾ ☾

Fifteen minutes later, Sian sped down the driveway, seething and doing her best to ignore her very imposing and greatly unwanted passenger. Diego was good as his word, refusing to budge until she'd had no choice but to take him with her. No way was she going to spend one more minute than she had to in his clothes, but she hated letting him know where she lived.

Her instincts, though, seemed to be firmly on Diego's side. Sian could've cursed them. She'd come to rely on her intuition, gut feelings, whatever she wanted to call it, and she didn't like its betrayal one bit. More times than she could count, her intuition had led her to the right place at the right time, or kept her from the wrong place at the wrong time. She'd learned to trust it implicitly.

All her instincts were telling her Diego was deadly dangerous, but not to her.

Yeah, right, she told her instincts. *The man kidnapped me and held me hostage, took off my clothes and refuses to let me out of his sight, not to mention he's apparently stolen my purse too. You want to explain how he's not dangerous to me?*

Her instincts paid no attention. They persisted on trusting him on a level that went far deeper than reason, reassuring her this man would rather die than harm her.

Sian ignored them with difficulty, keeping her guard up. She wasn't the only one in her family to have inherited this strange intuition. Her father had had it so strongly it bordered on precognition. His mother had been Cajun, a practicing voodoo priestess famous for her second sight. Her family had never been large and every member she'd ever known had possessed the same thing to varying degrees. She couldn't remember ever hearing one instance where anyone in her family had been in a similar predicament where they didn't dare trust it.

Which left her in a sticky situation. What to trust, a gut feeling that defied definition or the evidence of every other sense she possessed?

Diego stiffened beside her as she whipped around a corner, sending gravel flying. His driveway was full of switchbacks and false turns, as she'd found out earlier when she'd been trying to find her way out. "Must you go so fast?" he asked mildly.

She clenched her jaw. "You don't like the way I drive, I'm happy to let you out here and you can walk back to your house," she snapped.

"You won't get through the gate without me," Diego pointed out, still in the same mild tone.

She didn't need the reminder. It had been the only reason she'd agreed to his accompanying her on this little jaunt. She skidded around another turn and hit the brakes a little too hard when the gate loomed in the beam of her headlights. She opened her mouth to demand he open the gate but before she could even take a breath it was swinging open. She shot a glance at him.

The man hadn't moved a muscle.

Sian started to ask how he'd done that, but remembering how he'd healed her hands earlier she bit off the question. *You really don't want to know,* she told herself firmly. *He'll just tell you he's a vampire or a warlock or some nonsense.*

Her instincts tried to speak up again but she ignored them ruthlessly.

It took less than thirty minutes to get back to the city, the silence tense and awkward the entire time. Sian felt no desire to speak to her captor and Diego did nothing to relieve the tension. By the time she pulled into the tiny alley behind her apartment building, she was wound tighter than a guitar string, nerves snapping.

She dreaded walking up to her door wearing nothing but Diego's shirt.

Diego surprised her by shrugging off his jacket, no small feat in the confines of the Mini, and handing it to her. "Tie it around your waist," he advised. "No one will know if you're wearing shorts under it or not."

"Thanks," Sian said, trying not to notice how the material still held the heat from his body. She got out and quickly tied the jacket around her waist. It fell past her knees, covering her more than adequately. She locked Baby and turned toward the narrow staircase leading up to her second story apartment.

Diego stopped her with a hand on her arm.

Sian started to yank her arm away but stopped when she saw the look on his face. Eyes alert, every line of his face tense, his gaze was focused on the window of her apartment. She didn't even wonder how he knew which one it was as her own gut tightened with a feeling she'd come to know too well. It hadn't been the tension from the silence in the car that had been bothering her on the way over here.

The psychic echoes of fury and danger radiated from her apartment, fouling the night air.

Chapter Four

"Stay here," Diego said, the barest hint of a growl in his low voice, urging her gently back toward the car.

Sian planted her bare feet stubbornly. "No way. That's my home up there and you're not going inside without me."

He spared her a single glance. "You're not going one step closer until I make sure it's safe," he said, the growl much more than a hint now. "You feel it, too, I can tell. Don't be stupid, Sian. Stay here."

She lifted her chin. "We're wasting time arguing," she said, turning her back on him and starting for the stairs.

His arm went around her waist, stopping her forward momentum and bringing her hard against his chest. A jolt went through her at the intoxicating feel of his hard muscles pressing against her back. Sian hated herself for even noticing it right now while her nerves were clamoring with the surety of danger.

"You will stay behind me at all times," Diego breathed in her ear. She shivered and hoped he wouldn't notice. He plucked her keys from her suddenly nerveless fingers and picked her apartment key from the jumble unerringly. "Do you understand me, Sian? I have no qualms whatsoever about restraining you in the car."

She didn't even need gut instinct to know he was telling the truth about that. "Fine," she whispered, hating when the word came out breathless. She never sounded like that. "Now get your hands off me. There's no reason for you to touch me."

He laughed softly in her ear. "There's every reason for me to touch you," he murmured, his lips brushing her skin. Before she could think of any reply, he released her, surprising her so much she actually stumbled. He stepped around her and started up the stairs. His long legs took them two at a time and Sian hurried to catch up.

He stopped at the second floor landing abruptly. She ran into his back before she could stop. He reached back without even looking and steadied her as she teetered on the top stair. Sian leaned around him to try and see, ignoring that she had to press against him to do it—or at least, trying to ignore it. Diego was the kind of man who was difficult to ignore.

The sight of her shattered front door went a long way toward clearing her mind. Sian gasped and tried to push past him, fury bursting through her with brutal force. The only personal possessions she had left were in there. She felt violated to her very soul. Diego turned and caught her, restraining her easily when she would have charged inside.

"Let me go!"

He held her hard, backing her two steps down the stairs. "You will not go in there until I make sure whoever did this is gone." The words were spoken softly, but his tone made them a command.

She barely heard him. All she could think of was the one picture she had of her parents, her mother's wedding rings. It was all she had left of a family now gone.

"Sian!" Diego snapped, shaking her a little. "You can't run in there blind!"

Her rage eased a little but Sian still burned with it as she forced herself to stop fighting. He was right, much as she hated to admit it. She had no weapon and no plan. She didn't even know for sure whoever had broken down her door was gone. It was suicide to rush in.

"All right," she forced out, hardly recognizing her own voice as she wrestled herself back under control. "All right, you can let go of me now."

Diego loosened his grip but didn't release her completely. He cupped her cheek and tilted her face up until she met his gaze. The sympathy and understanding she read there stunned her. She never would have thought her captor would show such feeling. In that moment, she wished she could trust his promise that he had nothing to do with Santonyo.

But why else would he hold her prisoner like this?

"I'll make sure it's safe for you," Diego told her softly. "Will you wait for me here, at least until I can bring you some shoes? There's broken glass all over the place in there."

His gentleness disarmed her and she nodded silently. Her feet had been abused enough for one night. Diego gazed down at her for another moment, his fingers warm against her cheek, before nodding back at her. "I won't be long."

Diego left her on the landing and stepped through the shattered door, silently cursing whoever had done this. The impact of Sian's anger and pain still echoed through him and he burned with the desire for blood. No one hurt his mate and lived.

It took only a moment to confirm the apartment was empty. Diego walked carefully through the rooms, his rage building with every step. There wasn't a single piece of furniture left intact. Her couch had been smashed to kindling, her television shattered against the wall, her bookshelves in pieces and the books shredded. Her bed was wrecked. The mattress lay half on the floor, long gashes torn through the pillowtop and stuffing strewn everywhere. Every mirror was shattered, her dresser broken and her clothes torn to shreds. He looked for a pair of shoes for her even though he had no intention of bringing her in to witness this destruction, but even those had not been spared.

Only the paintings on the walls had escaped destruction. Diego looked carefully at them as he walked slowly through her rooms. He didn't need to read the small signature in the corner to know Sian had created them. Her touch still brought a lingering radiance to the canvases. The seascapes were incredibly realistic, almost eerie. It took a moment before he noticed what had been done to them.

In every painting a black figure had been added, scrawled in marker. A body lying on the beach, another tumbling from a cliff, one hanging from a noose from the top of a lighthouse. Every painting had been desecrated by the crude renderings of death.

A soft sound behind him made Diego whirl, fangs and claws out, ready for battle. He reined in his rage quickly when he saw Sian standing in the doorway with her hands pressed to her mouth. He crossed the devastation and took her arms, trying to steer her back outside. "You said you were going to wait for me," he told her, keeping the bite from his voice with difficulty.

The shock in her eyes killed his frustration with her at once. "My God," she breathed, staring in shock at the fractured remains of what had been her home. Her gaze fell on a painting of a sailboat and she paled when she saw what had been added to it. "My God."

Diego scooped her up in his arms, remembering the glass on the floor from the shattered mirrors. "It's time to go, Sian. There's nothing left here," he told her gently.

She pushed at his shoulders, trying to get away. "I have to get my things," she said, her voice no more than a stunned whisper.

"*Querida*, there's nothing left," Diego repeated, pulling her closer and wishing he could soothe her. "Whoever did this destroyed everything. I'll buy you more clothes—"

"No, I don't care about my damn clothes!" she exploded at him. "I had a picture of my parents, my mother's rings…" Her eyes beseeched him. "They can't have taken them!"

He rocked her gently. "All right," he murmured. "All right, *querida*, I'll look for those things. Tell me where they were."

"My bedroom. On the bedside table."

He felt a dangerous surge of anger at the thought of her witnessing what they'd done to her room, the violence unleashed on her bed, and tamped it down. She didn't need to see him in the grip of bloodlust right now. She was frightened enough of him as it was and didn't need anything else added on top of this trauma.

"I'll look," he said, turning toward the door again. "Wait for me in the car, Sian. You have no shoes, your feet would be cut to ribbons in moments in there."

"No," Sian said, and he wasn't surprised. "I want to see what they did. I need to see if there are any clues. They will have left me some clues."

He froze where he stood. "You know who did this, don't you?"

She looked away. "Put me down."

"Not a chance," Diego growled. "Who did this?"

A muscle twitched in her jaw but she remained stubbornly silent. Diego knew she wouldn't tell him until she was good and ready, and he burned with frustration. "Fine, keep it a secret. You're still not going in there."

Sian couldn't argue her way around him, though she tried. In the end Diego deposited her on the landing again and went into her bedroom by himself. She couldn't make herself stop looking at what they'd done to her living room. This had been no robbery, no random act of destruction. Whoever had been here had taken their sweet time. Her gaze kept going back to her paintings, pristine but for the black bodies they'd added, and a shudder worked its way down her spine.

Slowly her shock turned to anger. Santonyo must've done this. He'd left similar calling cards at her other residences, but never with this ferocity. What would it take for him to leave her alone? Her fists clenched and she wished she'd been here when they'd arrived. Up until James had taken it, Sian hadn't been without her gun once since moving in here six months ago, and she knew she wouldn't have hesitated to use it.

Her pulse kicked at the thought of putting a bullet into the man who had tormented her for years. Was that what it would take to finally get some peace? She was tired of running, tired of being hunted.

When Diego emerged from the bedroom a few minutes later, the surge of relief she felt to see him made her angry again, this time at herself. She didn't know this man from Adam. She didn't think he had anything to do with this, but he was still holding her hostage for some strange reasons of his own, and there was no reason at all she should be glad to see him.

"Find anything?" she asked to hide her own turmoil.

He was at her side almost at once and she jumped. She'd never seen anyone move so fast. "I didn't find any photographs," he said. "I'm sorry. If it's in there, they destroyed it."

Sian felt sick. That picture had been the only one she had ever seen of her mother and the last one she possessed of her father. "And the rings?" she forced out through numb lips.

Rather than answering, Diego held out his hand. She looked down and saw her mother's rings there in his palm. Tears of relief blurred her vision. Only when she blinked the moisture away did she notice what had been done to them.

Only when she picked them up did she see the gold bands were twisted out of shape and none of the stones remained in their settings. She clutched the broken rings to her chest and bent her head, not wanting a stranger to witness her tears.

She didn't expect to feel comforted when he put his arms around her. "I'm sorry, *querida*," he murmured, holding her tight. "I can have them repaired for you, but I know it's not the same."

She didn't speak, just stood there in the circle of his arms, trying not to cry. She hated to cry. Only weaklings cried and winners never showed weakness. It was a rule she'd learned in the cradle, but damn it, it felt like her heart had been ripped out.

At last Diego urged her down the stairs again and Sian let him, slipping the mutilated rings into the breast pocket of the shirt and feeling hollow inside. She needed to get away from Diego and run again, but where could she go now? How could any place be safe ever again?

Diego stopped and tilted her face up with a gentle hand until she met his gaze. "You don't have to run anymore," he said softly. "Believe it, Sian. I can keep you safe."

She stared at him, unable to shake the strange certainty that he'd read her mind again. It was insane to even consider it, but how else could he have known what she was thinking? She opened her mouth, not sure what she was going to say, when the sense of danger hit her with such force, every other thought in her mind was swept away.

"Get down!" Sian yelled, grabbing Diego and yanking him to the pavement. His weight drove the breath from her lungs a bare heartbeat before her beloved Mini Cooper exploded. Heat washed over her and something heavy drove into the wall beside her head, but before Sian could even take a breath, Diego leapt to his feet and pulled her swiftly down the alley. "What are you doing?" she gasped, trying her best to keep up with him.

"Getting you out of here. They'll be here soon if they're not already," Diego said. She stumbled and he scooped her into his arms without breaking stride.

Her heart froze at the thought of him getting hurt because of her. "Put me down!" she demanded. Santonyo's thugs wouldn't take another innocent life on her account, no matter what she thought of Diego personally. "Let go of me!"

He didn't even bother replying as he ran with a speed that made her head spin. If she'd thought he moved fast in the apartment it was nothing compared to this. Four blocks later he finally slowed, ducking into a dark doorway with her and pinning her to the wall so they looked like they were making out in the shadows instead of hiding. "Do you feel anything?" he asked, looking down at her urgently and not out of breath at all.

She was suddenly out of breath enough for both of them.

She felt something, all right, and it had nothing to do with any possible pursuit. Her nerves jangled with a purely feminine reaction to being trapped between a cold wall and his hot and completely male body. The adrenaline rush from the danger and his incredible speed morphed into desire in the space of a heartbeat. She couldn't take a breath without pressing more fully against him. Her hands were trapped between them, fingers splayed wide against his chest, and she felt his heart beating beneath her palm. His arms tightened around her and she wished suddenly they weren't pretending.

Belatedly she remembered his question and realized he knew she'd had a premonition. She stared up at him in shock, hardly able to believe his instant acceptance of a gift no one outside her family had ever believed in. She took a deep breath that was scented of him and closed her eyes, trying to block out the distraction he presented and concentrate on what her instincts were telling her.

"No," she whispered at last, opening her eyes again. "I think we're safe."

"Good."

His mouth came down, taking hers with such heat and hunger that she couldn't hold back a moan. He growled and tangled his fingers in her hair, nipping her lower lip until she opened for him. His tongue claimed hers as her arms went around his waist. Heat pooled low in her belly and she felt his arousal pressing against her. He pulled her hard against him as he took her apart piece by piece, each stroke of his tongue sending sparks through her, every nip of his teeth making her shiver. Never had anyone kissed her like this. His mouth was fierce and possessive and he drew a passion from her she'd never suspected she was capable of, and he showed no sign of stopping. He kissed her again and again—long, drugging kisses that stole her breath and her will to resist.

Sian had no idea how much time passed before Diego tore himself away, burying his face in the curve of her shoulder and breathing every bit as hard as she was.

"*Dios, querida,* you make me forget where I am." He breathed against her skin, sending a shiver through her when he nipped the side of her throat with teeth that felt much too sharp.

Sanity returned with a crash. She struggled out of his arms and pushed him away, shaking hard. How could she have let a complete stranger kiss her like that? How could she have reacted so wildly, as if she had no inhibitions at all?

"It was the danger," she said, pushing her hair back from her face and wishing her cheeks didn't feel quite so hot. Wishing her entire body didn't feel quite so hot. "It didn't mean anything. It was just because we almost died, that's all."

Diego stared at her, his broad shoulders blocking her view of the street behind them, his face shadowed, masking his expression. "Is that what you think it was?" he asked, his voice low and vibrating with suppressed emotion. It sent another shiver through her. "You think that was some meaningless reaction to what happened?"

"Yes!" Sian cried, wrapping her arms around herself. She wondered which one of them she was trying to convince. "That's all it was!"

He was silent for a moment and she knew she'd made him angry but she didn't care. "Fine," he snapped at last. He turned his back on her and gazed up and down the street before stepping out of the alcove and raising his arm. Sian stared stupidly at him for a moment, trying to figure out what he was doing, before a taxi stopped in front of him. He glared over his shoulder at her as he yanked open the door. "Coming?"

She wanted to say no, but she wasn't crazy enough to think staying half-dressed and alone downtown in the middle of the night was any better of an idea than going with him. She hurried after him, sliding into the taxi and slamming the door as the driver pulled away from the curb.

Diego gave the driver his address and sat back with his arms crossed, staying as far from Sian as the seat allowed. His fists clenched against the volatile emotions buffeting him. He burned with fury at what had been done to her home, with desire so potent he could hardly contain it, with frustration that she wouldn't tell him who was after her, and yes, with hurt that Sian had so coolly dismissed what had started between them. She was his mate, damn it, and for a few glorious minutes in that dark doorway she'd forgotten her distrust of him and acted like it.

He could have kicked himself for pulling away. It hadn't been the most romantic spot in the world but he knew that if he hadn't stopped kissing her when he had, he would be buried deep inside her right now. Sweet heaven, he ached for her. It wasn't their close call that made him kiss her, no matter what she told herself. He'd had thousands of close calls before this and hadn't fallen on the nearest female like a ravenous beast.

It was *her*. Sian. She'd looked lost, sexy, and vulnerable there in his arms and he'd wanted her so damn bad, he hadn't thought twice about their surroundings or the danger or anything else. All he'd known was he had to kiss her or lose his mind.

And he'd kissed her and promptly lost his mind anyway.

He didn't dare even look at her right now. Desire pounded through him with every heartbeat. He stared blankly out the window, trying to shut out the sound of her breathing and the faint trace of her soft scent in the nicotine-tinged air of the cab. How *dare* she tell him it hadn't meant anything?

When they pulled up in front of his gates, Diego reached for his wallet only to remember it was still in the pocket of the jacket still tied around Sian's waist. She jumped when he reached for her and he scowled. "I'm getting my wallet, not assaulting you," he bit out.

She blushed but didn't say a word as he dug it out of a pocket and handed the driver a credit card. She was out of the car by the time he'd signed the slip and Diego slammed the door behind him after getting out. The gates swung open at his mental command and he brushed past her, heading for the house without a word and angry enough in that moment not to care if she followed him or not.

That anger died when he finally gave in to the urge to glance back a few minutes later and saw Sian limping along the gravel road several yards behind him. He'd forgotten she was still barefoot. "Why didn't you say something?" he demanded, striding to her side and reaching for her.

She batted his hand away. "With you glaring out the window the whole way here like I'd just drowned your favorite pet, why do you think?"

Diego started to scowl at her again and caught himself. No matter how much right he had to be angry, nothing good could come from glaring at her. "All right, truce until we reach the house if you let me carry you," he said, keeping the anger in his voice to a bare minimum with an effort. "You won't get there until morning if you don't get a move on and I'm getting a little tired of healing you." It was a lie, but he was willing to try anything to get her back into his arms at this point.

She crossed her arms and leveled a glare of her own at him. "What makes you think getting hauled around by a caveman is preferable to walking on sharp rocks?"

That was it. Diego scooped her up and threw her over his shoulder, ignoring her outraged shriek of surprise, and set off down the drive. She pounded on his back with her fists, unerringly hitting his kidneys with every blow. "Let me go!"

He ground his teeth. "Don't call me a caveman unless you want me to start acting like one," he growled back at her.

"Look, I'm sorry I wounded your male pride or your libido or whatever, but it doesn't give you the right to—"

Diego resisted the urge to give her rear a good swat. "You think I believe the crap you gave me about that kiss? Wrong, princess. You were blown away whether you want to admit it or not."

"You egotistical—"

He swung her down onto her feet. "I didn't think cavemen could be egotistical. Besides, am I wrong?"

She glared at him but didn't say a word.

It was as good as an admission in his book. Diego smiled, knowing it would infuriate her. "If I'm wrong, prove it," he challenged softly.

Her eyes went wary again. "Prove it how?"

"How do you think?" He stepped closer, invading her space. "Kiss me. There's no danger here, Sian. Prove it was only the brush with death that had you clinging to me like a second skin."

She went scarlet but whether it was from embarrassment or rage was beyond Diego to decipher. "I was not!" she hissed.

He smiled again. "Prove it," he murmured. When she still hesitated he played his ace. "It's all right, Sian, I won't think less of you if you're afraid to kiss me."

It worked. A bare second later, she reached up and dragged him down, kissing him hard. Diego wrapped both arms around her and groaned as she kissed him with all the anger flashing through her. He took it gladly and gave back passion. His lips gentled hers, turning the kiss from an angry meeting of mouths to a slow, heady dance of seduction.

Had he thought there was no danger here? How wrong he'd been. Her taste intoxicated him, every sweep of her tongue against his sending heat spiraling through his body, and it wasn't long before she was every bit as lost in it as he was.

It lasted only moments before she wrenched herself away, stumbling back from him with her fingers pressed to her lips. "That was a dirty trick," she said, glaring at him, but she couldn't hide the bright desire in her eyes.

"Yes," he agreed. "And I'd do it again in a heartbeat."

"Well, I won't fall for it again," she muttered, turning her back on him and starting to walk again.

Diego swept her off her feet and back into his arms again before she'd taken two steps. "Enough wrecking your feet for one night," he told her, his tone brooking no argument.

"Fine, you want to throw your back out, be my guest," she said, surprising him with her easy acquiescence. Diego didn't say another word as he made his way back up the drive, simply enjoying the feel of her in his arms. Being mated to this woman would be incredible if she ever stopped fighting him, he thought in amusement. She did everything with such passion, she made him dizzy. He hardly dared to imagine what it would be like to make love to her.

He wasn't very successful at not imagining, though, and by the time they reached the house his jeans were feeling decidedly tight. He glanced down at her to see if she'd noticed and found to his complete surprise she'd fallen asleep. Something inside him melted at the sight of her face relaxed in slumber, her formidable defenses down.

On the heels of that thought came the familiar fear. What if he failed her, too? He knew she thought she was invincible, a fearsome fighter, but he'd overpowered her easily. Another vampire could do the same. Sian didn't believe the dangers he'd tried to warn her about and he knew she wouldn't do what he said and stay where he could keep her safe.

It wasn't that he thought a human had no chance against a vampire. He'd taught James how to fight practically from the cradle, teaching him the weaknesses of vampires and how to kill them. He had total confidence in his Steward's ability to defend himself should an Outcast attack him. Sian had no idea what she was facing.

Damn it, he didn't want another mortal to protect!

James opened the front door before Diego could reach for the handle, jolting him from his thoughts. "Why are you walking, Diego? Didn't you leave in a car?"

"Shh," he said, glancing back down to make sure Sian hadn't woken. "The car's toast, along with everything else she had. It's a long story and I'll tell you later." He brushed past his Steward and made his way up the stairs, heading for his bedroom.

"Yeah, but why were you walking?" James persisted. "Seems to me you know some faster ways to get around, and your ribs can't be fully healed yet."

Diego nudged open the bedroom door with his foot and gently lowered Sian to the bed. He hadn't thought about his ribs once that night, his frustration with Sian so intense that the ache of his ribs had completely slipped his mind. He covered Sian with the comforter and ushered James out before answering. "She doesn't believe in vampires."

James gaped at him for a moment before laughing. "Oh, man, this is priceless. You'd rather spend half the night walking around than show the woman you're supposed to spend the rest of your immortal life with that you're a vampire? I mean, it's a sweet thought and all, but don't you think she's going to figure it out eventually anyway?"

Diego sighed. "You'll forgive me if I don't find the humor in this particular situation," he said dryly. "Look, I need to go out for a while. Keep an eye on her, will you? Try not to let her jump out the window this time if you can possibly help it."

James scowled at him, clearly not thrilled with the reminder of how she'd escaped him before, and turned to go downstairs. "When I took this job, I never agreed to be a babysitter," he grumbled as he left.

Diego ignored him and went back into the bedroom, deliberately not looking at Sian sleeping soundly in his bed before going out the window, taking the form of the hawk once more. The woman was far too tempting, even asleep, and if he didn't feed soon his control would be nothing more than a memory.

Things between them were precarious enough as it was. He didn't need this craving for her blood complicating them further.

Chapter Five

Diego fluttered through the open window, transforming back into his human form before his feet silently touched the carpet. He'd fed well in the hopes that hunger had compounded his desire for Sian. Now that it was sated he should be able to talk to her without this overwhelming need to pull her into his arms and kiss her senseless.

As soon as his gaze fell on her, though, he knew it was a futile hope. She still slept, one arm thrown back over her head in a way that made her breasts press temptingly against the thin material of his shirt. One leg had escaped from beneath the covers, bare all the way to mid-thigh. His mouth went dry at the sight of her. Sweet heaven, what he wouldn't give to strip off his own clothes, slide into the bed beside her and wake her with slow kisses…

Diego cut the thought off with a sharp shake of his head. Bondmate or not, he had no business fantasizing about her like this. It only made him crazy and didn't help anything. Still, he couldn't stop looking at her, beautiful in his bed, soft and trusting in sleep, her ferocity hidden. Fragile compared to him.

So mortal.

He walked silently to the edge of the bed and sat beside her, unable to stop himself from reaching out and smoothing her hair back from her face. His mind knew she was neither soft nor fragile and she'd happily prove to anyone she had no need of protection. All he had to do was remember how she'd fought him to know that.

His heart, his fears, knew no such thing.

How could he convince her to let him protect her? He hadn't been able to save his Clan when the hunters had come. Guilt ignored the fact that he'd been only a boy and tormented him for his failure just the same. He'd been too weak, too late, and it was by the grace of a God he wasn't sure he believed in that he and Anton survived.

A century ago, Anton had needed him and Diego had failed him, too. This time he had no excuse of youth or weakness. He simply hadn't been there. Eli's intervention had ensured Diego couldn't even claim the small satisfaction of revenge for his brother's death.

He couldn't fail Sian.

The memory of the destruction of her apartment made him want to howl with rage. Someone was after his mate and she wouldn't tell him who it was. Didn't trust him enough to tell him why. He touched her cheek, wishing he could read more than her surface thoughts and find the answers for himself, but even in sleep her mental barriers didn't weaken.

As soon as he hit the psychic wall, he hated himself for trying to take something she didn't want to give. How could she trust him when he did something like this? Frustration and anger swirled together, a volatile mixture he couldn't hope to contain for long.

Sian sighed and turned her face toward him, pressing her cheek against his palm.

The gesture cooled his anger as nothing else could. His thumb caressed her full lower lip before he made himself pull away. The memory of her gorgeous mouth on his was enough to send hot blood rushing through his every nerve, but he couldn't let himself give in to desire. Not yet, not now, not while she still thought he was out to hurt her.

He had to woo her first, and he was a hundred years out of practice and on edge.

It seemed a monumental task. He really should move her to one of the other bedrooms until he found a way to do it, Diego thought with a sigh. She looked far too tempting there in his bed. But something inside him, something primal and completely unreasoning, demanded he keep her right where she was.

My mate.

My bed.

He didn't quite dare. It was the height of foolishness to keep her here. His emotions were already in an uproar, his body clamoring for a taste of her. Diego tore his eyes away from her lush mouth, her lips slightly parted in sleep, and caught sight of the tiny scratches marring the smooth skin of her exposed leg.

He'd forgotten to heal her before he left.

His fingertips touched her knee before he could stop himself. He could heal her without touching her, but it was much easier with the physical contact.

That's a lie and you know it, a little voice snorted derisively in his mind. The voice of reason, he assumed. *You're looking for an excuse to touch her and anything will do, aren't you?*

So what if I am? Diego thought back, then shut the little voice down before it started taunting him again. He slid his fingertips down her calf, the scratches disappearing as he went, before wrapping his fingers gently around her ankle. He sensed she'd twisted it at some point, probably during their mad dash down the alley, and hadn't even told him. He healed it with a caress and glanced at her foot.

The sole was covered in little cuts and bruises. Diego covered it with his palm and erased them, mourning the chips in her peach nail polish. The brief thought of repainting them for her flashed through his mind and was gone. When he was done with her sole, he gently brushed aside the comforter and exposed her other leg, repeating the process for it. One particularly deep scratch on her calf tempted him and he bent closer, running his tongue over it and hardening at the taste of her skin.

Finally he made himself pull away and draw the blankets back over her, trying to ignore the heat coursing through his veins. Good Lord, she was tempting, and his resistance to temptation was apparently at an all-time low. He had to get her out of here before he did something unforgivable. Trying to take her thoughts was bad enough. If he had any sense at all, he'd move her to another room and chain her down if that was what it took to keep her safe, even if she'd hate him for it. Diego stood and stretched before glancing back down at her, trying to remember if the bed in the guest bedroom across the hall from his was made up.

My mate, my bed. The instinct pounded in his brain, too insistent to ignore.

Diego bit back a groan. He definitely should not do this. Keeping her here was the height of folly. If he'd been afraid of what she would think if she'd woken alone and handcuffed to a strange bed, why would he even consider letting her wake up wrapped in his arms?

In the end, instinct won out over good sense. Diego kicked off his boots and dropped his shirt on the floor, keeping the jeans on despite his body's protests, before sliding into bed beside her and cautiously reaching for her.

Sian sighed in her sleep when his hand touched her and stunned him by rolling into his embrace. Diego hardly dared to breathe, praying she wouldn't wake up even as a wild, wicked part of him longed to wake her himself. She shifted closer, resting her head on his shoulder, and murmured something unintelligible before relaxing in his arms.

Diego stroked her hair and closed his eyes, trying to ignore the tight confinement of his jeans, and prayed for sleep. If only she would trust him like this when she was awake.

He finally drifted off as the sky lightened with the dawn. His last thought was a fervent hope she wouldn't awaken before sunset.

☾ ☾ ☾

Sian floated gently back to consciousness, fighting it every step of the way. She couldn't remember the last time she'd slept so well, warm and perfectly comfortable and steeped in a feeling of complete peace and safety she hadn't felt since childhood.

But wakefulness was winning the fight and she sighed, treating herself to a long, slow stretch. She froze when she identified the heavy warmth around her waist as a very muscular arm and her eyes flew open.

Diego's face filled her vision.

Instantly fully awake, she drew in a breath to demand he release her when she belatedly realized he was still deeply asleep. He hadn't even twitched when she'd woken and those hypnotic green eyes were closed. She stared, stunned at how peaceful he looked in sleep, and she imagined this was how he'd looked as a little boy. Her eyes traveled slowly down to find him bare-chested again and her breath caught. Dear Lord, but the man had a gorgeous body, and right now he was pressed close enough for her to appreciate every inch of it.

The roughness of denim whispered over her legs as Sian carefully disentangled herself from his embrace. Relief mixed with a strange disappointment at discovering he'd kept his jeans on. She was embarrassed that her arms had been around him, too—she'd been holding him close in her sleep. She couldn't believe it. She'd never been a snuggler in her life, but she'd just had the most restful, peaceful sleep of her life while draped all over a man who was practically a stranger to her.

She eased away from him, watching his face carefully the entire time and praying he wouldn't wake up. Sian grabbed a pillow and shoved it beneath his arm as she slipped out from under it, not expecting it to fool him if he reached out to search for her but hoping nonetheless. It apparently worked, though, because he still didn't move a muscle. Sian breathed a silent sigh of relief and tiptoed toward the door.

Only when she was out in the hall and walking normally did Sian notice that her feet, which had been aching miserably last night, no longer hurt at all. She leaned against the wall and lifted her foot to look at the sole. It was pristine, completely unmarked, but she knew for a fact it had been scratched up and bruised last night. Her sprained ankle didn't give even a twinge when she put her weight on it. She remembered how Diego had healed the burns on her palms and shivered. It was impossible for him to heal her like that—wasn't it?

What kind of man had the power to heal with a breath?

Pushing those disturbing thoughts out of her mind, Sian silently tiptoed down the stairs, but she froze when she saw the big blond man who'd tried to keep her from leaving the night before waiting at the bottom.

He looked up at her and sighed. "Come on down, I'm not going to do anything to you," he said, crossing his arms and looking greatly put-upon. "Diego would have my head if I even tried to touch you. I was about to make something to eat anyway."

Sian blinked at him. "Diego told you not to touch me?"

He gave a snort that might have been laughter and turned toward another doorway. "He doesn't need to tell me," he said, and when she followed him she found he'd led her into an enormous kitchen. "You're his bondmate. Any man who touches you is taking his life in his hands."

Sian stopped in the doorway, hesitant to get within reach of this man even though her gut instincts were still insisting he wasn't a threat. "You're not going to start with this mate thing, too, are you?" she asked wearily. "I've had about all I can stand of that nonsense."

He snorted again and took down a pan from the rack hanging from the ceiling. "Well, brace yourself, because I can guarantee it's not going away." He put the pan on the stove and turned to look at her again. "Look, you don't have to stand there looking at me like I'm a psycho killer," he said. "I work for Diego, so technically I guess I now work for you too, unless you try to hit me again. I'm James, Diego's Steward. How do you like your eggs? Please say scrambled because that's all I can make."

Sian edged into the room and sat down on the nearest barstool at the large center island. "What's a Steward?"

James pulled out a carton of eggs and started cracking them into a bowl. "A vampire's mortal servant and general gofer," he replied. He shot her a glance when she made a choked sound. "Oh, right, I forgot. Diego said you don't believe in vampires." The thought seemed to amuse him greatly.

"Of course I don't believe in vampires," Sian retorted automatically, trying to forget the nightmare she'd had of Diego with cat-like eyes and fangs and the way he'd healed her palms and feet. Something deep inside her tried to speak up with an opinion on the subject and she persistently ignored it. "I like a good vampire movie as much as the next person, but they're not real."

Oh yeah? the little inner voice murmured.

Shut up, she told it sternly. *I refuse to be delusional before breakfast.*

James laughed as he beat the eggs with a fork. "You want proof? Go wake Diego up," he said, turning on the fire under the pan. "On second thought, don't. Vampires really don't like getting woken up during the day and I'm sure he'd be very ticked if he found out I sent you up there to bother him."

Sian rolled her eyes. Apparently James had no problems being delusional on an empty stomach. "How long have you worked for Diego?" she asked, determined to turn the subject to something saner. It was hard to picture this man in any kind of menial role. At six feet tall and with broad shoulders and muscles to spare, he looked like he was no one's servant but his own.

"Officially, a little over five years now," he said as he sprinkled shredded cheese into the pan. Sian's stomach rumbled at the aroma coming from the stove. "But I've known him all my life. My father worked for him before me, and my grandfather too, and on down the line for several hundred years. You could say Diego's a family tradition—or a particularly lively heirloom." He glanced back at her. "If you're feeling useful, there's bread over there for toast."

She found the bread and the toaster and popped a couple of slices in. "Mmm hmm. You mean everyone in your family has suffered from this mental illness where you think you work for a vampire?"

James laughed again. "I'm not going to try to convince you, if that's what you're after," he said, turning off the burner and dumping the eggs onto a couple of plates. "I'll leave it for Diego. You'll see for yourself soon enough, I'm sure." He put her plate on the island and handed her a fork before snagging the first slices of toast as they popped up.

"Help yourself," Sian said sarcastically as she put some more bread in.

"Thanks, I will," James grinned. He pulled down two glasses and went to the fridge, but glanced back at her before opening it. "Um, if you want to keep living in your vampire-free fantasy world, I'd suggest you stay out of here."

Sian raised an eyebrow at him. "What, is it the secret entrance to his coffin or something?"

James shook his head and opened the refrigerator a crack, blocking her view inside with his body as he withdrew a carafe of orange juice. His shoulders were broad enough she didn't have a chance to peek past him. Why in the world did she have to get stuck with two lunatics who were this *massive?*

"Trust me on this one," he said, closing the door with his hip. She rolled her eyes and refused to question him further.

She accepted the juice from him and started in on her eggs in silence. From the first bite hunger overrode every other concern and she remembered belatedly it had been over twenty-four hours since the last time she'd eaten. James watched her in silence as she cleaned her plate in minutes. "Didn't he feed you something last night?" he asked as she took a big bite of her toast.

"There wasn't much of an opportunity for food," Sian admitted between bites.

James went back to the stove without another word and cracked a couple more eggs into the pan, leaving his own half-eaten breakfast on the counter as he made her a second helping. When he scooped them onto her plate, she met his eyes for the first time. "Thanks," she said.

He shrugged and went back to his own breakfast. "I suppose there wasn't time to get you anything else to wear, either?"

Sian tugged self-consciously at the hem of Diego's shirt. She was feeling decidedly grungy in it and wished James hadn't reminded her of what had happened to all the rest of her clothes. "No," she said, pushing her plate away, her appetite suddenly gone at the memory of those black figures scrawled on her paintings.

James pushed it right back at her. "Eat and don't think so much," he said and Sian glanced up at him, wondering if he had his boss's eerie ability to pick up her thoughts. "When you finish tell me your sizes and I'll go get you something to wear until Diego can take you shopping himself." He grinned at her look of surprise. "All part of the job, my lady. If you have a need, I take care of it. It's what I'm paid for."

She took another bite and chewed automatically, unsure what to think of this man. He had to be nuts if he thought Diego was really a vampire, but apart from that he seemed like a decent guy. Still, she was hesitant to take anything about this situation at face value. "What if I need to get out of here?"

His grin faded. "Please don't put me in that position," he said, suddenly serious. "Diego asked me to keep you here but if I lay a hand on you to restrain you he'll probably tear it off. If I let you leave I don't even want to think about what he'll do. Let me get you some clothes and you can talk about it with him when he wakes up, okay? Please?"

He was telling the truth, or at least he thought he was. Sian could catch a lie better than any lie detector and James honestly thought Diego would be furious with him if she left. She bit her lip and pushed what was left of her eggs around on her plate. Why she should care what happened to this man was beyond her, but she didn't feel right about making trouble for him. So far he hadn't done anything to her except make some killer eggs.

Apart from keeping her here against her will, that was.

Sian sighed. Who was she kidding? She had no clothes, no car, no house and no destination. It would be stupid to run right now. If Diego truly wasn't affiliated with Santonyo, it would take her enemy at least a little longer to track down where she'd gone. She would have to leave eventually, there was no doubt about it, but she had at least a little time to prepare before she did.

She would rather face Santonyo's wrath alone than bring a murderer down on Diego and James. No matter that they'd kidnapped her and were holding her for some bizarre reason of their own, they didn't deserve to die for it.

"All right, I won't go anywhere," she told James at last, and he relaxed visibly. *Yet,* she added silently.

"Thanks," he said. "Now, tell me what you need and what size to get it in and I'll go pick up something for you to wear."

Sian swallowed her embarrassment at the thought of a stranger picking out clothes for her and gave him her sizes. James left almost as soon as she was done speaking and she gathered up the dishes. When they were done she looked around the kitchen, wondering what she was going to do with herself until James got back.

She dried her hands on the dish towel and bit her lip. She knew exactly what she should do. James was gone and Diego was sleeping like the dead upstairs. There would never be a better opportunity to snoop around.

But something in her hesitated as she left the kitchen and glanced around. Her conscience didn't care that Diego was holding her hostage and James refused to help her leave, she still felt awkward as she stepped into the den and caught sight of an enormous desk in the corner. Why did it feel wrong to snoop on Diego?

She pushed the feeling away resolutely and turned on the computer. The login page came up and she hit enter out of reflex, used to her own personal computer which she'd never bothered to set up with a password. The screen briefly went blank and she swore softly under her breath, hoping she hadn't locked up the system.

To her complete shock the screen came back up, Windows booting almost instantly. She stared at the screen, too surprised for words. Diego didn't even have a password on his computer?

This certainly didn't fit his super bad-guy image.

She glanced over her shoulder at the door, wishing she had her watch back so she could keep track of how long James had been gone. The curtains in here were heavy and she couldn't tell if it was day or night outside. If Diego was really into this vampire fantasy, he probably wouldn't come downstairs until after the sun was down, but she didn't dare rely on that assumption too much. He might be crazy, but Diego had done nothing to indicate he was stupid.

Vampire fetish or not, he would probably be up and looking for her as soon as he realized she'd left the bedroom.

Sian opened up his word processing program, not sure what she was looking for but not having any better ideas of where to start. There wasn't much in there, just a few files that looked like personal letters. Sian opened the first one and started to read, turning the monitor to the side so she could glance between it and the doorway.

She was hardly aware of time passing and gasped when a hand fell on her shoulder. She jumped and spun around in the chair to find Diego leaning over her. He reached past her and eased the mouse from under her hand.

"There's nothing earth-shattering in there," Diego said mildly, closing the window and opening the Internet connection. He clicked on his favorites file and selected a webpage. "There," he said, stepping back again as it loaded. "This might be more along the lines of what you're looking for." And to her utter shock, he turned and walked back out of the den without another word.

Sian gaped after him for a long moment, too stunned for words. He'd caught her red-handed but not only hadn't been upset, he'd actually guided her to what she was looking for? It was too bizarre. She finally made herself look back at the screen and blinked at it for a long moment.

Diego's face stared back at her from the screen, the image as dark and forbidding as he was in person, only without the goatee.

It was some kind of genealogy site, she discerned after a moment, but unlike any she'd ever seen before. There were ancient-looking engravings of a castle, several different ones showing it gradually expanding from a simple stone keep to an impressive fortress. Next to the most elaborate one was a sepia-toned photo of an ancient-looking ruin. From the silhouette of the mountains behind it Sian knew she was looking at what remained of the once-proud castle. She scrolled down and the words "House of Leonides" appeared at the bottom of the page. She clicked them and a new page loaded almost instantly.

This time there were no photographs. Beside most names were exquisite paintings, each looking more ancient than the last. Her eyes traveled over the screen, scrutinizing the names and faces. Paintings and engravings were beside most of the names with a few exceptions. One had a photograph of a marble bust, weathered by time. Another showed a statue in a remarkable state of preservation. Several of the most ancient names had no image at all beside them.

Diego was there too, right at the very bottom of the family tree. There was a painting beside his name as well, a worn oval cameo of a boy of eight or nine. His name was listed "Diego Leonides, b. 997." Beside him was a cameo of another boy, his face a few years older—a boy on the threshold of manhood. His name was listed as "Anton Leonides, b. 992, d. 1899."

She stared. Of course it was hard to tell the authenticity of anything on a computer screen, but the paintings were amazing. The boy in the cameo beside Diego's name looked so much like him Sian couldn't imagine it being a portrait of anyone else. Even in the boyishly innocent face those green eyes were compelling, seeming to stare straight at her with a knowledge far beyond his years.

The cameo of Anton was just as impressive. The resemblance to Diego was incredible—the same straight nose, the same stubborn chin, the exact same eyes. She stared at the date of death listed and did a quick mental calculation.

If this was to be believed, Anton had been 907 when he died.

It was insane. Sian scanned the page again, noting similar ages for almost every name listed there. Yasina Gonzalo de Leonides, listed as Diego's mother, had died a few months shy of seven hundred years old. Claudio, his father, had apparently made it to the middle of his eighth century. The date shown for both their deaths was 1215. In fact, quite a few of the names had 1215 listed as the date of death and she absently wondered if a plague or something had hit around then before shaking her head sharply. Why would a plague wipe out someone who'd already lived a few hundred years? She kept looking, doing the math in her head, finding most names on the page averaging in the five- to eight-hundred year mark in age. She shook her head, bemused.

Diego's name was the only one without a date of death beside it. If this website was to be believed Diego had passed his thousandth birthday a few years ago, making him the oldest member of a family that gave new meaning to the word longevity.

"It wasn't a plague."

Sian jumped when Diego set a cup of coffee at her elbow, turning to stare up at him accusingly to hide how much she was shaken by the website. "This is a very well put-together prank," she said, crossing her arms over her chest and ignoring both the coffee he'd brought and the eerie way he seemed to know what she was thinking. "I'm surprised I don't see Methuselah on here. Isn't he your great-uncle or something?"

Diego's eyes lit with warm amusement. "I don't think he's one of my relations," he said. "Maybe you should check with Eli, though. I think he might *be* Methuselah."

"Surely you don't expect anyone to believe you're really a vampire. If you were, why would you post your family tree on the net for all to see?"

"Maybe because I'm proud of my heritage, or perhaps so any lost members of my family might find it and contact me?" Diego replied, leaning on the edge of the desk. "It's hard to be the last of your clan, Sian. I was a prince of Spain, though such titles are outdated now, and anyone of the Panther Clan who lived would naturally search for me, the Clan patriarch. I don't care who believes it or who thinks it's a joke—except for you, of course."

She was momentarily too taken aback to even laugh. "A prince?" she finally choked out. "Oh, this gets better and better. Tell me, Diego, do you honestly believe this fantasy?"

He didn't get upset with her as she'd expected him to. Instead he smiled and ran a gentle hand over her hair. "Not only do I believe it," he said, "I won't rest until you believe it, too." And he took her hand and dropped something into her palm.

Sian watched him walk out, almost mesmerized by the sexy way he moved, before looking at what he'd given her.

It was the cameo of himself as a boy.

Chapter Six

James returned an hour later, carrying three large shopping bags. He grinned at Diego when he passed him in the kitchen. "I take it she didn't run off," he said, raising an eyebrow as Diego absently drummed his fingers on the kitchen table.

Diego shook his head, glancing at the bags. "Did you buy the entire store?" he asked with only a trace of his old smile.

James shrugged. "I just did what any woman I know would've done and bought everything they had in her size. I assumed you'd tell me to spare no expense." He gave an exaggerated wink. "Damn shame to cover her up, though."

Diego sighed, not rising to the bait. "You'd better go give it to her," he said, resuming his finger-drumming and staring out the window again. "I think she'd rather go naked than take anything from me."

"Well then, by all means, you take this," James laughed, holding out the bags.

Diego only shook his head. "That's all I need, more frustration."

James's smile faded. "This is really getting to you, isn't it?"

Diego sighed. "Can you think of any reason why it shouldn't?" he asked, rubbing his eyes. "I've been ducking the Council's insistence that I take a bondmate since before your great-grandfather was born, and now I've not only lost the fight, I'm stuck with a woman not of my choosing who apparently has someone trying to kill her and doesn't even believe vampires are real. You might say it hasn't been the best few days."

James hesitated in the doorway. He'd only been officially working for Diego for five years but he'd known him all his life and had never seen anything get the vampire down. "There's bound to be an adjustment period," James said, knowing it sounded lame but unable to think of anything better to say.

Diego shrugged, still staring out the window. "Go give her the clothes," he said. "She's in the den. I'll be along in a while."

James left him in the kitchen, frowning. He didn't like to see Diego like this. He came from a long line of Stewards and he knew his duties practically from the cradle. Chief among them was keeping his vampire's spirits up.

Diego was already older than most vampires. There were older vampires in the League, but not many. Only Eli was truly ancient and he seemed to be immune to the cares that eventually wore down even the most resilient of their kind. Life eternal could wear on the spirit, leaving scars that would never show on the surface.

Sian looked up when he came in and her eyebrows raised at the sight of the bags. "You didn't have to get me all this," she said, breaking him from his dark thoughts. "A pair of jeans and a T-shirt would have been completely sufficient."

He shrugged. "Never let it be said Diego doesn't take care of his own," he said. "Completely sufficient is completely unacceptable when it comes to you."

She looked away as if unable to hold his gaze. "Look, I don't know what he's told you, but there's nothing going on between me and Diego."

He snorted. He knew it was rude, but honestly, if Sian thought she could protest her way out of this she was insane. "You keep living in that dream world," he said, turning to walk out. "Let me know how it works out for you."

"You know I'm not going to stay here."

Her words stopped him at the door. James turned and gave her a hard look, remembering Diego's slumped shoulders as he'd sat at the table. "You do what you think you have to do," he said, his tone cold, "but don't think for one second Diego's just going to walk away and forget about you. The two of you are bound now, whether you like it or not. You're in some kind of trouble and there's no way in hell he'll leave you to face it on your own. Maybe if you knew anything about honor you'd understand."

She stood, angry now too. "And what if I bring that trouble here?" she challenged, but he saw the sudden fear behind her eyes. "You don't know what's going on, James, and I don't expect you to understand. Diego may be a nice guy apart from his vampire delusions, but I'm not about to endanger him or anyone else by sticking around."

James laughed. "Lady, whatever trouble tries to follow you here will have to go through him first," he said. "It's no easy task whether you want to believe he's a vampire or not. But like I said, you do what you think you have to do. You'll see." He grabbed the bags and set off through the door.

"Where are you going with my clothes?" Sian protested.

"Putting them in your room," James said over his shoulder.

He heard her push the desk chair back and hurry after him. "I don't know what you're talking about. You people haven't given me a room!"

He laughed as he went up the stairs with Sian right on his heels. "If you don't know which room I'm talking about you're thicker than I thought, and babe, I thought you were pretty damn thick already."

He had to be kidding. Sian followed him up the stairs, trying to catch up and snatch one of the bags out of his hands, but James was fast. Her gasp of outrage when she saw him push open Diego's bedroom door made him laugh again. She followed him inside, hands planted on her hips. James dumped the bags on the bed and turned to leave but she blocked the door. "I am not staying in his bedroom!" she hissed.

He merely shrugged, stepping past her and heading out the door. "This one isn't open to debate, my lady."

Sian ground her teeth and drew in a breath for a scathing put-down but James closed the door behind him, cutting her off. She glared for a moment, wishing she'd hit him harder back when she'd escaped the first time.

Finally she glanced back at the bags and sighed. Regardless of how little she wanted to be stuck in Diego's room, she was very grateful at the prospect of putting on some real clothes at last. She looked at the open door to the bathroom and literally ached for a shower.

She up-ended the bags on the bed and searched through the pile of clothes, snagging a button-up blouse in her favorite shade of blue and digging around in search of some jeans. She frowned, not finding anything but skirts. Was James one of those old-fashioned guys who thought women in pants were unfeminine? Somehow it didn't fit what she knew of it, but after few minutes of searching, she gave up and pulled out a khaki skirt. It wasn't anything she would've bought for herself but at this point fashion was the least of her concerns. All she wanted was to be clean.

Sian tossed her new clothes on the counter and locked the bathroom door behind her. She carefully set her mother's twisted rings on the counter before she dropped Diego's shirt on the floor and peeled off her bra and panties, hesitating only a moment before turning to the sink and hand-washing them with a squirt of shampoo. It wasn't exactly the recommended detergent for silk but there was no way she could stand to wear them a minute longer without washing them. Besides, she'd given James all her sizes. Surely he'd gotten her something decent to wear while these dried. She hung the lingerie off the towel rack and turned on the shower, cranking the hot faucet to maximum.

She lingered under the spray, lathering her hair twice and trying not to notice how the sandalwood scent of the shampoo reminded her of Diego. The crisp scent of his soap reminded her of waking up in his arms and she breathed deeply, remembering. Annoyed at herself for it, Sian rinsed briskly and turned off the water, already feeling exponentially better.

She wrapped one thick towel around her body and another turban-style around her hair before reaching nervously for the doorknob. She hadn't thought to grab a bra or panties out of the mess on the bed before coming in here, so desperate had she been for a shower, and she hesitated to walk out wearing nothing but a towel.

A quick peek confirmed the room was just as she'd left it. Sian sighed in relief and stepped out an instant before the bedroom door opened and she came face-to-face with Diego.

They both froze. Diego's gaze went slowly over her, sending a blush over her entire body. His eyes darkened as he took a slow, deep breath that drew her gaze to his still-bare chest. The black panther on his biceps jumped as he clenched his fists. She couldn't stop herself from following the tapering line of the dark hairs sprinkled over his tense muscles down to the waistband of those jeans. Unbidden came the image of following the same path with her hands, her lips. Sian clutched the towel between her breasts, attempting to convince herself her own pulse hadn't just kicked into high gear. She tried desperately to make her feet move or think of anything to say.

Diego finally closed his eyes and turned his back, bracing a hand against the doorframe. "I came to see if there was anything you needed," he said in a low tone that skittered along her nerves like liquid heat.

Sian swallowed with an audible click. Turning around might have been the gentlemanly thing to do, but the view of Diego from behind was every bit as distracting as it had been from the front. His broad shoulders rippled with muscle when he released the doorframe and jammed his hands into his pockets. Those shoulders tapered down to a narrow waist and lean hips, his tight rear now even more defined because shoving his hands in his pockets had drawn his jeans almost skin-tight. She was suddenly hyperaware of the huge bed dominating the room.

He half turned his head, not looking back at her but giving her a glimpse of a profile that could make an angel weep with jealousy. "Well, do you have what you need?" he asked, and for a moment she couldn't think of any answer that didn't involve him and his enormous bed.

She tore her eyes away and tried desperately to find her voice. "Um, I think so," she mumbled, finally remembering her forgotten modesty, and hurried back into the bathroom. The sight of her lingerie hanging from the towel rack made her blush again and she quickly adjusted the towel on the rod above them, hiding them from view. "I'm fine, thanks for asking."

She heard the bedroom door close after a moment and dared another peek out, her heart still pounding. The room was empty again. Ignoring the strange feeling in her chest that felt almost like disappointment, Sian went to the bed and started going through the clothes again, this time trying to arrange them into some sort of order so she could see what she had.

James had assembled a decent collection for her. She had five or six blouses, most a clingy sort of material she rarely bought, and several skirts in different colors. There were several pairs of shoes ranging from comfortable looking flats to a pair of three inch spike heels that made her wince just to look at them. She found a package of socks, a short lavender satin nightgown and a matching robe, a new hairbrush and toothbrush and assorted toiletries.

She bit her lip, frowning. There was no lingerie.

Finally she spotted a smaller bag that had apparently fallen to the floor when she'd dumped everything out. She picked it up and tipped it onto the bed beside her now-neat stacks of clothes.

Her jaw dropped. Out came three bras, each flimsier and sexier than the last, and each with its own matching thong. Sian gaped, utterly taken aback as she stared at the altogether too-small heap of lace. "Good Lord," she whispered, lifting one bra by the strap and checking the tag. No way would this tiny scrap cover her. James had to have picked the wrong size.

At the thought, her mouth shut with a snap and she blushed all over again. She didn't even want to imagine a stranger, a strange *man* at that, choosing such sexy things for her. How dare he? Her hands shaking with anger, she chose the most modest of them—a fire-engine red bra that barely covered her nipples while still managing to make her cleavage look deep enough to drown in—and put it on with sharp jerks before pulling the blue blouse she'd grabbed earlier on over it. She lifted the matching thong and looked at it for a moment before throwing it back down.

She hated thongs. She'd rather go bare than walk around with a string up her butt. There was no way in hell she was wearing that thing.

She pulled on the khaki skirt, shivering as the material slid over her bare skin. The thought of Diego came unbidden and she shoved it away, even angrier. Had he put James up to this? She shoved her feet into a pair of flats and turned toward the door, ready to storm downstairs and go to war.

One glance in the mirror made her hesitate. The blouse, which looked modest in her hand, was anything but modest when on. Combined with the cleavage-enhancing bra, Sian's breasts looked ready to tumble out with every breath she took and the top button seemed in serious danger of bursting free. Her golden hair was still damp from the shower and fell around her shoulders in chaotic waves. The skirt rode low on her hips, exposing a sliver of skin at her waist and clinging in a way that made every move look like a come-on.

She'd never looked sexier in her life, and it made her furious.

Well, there was nothing in the pile that was any better. She'd already chosen what she thought were the most modest clothes in there. Sian squared her shoulders and jerked the door open, hoping she found James before she saw Diego.

☾ ☾ ☾

Diego hardly paid any attention to where he was going as he went back downstairs, his mind filled with the memory of Sian standing in his bedroom wearing a completely inadequate towel over a lot of wet, bare skin. He'd had to turn away before she saw his eyes change and his fangs come out with the hot surge of lust. Seeing her like that had awoken the wild, untamed side of his nature and he still fought to contain it again.

It didn't want to be contained, it wanted Sian. The woman was built like a goddess. Diego's mouth went dry as he wondered if she was still as he'd left her—short towel skimming over lush curves, tiny droplets of moisture still clinging to her skin, her legs bare all the way past mid-thigh. He swallowed hard, biting back a groan. Those legs had been bare a lot further up than that. He'd never been more jealous of anything in his life than he'd been of that lucky towel.

The temptation to turn around and snatch it away from her damp body still pounded through his brain.

Diego found himself in the den again with no idea whatsoever how he'd come to be there. He threw himself down on the couch and rubbed his eyes as though he could wipe Sian's too-tempting memory from them.

"So, how's married life treating you?"

Diego cursed and spun around, back on his feet in an instant. Eli lounged behind his desk, his feet propped up on the mahogany surface and a grin on his face.

"Have you ever heard of knocking?" Diego growled, striding over and reaching out to knock the other vampire's feet off the desk. "And get your damn feet off my desk. That's an antique, not that you care."

Eli grinned and dropped his boots to the floor before Diego touched him. "I'm an antique, too. Maybe I should worry about it scuffing me."

"I'm more than tempted to scuff you myself. What do you want?"

Eli didn't seem phased in the least by Diego's bad mood. "Cranky, aren't you? I expected you to be happily creating little Leonides heirs right now—unless you've already got one on the way. It's been, what, three nights now? More than enough time."

Diego scowled. "Two, and I don't perform on command for you, Eli." He instantly wished he hadn't risen to the bait when Eli laughed.

"Never thought I'd see the day when your legendary charm failed," he commented through an infuriating grin. "You were quite the ladies' man once, Diego. Surely your self-imposed avoidance of women this last century hasn't made you lose your touch completely."

Diego's frustration edged higher and he held onto his temper with both hands. "Is there a reason you're here or have you come to torment me some more?"

Eli stood with the lazy grace of a natural predator. "I thought you might like to know who trashed your mate's apartment," he said with studied casualness. He reached into the pocket of his leather jacket and tossed something to Diego.

He caught it out of reflex. It was an unmarked CD. He held it up and looked questioningly at Eli. "What's this?"

"All the help I'm giving you," Eli replied, already heading for the door. "Don't bother showing me out. I know the way."

Diego made a face at his back as he left. He knew it was childish but sometimes Eli absolutely infuriated him. There was no one he'd rather have at his back in a fight, but right now he was more than tempted to send Eli on his way with a good, swift kick in the rear.

Not that Eli would let him. He'd never seen anyone lay a hand on Eli, in battle or in any other way. He was fast as a cat and twice as mysterious.

Diego sighed and glanced back at the disk in his hand. Mysterious and annoying he might be, but Eli never did anything without a reason. He took Eli's vacated place behind the desk and plugged the CD into his computer, waiting impatiently as it loaded.

The screen blanked only to be filled a moment later with a scanned newspaper clipping. He frowned at the photo of a younger-looking Sian striding down the steps of what looked like a courthouse, her head held high despite the crush of reporters around her. Uniformed policemen surrounded her and an older man, perhaps a lawyer, held her elbow. Diego leaned forward and read, his frown deepening with every line.

"The jury returned a verdict of guilty today against Enrique Santonyo, a well-known Savannah businessman," the story read. "Santonyo is convicted of the murder of Mayor Kay Tripsan last October. He was also found guilty of the lesser charges of kidnapping, conspiracy to commit murder and drug trafficking. The state's case against Santonyo hinged on the testimony of Officer Sian Lazuro of the Savannah Police Department, who witnessed the slaying while off-duty.

"But only hours after the verdict was handed down, Santonyo escaped from the Savannah jail and is still at large. Police remain closed-mouthed about his disappearance although there is speculation that Santonyo had inside help in his escape.

"Judge Greene stated the sentencing phase of the trial will take place as planned despite Santonyo's disappearance. Officer Lazuro declined to comment on rumors that she has left the Savannah police force and gave no statement when asked about Santonyo's escape."

There was more, but Diego couldn't read it. He stared at the picture of Sian on the courthouse steps, her jaw tight and her eyes unreadable, her spine straight despite the danger she must have known she was in when this man escaped.

His blood boiled as he imagined this killer in her apartment, slashing the bed where she'd rested, shredding the clothes that had once caressed her body, destroying the photograph and rings that were all she had of her family. The thought of what Santonyo would have done to Sian had she been there made Diego shake with fury.

This man would pay. Diego would make sure of it.

A noise in the doorway caught his attention and Diego looked up to see Sian standing there. The towel had been replaced by a short khaki skirt and a blouse the exact shade of her eyes, both snug enough to make his mouth water. He quickly blanked the screen and motioned her inside, wondering at her uncertain and clearly uncomfortable expression and trying to keep his own from betraying his anger and desire. "Come in, sit," he invited, standing and gesturing at the couch.

She shifted from one foot to the other and didn't come any closer. "I was looking for James," she said, not meeting his eye and blushing.

Diego raised an eyebrow and left the desk, wanting to get a closer look at her delicious outfit. "He's gone out for the evening," he said, wondering where that blush had come from and trying not to notice how good it looked on her. "What do you need, Sian? Tell me and I'll take care of it."

Her blush deepened and the rush of hot blood called to the hungry vampire in him, reminding him he hadn't fed tonight. Diego pushed the need down, ignoring the ache in his mouth from the fangs he refused to let show.

"Never mind," Sian muttered, starting to turn away.

Diego reached for her before he could help himself, crossing the remaining distance between in three strides. She jumped when he caught her hand but he didn't let her go when she tried to pull it away.

"Tell me what you need," Diego said, cupping her cheek in his other hand and tilting her face up until she met his eyes. "Taking care of you is my job, not his."

Sian pulled away again. "I'm not anyone's job and I certainly don't need anyone to take care of me," she said with a hint of her old temper, and Diego smiled. She glared at him and finally managed to free her hand, crossing her arms over her chest. He tried his best not to stare at what the movement did to her already mind-blowing cleavage.

"Oh, fine," she snapped as though he'd insisted she tell him what was on her mind. "If you must know, he didn't get me certain necessities. Well, he got them, but they're completely wrong. I mean, they're the right size and all, but they're not—I mean, I can't use them. Okay?"

Diego raised an eyebrow. In the time she'd been with him she'd been angry, confused, frightened and upset, but never had she been reduced to gibberish. "You want to run that past me again?" he asked, keeping the laughter from his voice with an effort.

It must have shown in his eyes, though, because she glared at him again even as her blush deepened further. "Forget it," she said, spinning on her heel to walk out.

He gave in to the urge to slide his arm around her waist, stopping her in her tracks. "Whatever you need, I'll get for you," he said, closing his eyes as he inhaled the intoxicating aroma of her warm skin and his soap. There was something almost unbearably arousing about the knowledge that she'd used his shower. "Tell me what you need, Sian."

"I need you to let me go," she said, but he didn't miss the breathlessness of her voice.

It was as good as an invitation. Diego drew her closer until her back pressed against his chest. He ran his free hand down her hip, loving the way the skirt clung to her curves and aching to slide his hand up under it. He bent and nuzzled her still-damp hair, savoring his scent on her, marking her as his. It was a primal instinct he had no desire to fight.

"Where would you go if I did?" he asked, his voice a low purr behind her ear. "There's no place on Earth you'll be safer than where you are right now. And you certainly didn't seem to mind me holding you a few hours ago."

Sian stiffened in his arms but didn't pull away. "I had nothing to do with that," she protested. "I was asleep and you took advantage—"

His mouth found the side of her throat and her voice cut off as though he'd hit a switch. Diego smiled against her skin and nuzzled her ear again. "*Querida,* you snuggled up to me."

"I did not!"

He laughed and ran his hand over her hip again, enjoying this game she insisted on playing. "Protest your innocence all you want," he began, but paused when he noticed something. He caressed her hip once more, thinking he had to be mistaken, but there was no mistake.

This skirt fit her like a second skin, and he'd felt no panty-line.

Diego instantly went hard as a rock and when she gasped he knew she'd felt it. "Did you forget something when you were dressing, *querida?*" he asked, fighting the redoubled urge to slide his hands beneath her maddening little skirt and make sure. "I'm not complaining, understand, just curious."

And very, very turned on.

Sian shivered against him and it was all he could do not to toss her onto the couch and claim her in the most primitive of ways. "That's what I wanted to talk to James about," she whispered. "I can't wear what he got me."

God bless you, James, Diego thought vaguely, letting his mouth go exploring down the side of her throat again. She gasped and he tightened his arm around her waist, pulling her harder against him, needing her to have no doubt of how much he wanted her. His mouth found her pulse and he drew in a shaky breath as it fluttered much too fast under his lips. He gave in to the urge to run his tongue over it, wanting a taste of her more than he wanted his next breath.

Sian suddenly tore herself away. Diego let her even though it was the most difficult thing he'd ever done. She stared at him, breathing hard and blushing, and Diego took a step back in self-defense. He wouldn't take what she didn't wish to give, but no one said resisting temptation would be easy.

"I'll get you what you need," he said, the thought of buying panties for her sending another wave of desire through his already overheated body. He wondered what James had bought and hoped whatever it was, he could bring her exactly the same thing.

Knowing Sian was bare beneath her skirt was erotic as hell, and he didn't want to cover her any sooner than he absolutely had to.

She went crimson. "I prefer to choose my own lingerie, thank you very much."

"You let James do it," he pointed out, wondering if he should say something to his Steward about overstepping his bounds and deciding against it. He'd clearly done a perfect job.

"Yes, and see the trouble it's caused," she snapped back. "I don't want you to do it, Diego, and that's final."

He grinned and leaned against the back of the couch. "Well, I guess I'll have to take you shopping then." He imagined watching Sian make her selections, then trying them on for him. *Dios,* if he didn't get control of his thoughts he was going to spontaneously combust, but the devil was in him now and he couldn't stop. "Too bad all the shops are closed for the night. Oh, and tomorrow I'm likely to be busy. It'll have to be later in the week—if something else doesn't come up. And since I'm understandably concerned about your safety, I won't be able to let you out of my sight. Of course."

Her eyes narrowed dangerously. "You wouldn't."

He laughed. "Try me."

Sian opened her mouth as though to protest again but shut it with a snap, clearly seething. "Fine, you do it. But you'd better get me something decent this time."

He straightened and stepped toward her, noticing how her eyes widened as he stalked her. There was no other word for it and he didn't even try to hide his intentions. "I am consumed with curiosity," he said, bracing a hand on either side of her head as she pressed her back to the wall. "I'll need you to describe what James bought and why it's unsuitable. You'll have to tell me exactly what you want." He leaned closer until his elbows touched the wall and her body was only inches from his. Her tongue flicked out and moistened her lower lip, and Diego felt the nervous little movement all the way through his body. He bent until his mouth was a breath from hers. "In detail, *querida.* I'd hate to make the same mistake."

She ducked under his arm and danced away and Diego laughed. "Chicken," he taunted softly.

"Pervert," she shot back. "I'm not describing my underwear for you. Just get something you'd buy for your mother and you'll do fine."

"Will you let me put them on you when I get back?" She gasped in outrage and he couldn't resist needling her further. "To check the fit, of course."

She glared. "You'd better enjoy touching my panties when you buy them," she said, lifting her chin regally, "because it'll be the last time you'll ever get near them."

Diego watched her disappear through the door and laughed again even though he was so hard every movement was painful. There had been desire in her eyes. He'd seen it clearly before she'd escaped. His little wildcat wanted him, and that made all the difference in the world.

Suddenly this situation didn't seem quite so intolerable.

He sat back down at his desk, starting an internet search on Enrique Santonyo and assembling a mental list of excuses to put off this shopping trip as long as possible.

Chapter Seven

Sian yawned as she rinsed her dinner dishes hours later and tried to convince herself she wasn't tired. Diego was deeply into this vampire thing, staying up all night like it was nothing, and if he could do it, so could she.

She avoided him like the plague since the scene in the den. She closed her eyes, a wave of heat flooding her at the memory of his hand caressing her hip and the skin of his arm against the exposed strip of her waist. Why did she have to keep wanting him? It wasn't fair!

He certainly wanted her and made no bones about it. When he'd trapped her against the wall she'd had the craziest urge to lean into him and taste the passion his eyes had promised. Only a belated sense of self-preservation had made her pull away.

She still wasn't sure if she was glad she had or not.

She'd heard about captives being brainwashed to sympathize with their kidnappers, but she thought it should take more than two nights to accomplish. No, the man just possessed more raw sex appeal than the law allowed and he had no qualms about using it, and she was woman enough to notice. It was pheromones or something. Surely she could ignore it long enough to come up with an escape plan.

She yawned again and rubbed her eyes. She couldn't stay awake any longer. It was time to bite the bullet and demand Diego give her a room of her own. She hung up the dishtowel and left the kitchen, passing the flats she'd kicked off earlier without picking them up and heading for the den.

It was empty. She bit her lip. "Diego?" she called. There was no answer and she started to search the other rooms downstairs. There was no sign of him in the dining room or either of the living rooms. The library and the game room were also empty. Was he even home? She kept opening doors, wondering if she'd had a perfect chance to escape tonight and missed it because she'd been hiding from Diego.

When she turned up no sign of him, Sian strode back to her shoes, slipped them on and hurried resolutely to the front door. James was gone and Diego was nowhere to be found, and she was getting out of here.

She pulled open the front door and jumped when Diego strode up the steps. "Going somewhere?" he asked mildly, urging her back inside and closing the door behind her. "At least you wore shoes this time."

"I didn't have any shoes last time, and where were you?"

The moment the words were out of her mouth Sian regretted them. She sounded like a wife calling her man to task for being out late. Diego grinned at her and she stepped back again, suddenly desperate to put some distance between herself and his potent animal magnetism.

"You've had dinner?" he asked. She frowned at the random question but nodded. He smiled again. "So have I."

She was absolutely not going to ask what he meant by that, especially after finding a bag of whole blood in the back of the fresh vegetable compartment in the refrigerator. She knew now why James had recommended she stay out of there, but honestly, she had to eat. She really hadn't been snooping.

Really.

Diego urged her toward the stairs, his hand very large and very warm at the small of her back. "Dawn's near and you've been up all night. Time for bed."

Sian spun away from him, crossing her arms and raising her chin. "I'm not going to bed with you," she said. "If you insist on keeping me here, I want my own room."

Diego merely picked her up and carried her toward the stairs. "Too bad."

Sian shoved at his shoulders, trying without success to get away from him. Good Lord, the man was strong. She'd never encountered anyone who could hold her when she didn't want to be held. "What the hell is it with you and carrying me around?" she demanded, pushing at him again. "I'm perfectly capable of walking on my own, you know!"

"Yes, but you wouldn't go where I wanted you to if I let you," Diego replied as though this was the most reasonable argument in the world. "Besides, I love the way you feel in my arms."

That confession sent a totally unwelcome shiver through her body. "Well, I don't love it," she lied. "Put me down right now, you beast!"

He laughed and ignored her struggles. "Don't tire yourself out," he advised. His bedroom door opened as though it had been triggered by a switch but Sian hadn't seen him touch anything. The door closed behind them, also without anyone apparently touching it, and she heard the definitive snick of the lock.

Only then did Diego put her down. "Your nightgown is in the top drawer," he said, nodding toward the dresser.

She stared at him in shock, only now realizing the neat stacks she'd made of her clothes were gone. "What did you do with my clothes?"

He pulled off his shirt and tossed it at the hamper in the corner. "Put them up," he said. "Can't leave them out, can we?"

He reached for his belt and Sian spun around. "Keep your clothes on!" she cried, panicking.

He laughed again. "I've slept in jeans for two nights in a row," he said. She heard the distinctive sound of a zipper and closed her eyes, feeling her cheeks heat. "It's uncomfortable as hell and I'll be damned if I'm going to do it again. I normally sleep in the nude but if it'll make you feel better I'll put on some pajamas."

"You can sleep however you want because you'll be doing it alone. I refuse to stay in here!"

She didn't hear Diego move but suddenly his hands were on her shoulders. Sian stiffened, fighting the surge of desire that tried to drown her at his nearness.

"You're staying here with me today, Sian," Diego murmured in her ear. His warm breath caressed the sensitive skin and an answering shiver worked its way all the way down to her toes. "No trying to run while I'm sleeping. You're exhausted and you need the rest as much as I do."

His bare arm reached past her and pulled open the drawer he'd indicated. The gown James had picked out for her lay beside the pornographic lingerie he'd bought. Sian snatched it and slammed the drawer, almost catching Diego's fingers in it.

"I am not sleeping in that bed with you," she repeated stubbornly, afraid to turn around and deliver her ultimatum to his face in case he truly was nude now. Surely the man had some sense of modesty. He wouldn't really strip to the skin right in front of her, would he?

"Turn around and find out," he whispered, brushing her hair aside and nuzzling her ear. His rough whiskers tickled her earlobe just before he nibbled it. "Modesty's never held much appeal for me, *querida*, and if you don't want to sleep, that's more than fine with me, too."

Sian scooted away from him at top speed, not pausing until she was in the bathroom with the door firmly locked between them. The way he seemed to know exactly what she was thinking was downright eerie. "That isn't what I meant!" she protested. She heard him laugh again and wanted to throw something at him.

Even his laugh was sexy. It wasn't fair.

She sighed and scowled at the mirror. The man was pure sex from his head to his toes. She'd have to be a fool to even consider getting anywhere near a bed with him in the vicinity!

Another yawn surprised her and her shoulders slumped. She hated it but he was right. She was exhausted. She looked around the bathroom, briefly entertaining the idea of making a pallet of towels and sleeping in there, but there wasn't enough room. In the end, she pulled on the satin gown, too tired to hide any longer. She reached for the towel rack to retrieve her panties and blinked in confusion at the empty rod.

Her panties and bra were gone.

Sian ran a hand through her hair, wondering why she was even surprised. "Are you dressed out there?" she called through the door, preparing to give him hell for hiding the only decent panties she had.

"Come out and see for yourself."

Now that was less than comforting. Sian scowled at the door for a minute before Diego laughed again. "Oh, all right, I'm dressed," he reassured her. "For a wildcat, you can certainly be a chicken at times."

Sian opened the door and pointedly avoided looking at him just in case he'd been lying about his state of dress. "What did you do with the lingerie I had hanging up in there?" she asked, staring fixedly at the corner.

"What makes you think I did anything with them?"

Unwilling to chance looking at him, Sian gave the corner her evil glare of death. "Diego, don't make me hurt you. I hung them up in there to dry earlier and I doubt James messed with them. What happened to them?"

"Well, you see, there was a little problem," Diego said, and something in his tone made her heart sink. "I thought I would hurry the drying process for you and use a hair-dryer on them, and—"

"Oh, no," Sian groaned, covering her face with her hands. "Those were silk, Diego!" And she didn't want to imagine how the delicate fabric had reacted to the heat. She forgot her determination not to look at him and transferred the death glare to him. "I hope you don't want me to believe it was an accident."

He merely grinned at her and her heart turned over at the sight of him standing there in a pair of black silk pajama bottoms and nothing else. She'd never seen a more ripped set of washboard abs in her life and she hated herself for even noticing them. *Why* couldn't he be short, fat, and balding?

"I guess you won't believe me if I say I'm sorry, either," he said, not sounding apologetic in the least. His abs contracted enticingly beneath his tanned skin with every breath, distracting her wickedly. "And I guess you'd be right, because I'm really not."

She managed to tear her eyes away from his awe-inspiring body and tried to glare at him again, but something in his unrepentant expression made her want to laugh despite her anger. She rolled her eyes instead and marched to the bed, yanking the comforter down and starting to line up a row of pillows straight down the middle. Diego's gaze burned her and she did her best not to bend over too far. No point in giving the blasted man a free peep-show.

"And what is that for?" he asked at last, his amusement coming through loud and clear.

"If you won't be a gentleman and give me my own bed," Sian climbed into her side without looking at him, "the least you can do is divide this one."

Diego laughed. "Of course, now it makes perfect sense. That veritable mountain of pillows would certainly stop me if I decided to ravish you. There's no way in the world I could get past it. Good thinking, Sian."

"Shut up and turn off the light."

"Yes, ma'am. Absolutely, ma'am. Your word is law."

The mattress shifted as Diego lay down and Sian closed her eyes, trying to pretend he wasn't there. His quiet breathing wrecked any attempt she made to relax and she tossed fitfully, trying without success to block it out.

"You know," Diego said conversationally a few minutes later, "you seemed awfully comfortable in my arms yesterday."

"So what?" Sian snapped, hating the intimacy of his voice vibrating along her skin.

Or wishing she hated it was more accurate.

"Merely making an observation."

"Well, don't."

Sian rolled onto her side and punched the pillow, searching for a comfortable position and not finding one. She punched it again for good measure, just to let off steam.

Steamy pretty much described every thought in her head right now, too. She wished Diego hadn't reminded her of how good it had felt to snuggle up to him. She didn't want to remember the warmth of his body next to hers, the comforting weight of his arm around her waist, the slow lullaby of his heart beating beneath her ear.

She flopped back onto her back with a sigh. It was no use. There was no way she could sleep with Diego right beside her, not when she was so achingly aware of him.

"You know," Diego said again a minute later after she'd changed positions three more times, "I'd be happy to rub your back if it'd help." He paused. "I'll rub anything else you'd like, for that matter. I could even make suggestions."

Sian snatched a pillow off the stack she'd created between them and swung it blindly at him. He laughed and caught her arm, pulling the pillow from her hand and entwining his fingers with hers. "I want you to notice who breached the impenetrable wall of pillows first," he teased, bringing her hand to his lips. "I was being good. You're the one who can't stay away."

She tried to pull her hand back without success. "Would you stop?"

"No." His mouth found her palm and slid down to her wrist. Shivers chased up and down her spine when his tongue flicked across her pulse. "Do you really want me to?"

"Yes!"

He laughed softly again, nipping the sensitive skin of her inner wrist. "Liar." Before she could demand he stop again, he moved her hand down to his chest, trapping her palm against his bare skin and holding it there. "Go to sleep," he said, his tone still frustratingly amused. "Delightful as this game is, the sun's coming up and I can't stay awake any longer."

"Oh, bully for you," Sian grumbled, but he didn't reply. She risked raising her head a few inches and peeked over the pillows at him.

He was asleep.

She gaped at him. He'd dropped off just like that? How in the world could he go to sleep as though she wasn't even there?

Sian rolled onto her back again, trying one last time to reclaim her hand and failing. Even in sleep he kept his hold on her. She sighed and closed her eyes, trying to shut out the feel of his heart beating under her palm, the warmth of his bare skin against her fingers. There was no way she'd get a wink of sleep like this.

She sighed, staring at the dark ceiling and praying for sleep. Where had her exhaustion gone? She was wide awake. Finally she closed her eyes, wondering how long it would be before Diego shifted in his sleep and she could get away.

☪ ☪ ☪

Sian awoke disoriented, unsure what had jolted her out of her slumber. There was something warm under her cheek. She ran her hand over it, frowning at the strange ridges that didn't feel remotely like the pillow she remembered finally falling asleep on. She raised her head, trying to focus her blurry eyes.

She froze when she realized she was once again lying with her head pillowed on Diego's chest. Their legs were entwined and her arm was around his waist, her hand resting on the firm ridges of his abs. She hardly dared move for fear of waking him, but fury burned through her.

How dare he sneak up on her again? Did the man have no decency at all?

But when she drew in a breath to let him have it, she realized his hands were tucked behind his head. He wasn't touching her at all. She blushed to the roots of her hair when she felt the pillows at her back.

He hadn't crossed her barrier of pillows.

She had.

Sian was trying to think of how to get out of this without waking him when Diego broke the tense silence. "Don't get shy now, *querida*. Please, feel free to finish what you started."

She remembered running her hands over his chest in confusion when she'd woken and felt her face grow hotter. "I wasn't awake," she mumbled, wondering if it was possible to die of embarrassment. "I can't be held responsible for what I did when I was sleeping."

His deep chuckle sent a thrill down her spine. "If that's the case, I'm going back to sleep right now."

Sian scooted away from him, rolling over the pillows and almost falling off the bed in her haste to put some distance between her and the overwhelming temptation Diego represented. He laughed again and sat up. "Relax," he said, grinning at the panic she knew showed in her face. "Trust me, *querida*, I plan on being fully awake when I make love to you for the first time. I don't want to miss a second of it."

"Keep dreaming. I still haven't decided if I even like you and you already have us making love?"

His eyes were emerald fire. "Oh, you like me," he said with complete assurance. "You like me so much you have to run every time I get close to you. And the way you look at me sometimes—your eyes say you like me just fine."

"Your ego knows no bounds," Sian snapped, reaching for her robe and pulling it on as she fled the bed. "You're holding me prisoner here, or have you forgotten?"

He shrugged. "From what I remember, you were holding me prisoner there, not the other way around. Besides, if you left, where would you go?" he asked, also rising and stretching. She couldn't stop herself from admiring his lean body as he did, his every muscle defined and rippling. He gave her a grin that clearly said he'd noticed her interest and she marched to the bathroom, seething.

She didn't like him, no matter what he said. "Why do you insist on keeping me here?" she demanded through the door as she turned on the shower.

His voice was alarmingly close to the door when he replied. "I told you, you're my mate," he said. "Remember the mark on your arm? You belong with me. It is my duty and my pleasure to keep you safe and see to your needs."

Like my need for decent underwear? Sian thought sarcastically, but she didn't quite dare say it. "I'm not interested in being your duty or your pleasure, and where I come from both parties have to agree to a relationship," she said instead.

"Same here, but in this case Eli's will overrode both ours."

She frowned, shrugging off her robe. "You've mentioned Eli before," she said. "Who is he?"

There was a low sound from behind the door that might have been a groan or a growl. "I suppose you could say he's my boss," Diego replied after a long pause.

"And he's picking your girlfriends?" Sian asked when Diego didn't elaborate. "He's taking micro-management to the extreme, don't you think?"

There was a short snort of laughter. "I would have to agree with that statement whole-heartedly."

Sian hesitated before slipping off her gown. There was something incredibly intimate about talking with Diego through the door as she prepared for her shower. She almost expected him to come through the door at any moment and ask to join her.

"I definitely would if I thought there was any chance you'd let me," Diego said softly, and Sian spun around with a gasp.

"You can't read my mind," she snapped at the door, double-checking the lock. "It's impossible, and I want you to stop it!"

He laughed again. "I can only catch the odd thought from time to time, *querida*," he said. "I know I shouldn't answer, but I can't help myself."

"You should really make the effort," Sian said acidly before catching herself. "Stop that!"

"Stop what?" He sounded genuinely confused. "I'm not reading your mind right now, Sian, I promise."

"No, of course you're not, because it's impossible. Stop trying to suck me into your delusions! I don't believe one word of this vampire, psychic crap you keep telling me, so cut it out already, will you?"

His deep chuckle seemed to caress her right through the door. "If you don't believe a word of it," he murmured, "you won't be upset if I keep trying to prove it to you. Aren't you supposed to humor crazy people?"

"I am not humoring you!" she cried, clenching her fists in impotent rage. He was manipulating her again. She never acted like this! She was a cop, for God's sake. She never lost her head and she knew damn well he was trying to brainwash her. Heaven alone knew why he wanted her to believe this vampire soul-mate crap, but he wasn't giving up.

Well, she was too smart for this and she wasn't going to listen to it anymore. Sian dropped the gown and stepped into the shower, plunging her head under the spray and determined not to listen to another word he said.

Diego felt her anger and sighed, turning away from the door and going to the closet. Every time they connected on any level, she either got mad or got scared. It was getting frustrating.

Of course, frustrated didn't even begin to describe his feelings at the moment. Waking up with Sian's arms around him and her hand caressing its way over his chest was a slice of heaven, but watching her almost fall off the bed in her haste to get away from him was definitely a taste of hell. *Dios*, he was starting to wonder if an immortal could die of prolonged sexual frustration.

If there was a woman who could do it to him, it was Sian Lazuro.

Diego pulled on a pair of black jeans and paused, glancing at her things hanging neatly beside his clothes. Putting her new clothes in his closet had unleashed a fresh surge of possessiveness last night and he still wondered if it had been a smart thing to do. Still, he loved seeing her clothes beside his.

He laughed silently at himself. She would probably find a way to move them out of his closet by the end of the night if he knew anything about his wildcat. She was so fiercely independent he was starting to wonder if she would ever trust him in anything. He imagined her standing there in the shower, rehearsing her arguments to convince him to give her a room of her own.

Well, that was definitely not going to happen. It might have made her supremely uncomfortable to wake up draped over him, but he wouldn't miss an instant of it for the world.

He looked back at his shirts, remembering how her eyes had caressed his bare chest last night. No matter what she might think of him personally, Sian certainly had no complaints with his body. Finally Diego pulled out a platinum silk shirt, putting it on and leaving it open to show his chest and abs. There was no need to help Sian ignore him, after all.

He heard the water turn off and glanced back at the door. His groin tightened at the memory of Sian stepping out of his bathroom yesterday wearing nothing but a towel and a lot of bare, damp skin. What he wouldn't give to capture every one of those tiny clinging droplets with his tongue…

Diego shook his head sharply and forced himself to walk out of the bedroom. There would be time for that once she trusted him. It was one thing to flirt with her, to try unrepentantly to seduce her, but to stay in here and watch her dress was crossing the line.

He heard James typing in the den and headed toward the sound. "What's up?" he asked, wondering at the frown on his Steward's face.

James spared him a glance before turning back to the computer. "Someone's trying to buy your old stomping grounds again," he said, pushing a FedEx package across the desk. "They want to turn it into a fairgrounds, sort of a Renaissance fair kind of thing."

Diego picked up the package, all thought of Sian evaporating in a surge of anger. He'd bought the ruins of the castle where he'd been born several hundred years ago and had willed it to his first Steward. The deed had been passed down through the generations, each Steward doing whatever they had to do to keep it safe for Diego.

At the end of James's father's career, however, a legal challenge had been filed in a Spanish court by a development company. They challenged the veracity of the ancient deed and wanted a judgment to allow them to buy Diego's land at auction prices.

Diego had spared no expense for the case, hiring the most brilliant and vicious legal team money could buy to fight the development company off. He'd won, but the challenges had continued after the first case. First had come a vineyard, tempted by the lush hills around the ruined castle. After that had come a wealthy recluse who'd wanted to bulldoze the remains of the castle and build his own ultra posh mansion there.

Diego had visited the man in the middle of the night and frightened him so badly he'd ended up building in a part of Alaska so remote he didn't even have a road.

The Leonides family was gone, his Clan massacred. All Diego had left of them was a few hundred acres of land and a ruined castle, and now they were trying to take even that away from him.

Diego couldn't understand why it kept happening. Yes, the ruined castle was in a prime vineyard region, but he had three judgments in his favor now and yet the new challenges to his ownership—or rather, James's—kept on coming. His scowl deepened as he read this latest one. This land was all he had left of his family heritage and he'd be damned if he would ever stop fighting for it. He'd done it more than once with a sword, then with cannon and musket, and now in the courts where blood still flowed in the color of money.

Money was no object. The land was his. He'd do anything it took to keep it.

"I am more than tempted to pay a few midnight visits to these people," Diego growled, scanning the artist's conceptions of what his castle would look like when they were done with it. It looked like a bloody cartoon, nothing at all like the proud fortress it had once been.

James leaned back in the desk chair and crossed his arms over his chest. "These people have the legal team from hell," he said. "They've got reports from the surrounding villages on the fiscal advantages of their plan and environmental surveys proving they won't wreck the landscape with their little park. They're well prepared to argue their case."

Diego threw the papers down. "However much they spent on their lawyers, I can spend twice as much," he said through gritted teeth. "And all the studies and surveys and public opinion in the world doesn't change that the land is mine."

James gave him a ghost of a grin. "Don't you mean mine?"

Diego raised an eyebrow at him. "Unless your name is Leonides, that castle will never belong to you no matter what I put on a paper a few hundred years ago."

James's grin widened. "Like I'd try to take your land away from you," he laughed. "You're just way too much fun to wind up about it, though."

Diego shoved his hands in his pockets and didn't smile back. He was feeling decidedly unamused by the last decade of legal maneuverings to simply keep what was his. "Are you ready to go now or do you need to pack?"

James stood and stretched. "I just finished booking my flight," he said, rotating his neck and wincing in pleasure at the pops that resulted. "I packed while you were still up there snoozing with the hottie."

Diego gave James a look of amused surprise. "*Hottie*, is she now?" he asked. "What happened to *psycho?*"

"Well, she's actually pretty decent if you can get past the fact she thinks we've kidnapped her for some nefarious purpose," James replied with a shrug. "And *we* haven't kidnapped her. That's all you."

"My purpose isn't nefarious!"

James laughed. "When you convince her of that, let me know, will you?"

Diego shook his head and changed the subject. He didn't want to think about Sian right now. It would only lead to wondering if she was dressed or not yet, and if she'd broken down and put on one of those tiny little thongs or was going bare again. He wasn't sure which thought was sexier, but neither was conducive to rational thought. "When do you think you'll be back?"

James shrugged. "I have meetings with the lawyers tomorrow and the next day," he said. "I went ahead and booked my return flight, but you know how these things go. If the lawyers say I need to stay, I'll stay."

Diego nodded. "Keep me updated."

"Of course." James headed for the front door where two suitcases were already waiting. "I went to the blood bank today so you're all restocked. I also stuck a few extra things in the first aid kit. Do you think Sian would help you out if you needed it or do I need to call in someone just in case?"

Diego raised an eyebrow at his Steward in amusement. "I've been taking care of myself for a few years now, Mom. I'm sure I'll be fine without you for a couple of days, but I'll promise to miss you if it'll make you feel better."

James made a face at him and grabbed a suitcase and went out. Diego followed him with the second one. "Do you want a ride to the airport? I thought you hated leaving your car in the lot."

James shrugged. "I figured you'd offer, and I appreciate it, but don't you think it would be better if you don't let your woman anywhere near the airport? If she decides to make a break for it, all she'd have to do is evade you until dawn and she's gone."

Diego knew the Steward was right, but hated feeling like he was holding Sian hostage. It was the only way he could be sure of keeping her safe, but the rationale didn't keep him from feeling like an ass. "All right," he said. "Let me know when you get there. With the time difference I can talk to the lawyers by phone if you need me to."

A few minutes later, Diego watched James drive away and went back into the house, frowning. Something had to be different this time. No company put out the money on environmental studies and fiscal plans unless they were damn sure they'd win their case.

No, something didn't feel right here. Diego had learned long ago to trust his gut instincts and they were screaming at him right now. This wasn't about land.

This was something personal.

☾ ☾ ☾

Sian was surprised to find the bedroom empty when she finally worked up the nerve to emerge from the bathroom twenty minutes later. She'd fully expected Diego to still be there lounging on the bed, ready to get a voyeuristic thrill out of watching her get dressed. She even had a host of scathing put-downs ready to use to chase him out of the room if he'd tried to talk his way into staying. He was gorgeous and he was charming, but he was also starting to get on her nerves in a big way with his confident assurance that it was only a matter of time before she fell into his arms.

The most galling part was that he just might be right.

She breathed a sigh of relief to find herself alone. She padded to the closet and pulled out a shimmery sage green T-shirt that looked great with her blonde hair and after much debate decided on a black denim skirt to go with it. When she put them on the shirt clung to her breasts and the skirt came only to mid-thigh. She looked at herself in the mirror, sighing.

It was clear her normally conservative style of dress would be impossible to maintain if she let James or Diego keep choosing her clothes. This shirt was positively decadent. Sian plucked at it for a moment, trying without much hope to keep it from clinging like a second skin before giving it up as a lost cause.

She glanced back at Diego's shirts hanging in the closet, wondering what Diego would say if she asked to use one. All she saw in there were button-up shirts that would swallow her whole. Sian turned to the dresser, biting her lip. The man had to have some T-shirts. Surely he wouldn't mind if she borrowed one.

She started opening drawers at random, slamming the first one when she glimpsed a pair of black silk boxers. She absolutely did not want to know kind of underwear Diego wore, she told herself firmly as she opened the next drawer.

In the bottom one, she finally found a stack of neatly folded T-shirts. She pulled out a black one and was about to slide the drawer shut again when she noticed something out of place.

There was a red leather strap peeking from between his shirts. Cherry red, to be precise. The exact shade of her purse, in fact.

Sian reached for it, her blood boiling when she pulled out her missing purse. How dare he hide her things from her? She looked inside, wondering if he'd gone through it and if she had anything left of her own in there.

She was surprised to see the soft sheen of metal. She pulled out her gun and checked the clip, her surprise growing to find it still fully loaded. She set the gun aside and pulled out her wallet. Her cash was still there, along with all her ATM and credit cards.

He'd hidden her purse from her but hadn't bothered to look inside it?

It seemed incredible but Sian didn't question her good fortune. She slid her wallet and gun back inside and snapped it closed before pulling on Diego's shirt. She put on a pair of black sandals, her mind racing.

This purse was all she needed to make her escape. She had five thousand dollars sewn into the lining, and she had ATM cards available to clean out her accounts. With what she had in there she could get a car—she briefly mourned the loss of her Mini—and get out of here and away from Santonyo's hired killers again.

Not to mention getting away from Diego and his vampire fetish.

Sian opened the bedroom door and glanced up and down the hall. Not wanting to run into James or Diego, she only left the room when she was sure the coast was clear. She hurried down the hall with her purse behind her back until she reached the top of the stairs, pausing to listen.

She heard voices downstairs, followed by the distinct sound of the front door opening and closing again. Gambling that both of them had gone out, Sian darted down the stairs, rushed past the den and kitchen and out the sliding doors to the back yard. She silently slid it closed, wincing at the click when the latch caught. In the silent dark, it sounded loud as a gunshot, but one tense minute passed and then another, and no one came to investigate.

She heard a car start and pull away and started around the side of the house. She wished she'd had a chance to grab some keys, but she'd never seen where Diego kept his. Besides, she wasn't exactly sure how to open the gate. On foot she had a chance of scaling it, and Diego would definitely hear a car starting in his garage.

Sian reached the front of the house and crouched in the bushes for a long moment, making sure no one remained outside before dashing for the trees. Once there she didn't dare slow down. Keeping to the shadows of the trees and making sure the twisting drive was always in sight, Sian fled as though the hounds of hell were on her heels.

A few minutes passed before she heard a loud bang and hit the ground, breathing hard. There was a noise of tires skidding in gravel and the thunk of a car door slamming. Belatedly Sian realized what she'd heard wasn't a gunshot, but the sound of a tire blowing out. She eased to her feet and crept along the road until she saw the car.

James knelt beside one of the back tires, cursing as he worked to lift the car up on a jack. She backed up just as quietly. She would have to be twice as careful now that she knew James was still around, but she couldn't let it stop her. Since her last escape attempt Diego had kept an incredibly tight watch on her. If he caught her again, she wouldn't put it past him to tie her to him or something.

She had almost reached the gate when she heard the car approaching and ducked behind a tree an instant before the headlights washed over her. She hurried when the car passed and when James opened the gate and sped through she rushed through after him, praying he wouldn't choose this moment to look in his rearview mirror.

The car sped off, though, and Sian breathed a sigh of relief. She started down the road, ready to flag down the first car she saw and beg a ride.

Chapter Eight

The house was too quiet.

Diego drummed his fingers on the desk, his anger growing the more he researched this latest company trying to take his land from him. He couldn't find out a thing and he wondered abruptly how long he'd been at it. Surely Sian had to be done showering and dressing by now. He'd known women who took forever to accomplish the most basic tasks of dressing but Sian certainly wasn't one of them.

He glanced at his watch—three hours had gone by since James had left. He stood and stretched muscles cramping from the extended time at the computer. Three hours and he hadn't heard a thing from Sian. She should have come downstairs to eat something by now.

Diego closed his eyes and sent his senses through the house, scanning for her. He almost wasn't surprised to find the house deserted. Sian had escaped right under his nose and he hadn't even noticed.

He should never have underestimated his wildcat.

Less than a minute later, he was outside and airborne, an enormous hawk soaring through the night. The exhilaration he normally felt in this form didn't touch him this time. Fear for Sian threatened to choke him. A scan with his senses showed she wasn't on his land. He followed the road, using the great bird's superior vision to look for her even as he kept scanning, fear goading him to greater speed. He caught her scent on the wind and circled down, hovering at last over a nondescript spot on the shoulder of the road. The bird's sharp eyes picked out her footprints leading to this spot and abruptly vanishing.

She'd hitched a ride. She could be anywhere. His heart thudded in his chest. Anyone might have picked her up, and people who picked up hitchhikers in the middle of the night were rarely the trustworthy, Good Samaritan type.

Anything could happen to her, and he wasn't there to keep her safe.

Diego wheeled in the air and raced toward the city, praying she'd headed in this direction and wishing bitterly that he'd taken her blood. Why hadn't he done it the last time she'd run away?

But he knew exactly why he hadn't done it. The terrified look in her eyes when he'd showed her his fangs still lived vividly in his memory and he would do anything never to see such fear on her face again. It was bad enough being mated to a woman who hadn't wanted it any more than he had. He couldn't imagine what it would be like if she were terrified of him. Sian had more fight in her than any mortal he'd ever known. The last thing he wanted was to see that warrior's spirit crushed by fear.

At least he knew her scent. He transformed from the hawk to a turkey vulture. It wasn't the most elegant of beasts but it possessed the most acute sense of smell of any animal on earth. He pushed the bird to its top limit of speed, his instincts starting to clamor again.

This time they were telling him to find her fast before it was too late.

C C C

Sian thanked the truck driver and hopped out, greatly relieved that the man who'd picked her up hadn't wanted anything more from her than conversation. She'd heard way too many horror stories about hitchhiking to be comfortable doing it but at this point she'd had little choice. The driver had even refused her offer of payment for the ride.

"Keep your money, little missy," he'd said, smiling at her in a fatherly way. "Use it for a taxi next time, all right? There's crazies on these roads at night."

She watched the rig pull away and walked toward the twenty-four hour variety store where she'd asked him to drop her. He'd been right about the crazies on the roads, but desperation had shifted her priorities a little. She'd gotten lucky this time.

Still, she had no intention of hitchhiking further tonight. Her gun was good protection, but she would rather not have to use it. No, she'd wait here at the shopping center until the used car dealerships opened in the morning. Five thousand in cash should get her something that would last as long as she needed it to, as long as she wasn't picky.

And picky was just about the last thing on her mind.

Sian squinted for a moment against the bright florescent lights as she walked inside the store. After distracting the clerk from her phone call to ask where the ladies' section was, Sian grabbed a pair of sweatpants, the only thing they had in her size, and a package of plain cotton panties. At the register she added a bottle of water and some jerky as her stomach growled and reminded her she hadn't eaten yet.

The clerk finally hung up the phone and started scanning Sian's things and dropping them into a plastic bag. "Can I use your restroom?" Sian asked the clerk, aching to get out of this miniskirt and into the sweatpants. They weren't the most fashionable things in the world, but at least they'd cover her.

The clerk snapped her gum, giving her a bored look. "Restrooms are for employees only," she said. "You can go to the pancake place around the corner if you want. Cut through the alley in back and go down two blocks."

Sian started to argue but the thought of a real meal instead of jerky and water made her change her mind. She paid and walked out, going around the back as the clerk had recommended and eyeing the alley nervously.

She'd already tested her luck once tonight by hitching a ride. Was she really going to test it again by walking down a dark alley at one in the morning?

She looked around. There wasn't any other way to get there unless she went all the way around the shopping center, and that would add at least a block to her walk. The alley wasn't that dark, either—one of those orange sodium lights illuminated the dumpsters beside the back door of the variety shop.

What was more dangerous—a long walk in plain sight down a highway at two a.m., or a short run down a well-lit alley?

The thought of pancakes spurred her on. If she took the shortcut she'd get there faster and she was starving. Sian slipped her hand into her purse, her fingers curling around the reassuring shape of her gun, and strode into the alley.

She'd made it almost halfway through before her instincts started screaming and she knew she'd made a mistake. She didn't see or hear anything, but her gut tightened and the hair on the back of her neck stood up. She drew the gun from her purse and quickened her pace as the sense of being watched grew stronger. "I have a gun," she announced to the alley and whoever might be listening.

There was an unsettling laugh from behind her. Sian spun, bringing up her gun, but no one was there. She was halfway through now and nearing the dumpsters. She turned and resolutely strode forward again, making sure the gun was visible.

The laugh echoed down the alley again, this time sounding like it came from right behind her. Sian whirled again and again faced emptiness. "Keep away from me," she said through clenched teeth. "This is a real gun and I won't hesitate to use it."

"Shoot if you want, Slayer's whore," a voice taunted from overhead. "It won't do you any good."

A shiver went up Sian's spine as her head snapped up, searching in vain for the owner of the voice. What the hell was a Slayer? More laughter mocked her, this time echoing all around her. She couldn't tell where it came from. Sian stopped and turned back the way she'd come. She hadn't seen anyone when she'd entered the alley and she would have to be stupid to keep pressing on when there was clearly someone in the there with her. Footsteps sounded behind her and Sian quickened her pace. The mouth of the alley was only yards away.

A hand fell on her shoulder and she whirled, knocking it away and bringing her gun up again. Her skin crawled when she found no one behind her.

"Oh, she likes that gun," the voice laughed.

"Maybe she'd like *my* gun," another answered.

A shadow fell over her and she gasped, spinning around again, and the laughter echoed around her. "Spooks easy, doesn't she?" a third voice said.

"Too easy for a Slayer's whore, if you ask me," the second voice replied with a hint of a growl. "Where's the Slayer?"

"Poor little girl, all alone in the night," the first one taunted. "Want someone to hold your hand and make the monsters go away?"

The third one gave a low, dirty laugh that was somehow more threatening than anything she'd heard before. Sian turned again and hurried for the parking lot at the end of the alley, truly terrified now and wishing she'd been less concerned with her stomach and taken the long route around the block.

She hoped it wouldn't be the last mistake she ever made.

She had almost reached the parking lot when a man dropped in front of her. She jumped back, colliding with someone else and ducking away before he could grab her. Sian aimed her gun at the two huge men who had materialized from nowhere, wondering where the third was as she backed away. "Keep away from me," she warned, her finger trembling on the trigger.

They laughed.

"Boo," said a voice right behind her, and Sian was caught before she could move a muscle. She fought the arm around her with all her might but it was like trying to move a stone wall. One of the others came up and effortlessly twisted her gun out of her hand, throwing it carelessly over his shoulder.

"Slayer has good taste," he said, surveying her critically. Sian's skin crawled when his eyes moved over her breasts and his grin widened. "Very nice. I'll have to send him my compliments after I thoroughly enjoy his little mate here."

Sian drew in a breath to tell him exactly what he could do with his compliments when all hell broke loose.

A huge bird screamed as it dove into the alley, catching the man who'd been ogling her full in the face with its talons. The one holding her cursed viciously. Sian used his momentary lapse of attention to drive her elbow back into his ribs before dropping like a weight in his arms, throwing him off balance.

Something shiny whirled past her face and Sian stumbled as the man holding her collapsed. Before she could regain her balance, someone else grabbed her. She screamed, clawing at him.

Her wrists were captured in one large hand as her attacker's other arm locked around her waist. "Stop it," a familiar voice growled in her ear as she was steered behind one of the dumpsters and pushed down into a crouch there. "Don't move, do you understand me? Stay here!"

Sian gasped as Diego spun away and disappeared back into the alley. How had he found her? She wrapped her arms around her legs, shaking and wondering why she was doing what he'd said instead of running down the alley and back to the highway. Wasn't she trying to get away from him?

She heard a sudden scream and a vicious snarl. The scream cut off almost at once and she shivered, afraid to look around the edge of the dumpster. The snarls redoubled and there was a crash against the dumpster which made it shake and bang against the wall. Sian pressed her back against the wall, fighting the urge to cover her ears. Someone growled and someone else laughed, and there was the sound of metal on metal and a thick gurgle she didn't want to think about too closely.

Suddenly the night was shattered by a gunshot.

Sian was on her feet in an instant, remembering how her attackers had taken her gun. She hadn't even stepped around the dumpster, though, when Diego was back.

He caught her around the waist and walked her back to where he'd put her, breathing fast and clearly furious. "I told you not to move, damn it," he growled. "Can't you do one single thing I ask?"

The tightness in her chest eased with a rush of relief she didn't want to examine. She started to ask him if he was hurt when she noticed his eyes.

They were too dark, the normally vivid green showing up black in the orange lights, his pupils elongated into cat-like slits.

Sian just stared, unable to breathe. She remembered the nightmare where he'd looked like this, where he'd claimed to be a vampire and showed her fangs too incredibly realistic to rationalize away.

Diego groaned and pulled her hard against him, burying his face in her hair and holding her tight as he let loose with a long and vehement string of Spanish.

"You scared me to death," he whispered a few moments later when he'd finished cursing, and the pounding of his heart beneath her cheek convinced her of the truth of his words. "For God's sake, Sian, what were you thinking, walking down a dark alley in the middle of the night?"

She let herself melt against him, her own fear slowly leaving her as his strength surrounded her. She'd imagined his eyes. It had to be imagination. "I was stupid," she admitted before realizing she was clinging to him.

She wasn't the clinging type. Embarrassed for acting like this, she tried to pull away. Diego didn't let her, completely ignoring her not-so-subtle push against his chest. "We should call the police to come get those men," she said, trying to fight her way back to reality again.

Reality was police and jails and statements given to a bored cop while drinking stale coffee. Reality was not Diego falling out of the sky in the nick of time with some kind of attack bird and saving her from rape and she didn't want to think what else.

Reality was not vampires and weird eyes.

He laughed softly and pressed a kiss to her forehead. "The police wouldn't know what to do with an Outcast," he said gently. "Taking care of them is my job, Sian, and I've done it. Now you need to tell me who sent you back here."

She wasn't going to touch any of that, whatever the heck it meant. Sian pushed at his shoulders again, trying without luck to get him to release her. "Will you let go of me?" she finally asked in exasperation.

Diego stroked her hair and kept his arm around her waist. "I don't want you to look at me yet, *querida*. You wouldn't like it. Now tell me who sent you back here."

"Why?" she asked, wondering what exactly he thought she wouldn't like. Her mind skittered away from the memory of her nightmare and the glimpse she'd gotten of his eyes a moment ago. "Are you hurt?"

He sighed, not answering her. She had the sudden and very disconcerting sensation of gentle fingers probing her mind. She shoved at him, terrified at the strange feeling.

"What do you think you're doing?" she demanded, still unsuccessful in her attempts to break free of his embrace.

He growled and she went utterly still. She'd never heard anyone make such a feral sound. A shiver worked its way down her spine as she remembered the horrible noises of the fight while she'd hidden behind the dumpster. "The clerk set you up," he said, his voice very low and very angry. "Stay here, Sian, while I take care of this."

He released her abruptly and turned to stride away, but Sian caught his arm in both hands. "What are you talking about? She was only giving me directions to a restaurant! What are you going to do?"

"What I have to do."

He didn't look at her and she wasn't quite brave enough to step around him and confront him face to face. "Answer me, damn it," she demanded, refusing to let go of him.

His arm was tense under her fingers and she sensed the rage still boiling inside him. "She saw my mark on you and called them," he finally replied in a voice that was little more than a snarl. "I can't let that slide, Sian. If she's not an Outcast herself, she's at least working for them."

"Stop talking in riddles, will you?" she snapped, exasperated. "She didn't do anything but refuse to let me use her bathroom. What's an Outcast, anyway?"

He turned slowly and she was almost afraid to meet his eyes, but when he faced her, his face was concealed by shadows. "Outcasts are lawless vampires," he said, taking a step toward her. Sian stepped back and hated herself for it. "Vampires who kill their prey. I am sworn to hunt them down and protect humans from them."

Sian wanted to shoot back some snappy comment about what nonsense he was spouting when she remembered the eerie laughter and the way her attackers had taunted her. How could anyone touch her and vanish so fast she hadn't even seen them?

Diego watched her in silence for a moment, seeing her fight to rationalize what had just happened. He fought the urge to step into the light and show her the truth of his words. Now wasn't the time. He didn't want to frighten her again and right now he was enraged, his fangs out and his fingernails elongated into killing talons. He wasn't exactly a reassuring sight.

But damn it all, she *should* be frightened. She'd almost died tonight and she had no idea how horrible her death would've been. She should be terrified, not standing up to him with the light of battle in her eyes and plans to evade him again running through her mind.

He took a deep breath, trying again to rein in his temper. Sian wasn't a prisoner to be kept safe on a shelf for his pleasure. Why had he thought he could win her trust and passion with chains? If he'd been doing his job as her mate, she wouldn't *want* to run away. Yes, Sian should be frightened tonight, but not of him. Never of him.

For the first time, he wondered if he'd been doing this all wrong from the start.

Finally she looked back up at him, searching for his eyes through the shadows. "I don't want you to hurt the clerk," she said quietly. "What happened back here isn't her fault, no matter what you think. She's just trying to make a living."

"And she would've received quite a payoff for delivering a Slayer's mate to a pack of Outcasts," he snarled. The mere thought of it was enough to negate any small progress he'd made in containing his temper.

She stepped back again. "They called me the same thing. I'm no one's *mate*, and do I even want to know what a Slayer is?"

"I'm a Slayer," he replied softly, seeing her alarm and trying again to get hold of his fury. "It means I'm a member of an organization called the Guardian's League. We dedicate our lives to keeping humans safe from the Outcasts, and keeping vampires safe from humans. We're protectors, lawkeepers." She'd understand that. He hoped. "Those of us who actively battle the Outcasts are called Slayers."

Her back was pressed to the dumpster now, putting her as far from him as she could get. She didn't look very understanding. His heart sank.

"And you're going to go in there and—and *slay* that poor woman?" she asked in horror. "Just because she told me to take a shortcut to the pancake place?"

The look on her face tore at him and he ran a hand through his hair with a sigh. He hated it, but he knew he was going to give in to her on this and leave the clerk alone despite every instinct demanding retribution. His need for revenge paled beside his desire to wipe the horror from Sian's eyes.

Revenge would have to wait. Sian came first.

He took a deep breath and forced his rage away, feeling his fangs and claws slowly retract. Only when he was sure all traces of his vampire nature were gone did he step into the light and reach for Sian's hand. "I wasn't going to kill her," he said quietly, wondering if he was lying. "I'd planned on giving her a good scare to keep her from associating with Outcasts. But if you wish it, Sian, I will leave her alone. On one condition."

Sian's hand was cold in his but she met his eyes squarely. "Let me guess," she said, her tone resigned. "You want me to go back home with you."

He smiled a little, trying to lighten the bleakness in her eyes. "I was planning on asking for a thank you kiss for saving you, but your idea is much better," he teased.

Sian didn't smile back. "Did they get away with my purse?"

Diego reached out and caressed her cheek. "They didn't get away at all," he said gently. "I can't allow anyone to threaten you, Sian. I won't." It was a promise and a warning all in one.

She shivered and he turned to gather up her purse, giving her a moment to pull herself together. When he handed her things to her she took them as if on auto-pilot. Only when he held out her little gun did her expression change.

Sian looked at him in surprise as she accepted it from him. She checked the clip and frowned to find it still loaded, minus the single shot the Outcast had fired at him in desperation during their fight. "Why would you give me this back?" she asked, confusion evident in her eyes.

Diego tucked it into her purse and slipped the strap over her shoulder. "You're not my prisoner, Sian, despite what you think," he said, wishing he knew how to make her believe it. "You are the most important person in the world to me. Whatever you want is yours for the asking. You won't have a reason to shoot me and I want you to have all the protection you can get. Why shouldn't I let you have your gun?"

"If I'm not your prisoner, why did you follow me tonight?"

He shook his head in exasperation. "Would you rather I hadn't? Honestly, Sian, you drive me crazy. Can I do nothing right?"

Sian started to answer but stopped herself. When had she become such a shrew? If Diego hadn't arrived when he had, she'd still be at the mercy of three men who looked like they had none. She blushed and looked at her feet.

"Thank you for saving me." The words were difficult for her, but she knew she owed him at least that much.

"You're very welcome," Diego replied, and she heard the smile in his voice as he draped an arm over her shoulders. "Now, can I take you home or did you have your heart set on eating at the pancake place?"

She blinked in surprise. He was willing to take her to a restaurant, a very public place where she could speak to people and ask for help? She didn't know what had caused this sudden change of attitude and she wasn't sure she trusted it yet. After all, what sane woman would trust a man who called himself a Slayer?

"I've lost my appetite," she said, and it was true. Reaction was setting in and all she wanted was to sleep off the adrenaline letdown. "I guess I'll go back to your house since I don't have a home of my own anymore."

"My home is your home. Everything in it is yours," Diego said, running a gentle fingertip down her cheek. "Next time you want to go to the city, why don't you take a car? I think I had a heart attack at the thought of you hitchhiking."

She laughed a little. "Hard to take a car without keys," she pointed out.

Diego reached into his pocket and pulled out his own keys, dropping them into her hand without hesitation. Sian stared stupidly at them for a moment. "You were serious?"

He sighed. "Of course I was serious. One of these days you'll learn I can't lie to you. Now close your eyes."

"Why?"

"Because I asked you to."

Sian looked at him for a long moment before complying. After what he'd done for her tonight, hesitating to trust him enough to close her eyes seemed petty. Diego lifted her in his arms and she didn't bother to protest. She started to open her eyes at the sudden feel of incredible speed and wind rushing past her, but Diego bent and murmured in her ear as though he truly was reading her mind.

"Keep them closed, *querida*. If I see those gorgeous baby blues I swear I'm going to kiss you senseless." She squeezed her eyes shut and he chuckled softly. "I'm starting to think you don't like my kisses," he teased.

"You can keep your lips to yourself." Still, she clutched his shoulders hard as the bottom seemed to fall out of her stomach. It felt like she was falling from a great height, almost like flying—but that was madness. She'd seen him run fast the night they'd found her apartment trashed. Surely running was all he was doing now.

But why would he want her to close her eyes for it?

"I'm losing my mind," Sian mumbled, holding onto his shoulders tight. "And you're not helping."

Diego laughed as he glided down and landed softly on the porch. He should've known better than to try to hide the flight from her, should've called a taxi again, but if she didn't know what he was after what had happened in the alley, she was truly insane. Besides, he'd needed the freedom of flight to help clear the last traces of fear from his mind.

"All right, we're here," he said, setting her gently on her feet but keeping his arms around her.

As soon as Sian opened her eyes, Diego made good on his promise and gave in to the need to claim her mouth. She gasped in surprise and he used the opening to sweep his tongue inside, catching fire at once and growling at the intoxicating taste of her lips. *Dios*, he'd been worried sick about her! He pulled her fully into his arms as he walked her back until her back was pressed to the front door. The feel of her body pressed hard against his only spurred him on. Her hands tightened on his shoulders and she kissed him back, tentatively at first and then more eagerly. Diego threaded his fingers into her hair, loving the way she responded to him and determined to make her as wild with need as he was.

She made a needy sound into his mouth and he kissed her again, a long, slow kiss that made him burn. She clung to him with a desire she wouldn't admit and his frustration reached new heights. Her eyes caressed him when she thought he wasn't looking and she responded to his kisses like a starving woman at a feast, but she still refused to acknowledge what was between them. She still ran away.

He wanted her to admit she wanted him, damn it. He was getting tired of having to steal kisses from her.

He forced himself to pull away despite the raw desire pounding through his body. The sight of Sian looking up at him, her aquamarine eyes misty with passion, was almost enough to make him forget his resolve to stop. He forced himself to step back, releasing her completely.

Sian pressed her fingers to her lips, still looking at him with dazed eyes. He gave her a smile that felt false on his lips.

"Forgive me," he said, reaching past her and opening the door. "I forgot you wanted me to keep my lips to myself."

Sian stared at him as he brushed past her and went inside without another word, too stunned to move. He'd been angry just now. She'd seen it in his face and heard it in his voice. How could he kiss her like that and be angry a second later?

"Diego?" she said, following him through the open door hesitantly and only now realizing they were back at his house. How had he gotten them home this fast? She'd seen him run fast before but it hadn't felt like he'd been running—

"You need something?" he asked over his shoulder.

She followed him into the kitchen but stopped dead in her tracks when she saw the red stain on the back of his platinum shirt. Every other thought evaporated.

"Diego, you're hurt!" she cried, hurrying to him and pushing up the back of his shirt, searching for his wound.

He brushed her hands away and shrugged his shirt off himself. "The bullet grazed my shoulder," he said calmly. She watched him pull the dishtowel off its hook and press it to a raw, painful-looking gouge on the back of his shoulder. "It's nothing," he added, glancing at her face. The anger melted from his eyes and he gave her a concerned look. "It'll be gone tomorrow night, Sian. There's no need to look like that."

She didn't know how she looked, but she felt horrified, and she thought she had every reason to be that way. He'd actually gotten *shot* while fighting for her tonight. She watched a blossom of red appear on the white dishtowel and clutched the back of one of the chairs.

"Diego, you're bleeding," she said, telling herself resolutely she wasn't going to be sick despite the queasy feeling in her stomach. This was crazy. She had no problem with the sight of blood and never had. Why should she feel like passing out at the sight of it now?

Because it's Diego who's sitting there bleeding, a little voice in her mind piped up, and much as Sian wanted to deny it, she couldn't.

"Where's your first aid kit, or do you even have one?" she asked, turning and starting to go through the cabinets, anything to keep herself from staring at his bloodstained shirt or the little red blossom on the towel. Her lips felt numb and her ears were ringing. She was on the verge of passing out and hated herself for it. "You shouldn't use a kitchen towel, it's not sterile, you'll get an infection—no, forget the first aid kit, you should go to the hospital, you probably need stitches or something, a tetanus shot or—"

She stopped babbling when she felt his hands on her shoulders. "Calm down," Diego said softly. "I'm fine, Sian."

She whirled on him. "Sit down!" she snapped, pushing him back toward a chair. "And keep pressure on that!" He looked like he was going to argue for a moment and she pushed him again. What if he passed out? How in the world would she move him to a bed? The man outweighed her by a hundred pounds if he weighed an ounce. "*Sit!*"

He obeyed with the merest hint of amusement on his face, spinning a chair around and straddling it backwards. "The first aid kit is on top of the refrigerator," he told her, pointing. "If you're feeling medical, I'd let you put some butterflies on this. It'll heal without them, but I think I have enough scars already."

She glared at him even as she went to pull down the kit. "You need stitches, not butterfly bandages," she repeated as she slammed the kit down on the table, letting her anger wash away the dizziness. This was stupid, completely and utterly ridiculous. She should use this opportunity and the keys he'd given her to get out of here, and yet here she was, playing nurse. It made no sense.

She refused to analyze it further and opened the first aid kit. Her eyes widened as she looked over the contents. "Are you setting up your own hospital here or something?" she asked, incredulous. He had everything she could possibly think of in here and some things she didn't even want to know the uses of. "Good Lord, Diego, do you get hurt a lot?"

He laughed at her. "You saw tonight what I do on a nightly basis," he said. "What do you think?"

She wasn't touching that one. She dug through the kit and pulled out a suture kit wrapped in plastic. She looked at it for a long moment, trying to figure out if she could bring herself to use it, when Diego spoke again.

"I don't need stitches, Sian. Just slap some tape over this and I'll be good as new, I promise."

"That's good, because I don't think I can do stitches without passing out on you," Sian admitted, exchanging the suture kit for a little package of butterfly closures. "Do you have something for pain? This is going to hurt."

He shrugged. "Chemicals don't go well with my system," he said. "It's best if you just do it fast and get it over with."

Sian bit her lip to keep from arguing. If he wanted to be a manly man and take the pain, who was she to try to dissuade him? She wet another dish towel and cleaned around the towel Diego still held. He moved it and she sucked in a breath at the sight of the raw wound, but she fought down the queasiness that tried to overcome her, she gently cleaned the area, wincing with sympathetic pain the entire time. She hesitated once more after opening the butterflies. "Are you sure you won't take anything before I do this?"

He raised an eyebrow at her. "Why, if I didn't know you better I'd swear you were concerned about me."

"I just don't want to hurt anyone," Sian snapped, feeling her cheeks heat and knowing she hadn't fooled him. "Not even someone as arrogant as you."

He laughed. "Just do it, Sian," he told her gently. "They haven't invented a pain medicine yet that will work on a vampire. I'll be fine."

"There you go with the vampire stuff again," Sian grumbled, hoping he didn't see how her hands trembled. "At least you're not suggesting I think of another way to distract you."

He leaned his forehead against the back of the chair. "Trust me, the thought crossed my mind. Unfortunately I have a good imagination and I'm sure I can picture exactly how receptive you'd be to the suggestion, and I have no desire to add another wound to my collection."

Sian drew the first butterfly across the wound, pinching it together until the edges touched. Diego didn't wince or move, but she knew it had to hurt, and she hurried with the rest of them. He was so still she wondered for a moment if he'd passed out. The only movement was the gentle rise and fall of his chest as he breathed. When she finished with the last one, she touched his other shoulder gently.

"Diego, are you all right?"

He turned his head and gave her a little smile, his eyes still closed, and she breathed a sigh of relief and turned back to the kit. "You have a much gentler touch than James," Diego said. "I think I'll keep you."

She laughed more from nervousness than humor. Tears came to her eyes for no explainable reason and she blinked them away. "I don't know if my first-aid training extends to vampires. Maybe you'd better stick with James."

She heard him move behind her and shivered when his fingertips brushed her hair. "Yes, but you're much better looking than James."

She fought the urge to turn and wrap her arms around him, to run her hands over him and reassure herself that he was truly all right. What was wrong with her tonight?

"Oh, I don't know," she said, babbling the first thing that came to mind to distract her thoughts from that dangerous path. "Dress him up in a skirt and who knows?"

Diego chuckled and moved away. She wasn't sure if she was disappointed or relieved when he left the kitchen. She dropped into the chair he'd vacated, wrapping her arms around herself as reaction from this crazy night crashed in on her.

She might have died tonight, died in some random alley for no reason at all. It wasn't Santonyo's thugs who'd attacked her tonight. Her death would've been a random act of violence, another statistic at the hands of some faceless street punks who'd been at the right place at the wrong time. Diego had incredibly shown up in the nick of time and saved her, but he'd gotten shot in the process and it was only due to simple luck he hadn't been seriously hurt.

Diego could have died for her.

Sian shuddered at the thought of another innocent life being lost because of her. As much as Diego annoyed her, she didn't want him to die because of her. The memory of his bloodstained shirt shot through her and she drew her legs up, pressing her forehead to her knees and wishing she could disappear. She couldn't stop shaking, wanting nothing more than to curl up in a ball somewhere and hide.

She wasn't a cop anymore. She wasn't the tough cookie who had taken on one of Savannah's biggest drug lords. She wasn't the brave woman who had ditched the Witness Protection Program and decided to take her chances with her safety on her own. She was just a woman now, and she felt incredibly alone and terribly afraid she would never feel safe again.

Chapter Nine

Strong arms suddenly came around her and held her close. "Easy," Diego murmured, rocking her gently. "It's all right now. I've got you. It's over."

Sian forgot her pride and wrapped her arms around his waist, holding him tight and hiding her face against his chest. She didn't care right now that she didn't dare trust him and couldn't protect him. She wanted comfort and he was offering it.

"You might have died," she whispered, squeezing her eyes shut against the tears threatening to escape. "And it would have been my fault!"

"Shh," he soothed, stroking her hair. "I'm not that easy to kill, *querida*."

She shook her head, wanting to believe him but knowing it wasn't true. Everyone thought they were hard to kill right up until they were staring down the barrel of a gun. She held him tighter and tried to pull herself back together, but inside she was falling apart. She hated for anyone to see her like this but she couldn't stop clinging to him, taking the comfort he offered as she tried not to break down completely.

Diego stroked her hair again, reassuring her without words, rocking her until her trembling eased and her silent tears stopped. "I know you don't believe many things I've told you," he murmured when she quieted at last, "but if you believe nothing else I ever say, believe this. I will keep you safe, Sian. I swear on my life I will."

His quiet declaration brought tears back to her eyes and she blinked rapidly, trying to keep them from falling. "You don't know anything about me," she whispered.

"I know about Enrique Santonyo."

She gasped and jerked back, staring up at him in shock. Never in her wildest dreams had she imagined he would say such a thing. For a moment she couldn't find her voice and when she did she could only manage one word. "How?"

He gave her a little smile but his eyes were steely. "I would have liked you to tell me, but it's enough that I know," he said as he wiped the tears from her cheeks with gentle fingers. "I know what happened in Savannah and I know why you want to run again now. Santonyo won't touch you ever again. I won't let him get within a mile of you. If he tries, I'll make him wish he'd never drawn breath, and that's a promise."

She shivered at both the mention of her enemy's name and the dark threat in Diego's voice. "You're only one man," she said, trying to be reasonable when everything inside her ached to grab the security he offered. "He has a hundred or more at his disposal. You don't understand how he thinks, how seriously he takes revenge. He'll stop at nothing to get to me, Diego, and he won't hesitate to go through you to do it."

"I'd love for him to try." Diego brushed her hair back from her face, a tender gesture that touched her all the way to the heart despite her resolve not to let it. "*Querida,* I think I know more about revenge than he could even imagine, and I will stop at nothing to keep you safe. He has terrorized you long enough and it ends here. You don't have to run anymore."

Sian wanted to throw herself back into his arms, but pulled away instead. She wanted to believe him. God, how she wanted to have a safe haven, a place where her past couldn't touch her, but it was selfish to lead Santonyo to Diego. She'd already almost gotten him killed once. She couldn't live with herself if Santonyo found out where she was and hurt Diego or James.

Diego let her go but gently pressed her back into the chair when she started to get up to leave. "You need to eat," he said, turning to the refrigerator. "I'll make you something."

She watched him pull out a handful of vegetables and start to put together a salad for her. "I thought you said you were a vampire," she said, trying for humor to hide how scattered she still felt. "Why do you know how to cook? I thought the occasional Bloody Mary would be the extent of your culinary skills."

He gave her a grin over his shoulder as he chopped a carrot, and she could have kissed him for embracing the lighter mood she was trying to set. "Someone has to take care of James when he gets sick and stays in bed, whining that he's too weak to come to the kitchen and fend for himself." He brandished the knife like Zorro. "I make a mean chicken noodle soup."

That grin should be outlawed, Sian thought as she tried to focus on what Diego had said. "I thought he was your servant," she said.

Diego shrugged. It sent muscles rippling all the way down his back. "Technically that's true, but you try convincing him he's a servant," he replied, tossing everything into a bowl and pouring dressing on for her. "When I need him, he takes care of me, and vice versa. In the end, we're both better off for the arrangement."

Sian stared at the salad he put in front of her. It looked delicious but her stomach clenched at the thought of eating anything. Diego nudged her fork closer. "You'll feel better if you eat."

"Aren't you having anything?"

He gave her another smile and sent her thoughts scattering. "I think I'll live without feeding for one night," he replied lightly. "Now eat."

She opened her mouth to ask him what he meant by "feeding" but thought better of it when he gave her a knowing smile. She might be exhausted and scattered, but she wasn't stupid enough to walk into that one.

When she finished the salad, Diego took the bowl and put it in the sink before taking both her hands and drawing her to her feet. "You're not used to staying up all night," he said as he urged her out of the kitchen and toward the stairs. "And I know you didn't sleep well yesterday. I'm putting you to bed early tonight, wildcat."

Sian thought about digging in her heels and protesting, but he was right. She was completely wiped out. Still, she couldn't let that "wildcat" remark slide. "I don't need you to put me to bed, caveman."

He laughed. "Are you trying to get tossed over my shoulder again?"

Sian quickened her pace to put some distance between them and Diego laughed again. "I think your shoulder's had all the excitement it can stand for one night," she said as she hurried up the stairs in front of him. "And speaking of beds, I want my own."

Diego didn't reply until they reached his door. Sian turned to face him instead of opening the door, her chin raised stubbornly. "Diego, I want my own bed," she repeated.

"I heard you the first time."

He reached past her and opened the door. Sian didn't go through it. "I know you're hung up on this 'bondmate' nonsense," she said, crossing her arms and glaring despite her fatigue, "but it's not true. I am not your wife. I'm not even your girlfriend. I don't want to sleep in the same bed with you. Now are you going to give me a place of my own to sleep or am I going to take you up on your offer of a car to drive away in?"

Diego sighed. "Just because you don't want to believe something doesn't make it untrue," he murmured, reaching up and touching her cheek lightly. "I know you don't understand anything about bonding or my people and I know this is hard for you. Give it some time, Sian. Give me a chance. That's all I'm asking."

She realized she should have knocked his hand away before he dropped it on his own and was furious with herself for not beating him to it. "And all I'm asking is for a little space and a little privacy," she replied. "You've put a weird tattoo on me without my consent, given me clothes that make me look like a slut, refused to even let me have any decent underwear, and I think I've been a damn good sport about all of this. Is it too much to ask for you leave me alone while I sleep?"

Diego sighed and stepped back. "You have never looked like a slut and I don't think I'm the one responsible for the positions you manage to wake up in," he said, but before she could snap at him he waved a hand at the hall. "All right, you win. Pick a room."

"Thank you." Sian stepped past him and opened the first door she came to. The room behind it was enormous, almost a suite in itself, with a couch and armchair grouped at one end and a tall bed almost as large as Diego's on a raised dais at the other. She glimpsed a door to a bathroom across from the little living area. "This one," she said, overwhelmed by the luxury of this guest room and too tired to look any farther.

"It's yours."

Sian turned to get her gown and robe from Diego's room and found him holding them out to her. She hadn't even heard him move. "Thanks," she said as she took them from him. Then she groaned, remembering the things she'd bought at the variety store. Yet again she was stuck with no underwear. "I forgot my shopping bag," she said when Diego looked at her in concern.

He smiled at her. "I will get you something to wear, Sian, I promise."

"Yeah, yeah," she grumbled, turning and going into her new room. "Right after hell freezes over, right?"

She started to close the door but Diego stopped her. "Don't I get a goodnight kiss?" he asked, clearly trying to look as pitiful as possible.

Sian laughed. Beneath the hangdog expression, his eyes were positively sinful. "You're hopeless. Do you never give up?"

"Not when I see something I want." A little thrill went through her as he looked at her, leaving her no doubt exactly what he meant. He leaned closer, a hand braced on the doorframe and a clear challenge in his tone. "I've given you what you wanted, *querida*. Is it too much to ask for you to do the same for me?"

She caught herself twisting her nightgown into knots and made herself stop it. "I have a feeling that if I gave you what you wanted, I'd be right back in your bed, and my lack of panties wouldn't be an issue." Dear Lord, had that really just come out of her mouth?

He dropped all attempts to look innocent and grinned. "You said it, not me."

Sian knew she should tell him no, slam the door in his face and lock it, but she couldn't make herself do it. He stood there looking like pure sin, his lips more tempting than Godiva chocolate. Despite her resolve not to respond, everything female in her rose up and demanded a taste. Surely one little goodnight kiss couldn't hurt.

Sian leaned up and pressed her lips to his before she could chicken out. His lips were firm, the roughness of his goatee abrading her cheek in a way that was entirely too pleasant. He didn't try to take control of the kiss even when she hesitantly ran her tongue over his lower lip, asking for entrance. When his tongue touched hers, hot desire shot through her to pool low in her belly. He tasted like everything she'd ever been warned against and she couldn't resist going back for more, another soft, slow kiss that seemed to spin on forever.

When she realized what she was doing, Sian pulled back. He let her go, but when she looked back up at him his eyes were burning and his breath came fast against her mouth. The thought that she'd done this to him with a simple kiss sent heat washing through her and she almost leaned up to do it again.

She caught herself just in time. "Goodnight," she whispered, scooting back at top speed and closing the door in his face. She didn't care if she was rude. This was about self-preservation, not politeness.

She heard his deep chuckle through the door and bit her lip. "Sleep well," he murmured, and despite the softness of his voice she had no problem hearing him. His words seemed to caress her despite the solid wood between them. "Dream of me."

Sian sincerely hoped she wouldn't.

But she did anyway.

☪ ☪ ☪

Sian woke some unknown time later and stretched lazily. She felt about a thousand percent better. Much as she hated to admit it, Diego had been right. She'd needed this.

Remembering the last time she'd woken with this feeling of peace and contentment, Sian slowly reached out and patted the bed beside her, almost expecting to find Diego there. The bed was empty. Sian opened her eyes and pushed down a strange feeling of disappointment as she threw the covers back. After the wildly erotic dreams she'd had all night—dreams which had all starred Diego, featured slow, hot kisses, and ended in heights too amazing to possibly be real—she would've killed him had she woken to find him beside her. She was clearly still half-asleep, that's all. No way she missed the feeling of lying in his arms.

Sian stood. Halfway to the bathroom, she realized she hadn't brought a change of clothes from Diego's room last night, and headed toward the bedroom door instead. She'd sneak into his room, snag a change of clothes, and be out of there quiet as a mouse. She turned the doorknob slowly, trying to be as quiet as possible—

It didn't turn.

Disbelief wiped away the last of the contentment she'd woken with. Sian stared at the door, trying the knob again as anger started to overtake her. How dare he lock her in? He had sworn repeatedly last night she wasn't a prisoner, and now he locked her in her room?

Sian pounded on the door and shouted for a few minutes before giving up angrily. She spun around and stared at the heavy curtains covering the windows, thinking of trying to escape through there again. She'd had enough of this. She didn't like games. But something on the couch caught her eye when she started toward the window.

Diego lay on her couch, sleeping deeply, his bare chest magnificently displayed and a black satin sheet covering him from the waist down.

Sian stared for a minute, completely taken aback. He must sleep like the dead not to have awakened with all the racket she'd made pounding on the door. She walked over and hesitated, trying to get up the nerve to reach out and shake him awake. His bare skin looked entirely too inviting. Did she dare to touch him right now after having such erotic dreams about him all night?

She shook herself, reaching for her anger again and trying not to stare, but good Lord, the man was gorgeous. What harm would a little staring do before she woke him up and gave him a tongue-lashing he'd never forget?

Her thoughts were cut short when she realized he hadn't taken a breath the entire time she'd been standing there.

"Diego!" Sian cried, forgetting all the mean things she'd been planning to say to him and shaking him by his shoulders. That gunshot wound last night hadn't been enough to kill him, she was sure of it. Had he been injured somewhere else and hadn't told her? Had he been coming to her for help and collapsed on the couch before he could reach her? "Diego, wake up!"

Nothing. Fighting down panic, Sian pressed her ear to his chest and prayed to hear a heartbeat. "Don't you dare die on me or I swear I'll kill you," she whispered, closing her eyes and listening hard.

Finally she heard it. His heart was still beating, it was just beating so slowly she'd missed it at first. Pressed against his chest like this, she was barely able to discern the faint rise and fall of his slow breaths. Sian wanted to cry with relief and hated herself for it.

It's just relief that I'm not stuck in here with a dead body, she told herself firmly as she sniffled, ignoring that she was still sitting here on the edge of the couch with her head on his chest and her hands clutching his shoulders for dear life.

Finally Sian managed to raise her head, making sure his eyes were still closed before wiping her eyes with the hem of her robe. He didn't move a muscle. She frowned. She'd never in her life encountered anyone who slept this deeply.

Was he only sleeping or was he unconscious?

Sian reached up and ran her hands through his hair, checking his head for any signs he'd been knocked out. Almost at once her thoughts were derailed by the silky texture of his hair sliding through her fingers. She'd never known a man with such thick, satiny hair. It was enough to make a girl jealous. She slid her hand through his hair again, more slowly this time, her fingertips lightly brushing his scalp before trailing down the back of his neck.

His skin was warm beneath her fingers, his muscles firm as she ran her palms across his shoulders. Sian's mouth went dry and she bit her lip, trying to focus. Injuries. She was looking for injuries, not copping a feel!

But maintaining her focus was a challenge as she glanced back down at his chest. She'd touched him before, but she'd been mostly asleep at the time. The thought of sliding her hands over those curling dark hairs and all that lush skin while she was awake enough to appreciate it was enough to make her pulse kick into high gear. She hesitated a moment before pressing her palms to his chest, biting her lip again. The man had muscles to spare, and even relaxed in sleep he looked like a master's sculpture come to life.

Sian took a deep breath to steady herself and ran her hands down his sides, trying to ignore how very good he felt and concentrate on checking for hidden wounds. She didn't find anything amiss, but for some reason her hands didn't stop sliding back over his ribs. The ridges of his muscles teased her palms. Her gaze traveled over his flat stomach, his abs defined even in sleep, and her fingers smoothed over them of their own accord.

Her breath caught. She could see his abdomen just fine. There was no need to check for injuries with her hands. Her mind knew it was the truth, but her hands weren't listening. They were telling her every inch of him needed to be thoroughly explored and were itching to get started.

And her mind was apparently checking out of the conversation, leaving her hands in charge.

Her hands were not shy at all. They wanted to explore his incredible chest and did so, reveling in the breadth of his muscles, their solid strength beneath her palms. One fingertip circled his nipple and she bit her lip as it hardened, unable—or unwilling—to bring her wayward hands back under control. Sian watched them glide down toward his hips and over his thighs through the sheet. She felt the heat of his body even through the cloth and it awoke an answering heat in her, especially when she saw that while the rest of his body was apparently sleeping like the dead, one certain part of him was entirely awake. Her cheeks heated but she couldn't make herself glance away, a wicked urge to cup him through the sheet making her hands tremble.

She shook her head sharply and tried again to focus on what she was supposed to be doing. If she was looking for wounds, how was she going to find them through a sheet and his pajamas? Her shameless hands went at once to the top of the sheet, but she stopped herself before she could rip it away.

Was she really going to undress him in his sleep?

Sian glanced back up at his face and the sight of him was enough to make her heart skip a beat. Those incredible emerald eyes were closed, his full lips slightly parted in sleep, his black goatee lending him the look of a devil in repose. He still showed no signs of waking.

"Diego?" she murmured. "Are you awake?"

Nothing. Not even a snore.

She leaned closer, close enough to feel his faint breath caress her lips when he exhaled. She closed her eyes and fought the urge to kiss those sleeping lips.

"Diego?" she whispered again, and somehow despite her resolve not to do it, her lips were brushing his. She forced herself to pull away before she gave in to the desire to part his lips and taste him. The memory of his hot kisses was more than enough.

She started to call louder but her voice didn't seem to want to work anymore. Her fingers curled around the top of the sheet and started to slide it away. Sian bit her lip and rationalized like mad, still carefully watching his face for signs of waking. Just because she was taking off his sheet didn't mean she was going to take off his pajamas. She was only doing this because of his unnaturally deep sleep. She had to make sure he was all right so she could give him hell for locking her in here when he finally woke up.

Only when she had the sheet down to his knees and dared at last to look away from his face did Sian realize he wasn't *wearing* pajamas.

She gasped, every moral and respectable bone in her body screaming in her mother's voice for her to stop staring and pull the sheet back up *right now*, but her arms weren't listening and her eyes didn't seem to want to hear it either. Her gaze stayed glued to his body as her fingers splayed on his bare thighs. She'd never had a great deal of experience with men, but she knew magnificence when she saw it.

And she was looking at it right now.

Her traitorous fingers tried to head in that direction again and Sian finally got control of them and jerked the sheet back up, breathing as though she'd just run a marathon. Good God, he was incredible all over. She tried to muster up some outrage that Diego had come into her room, *nude*, and collapsed on her couch, but all she could find was a lot of heat and a totally unwelcome urge to try to wake him up in an entirely different way.

Sian stood and backed away from the couch, pressing her hands to her cheeks as if the gesture could cool their burning. Outrage wasn't saving her. It'd be a little too hypocritical to be outraged at his nakedness when she'd spent the last ten minutes with her hands all over him.

Not to mention that she was shaking with the desire to toss her gown aside and feel all his hard male glory pressed against her, skin to skin, from her head to her toes.

She shuddered at the mental image and made herself turn away. This wasn't like her at all. She enjoyed sex as much as the next woman but she never lusted over men, and never in her life would she have imagined she would actually do what she'd just done to Diego while he slept. She walked resolutely to the bathroom, determined to put some distance between them and regain her composure.

A cold shower might help, too. She'd never tried it, had never been in a situation where she thought she *needed* to try it, but now definitely seemed like the time to find out if icy water truly did quench burning lust.

Almost twenty minutes later, Sian was soaking wet, shivering, and every bit as turned on as she'd been before. Every time she thought back to what was waiting in the bedroom, any progress she'd been making toward cooling off evaporated. She wouldn't have been surprised to see steam rising from her skin. She sighed in resignation as she turned off the shower and reached for a towel. There was no need to freeze herself to death. If the shower hadn't worked yet, it wasn't going to.

She looked at the clothes she'd had on last night and couldn't make herself put them back on. The back of the T-shirt was sticky with some sort of unidentifiable slime from when she'd pressed against the dumpster and her skirt was smudged with dirt. Both still seemed to hold the scent of fear. She dropped them and instead pulled her gown back on, cinching her robe tight around her. The satin on her skin was incredibly sensual, reminding her of the feel of Diego's lips against hers, but she wasn't about to take it off. She needed all the clothes she could get.

Sian forced the thought away and left the bathroom, wondering belatedly what time it was. She had no idea how long she'd slept but she was still tired. Diego was right, this nocturnal schedule combined with the terrifying events of last night had worn her out. She went back to bed, resolutely avoiding looking at the couch, and snuggled down beneath the covers again. She didn't expect to sleep again after what had just happened, but there wasn't anything else to do until Diego woke up and unlocked the door.

She was asleep almost as soon as her head touched the pillow.

☾ ☾ ☾

It wasn't long before the erotic dreams were back. Sian arched with a breathy sigh, her body already hot and aching for satisfaction. Gentle fingers trailed across her cheek before threading through her hair, rubbing her scalp in a sensual massage. The heat blossomed, building until Sian wanted to throw off the comforter. She was burning up. She pushed at the bedding and it was suddenly gone, replaced by a lean body pressing against her side from knee to chest.

Lips found her ear and nibbled for a moment. The soft rasp of whiskers on her sensitive skin sent shivers down her spine. Warm breath caressed her throat as those fingers trailed down the back of her neck and Sian moaned.

"Wake up, sleeping beauty," a deep voice murmured in her ear. "I want you awake so you can enjoy me touching you as much as I enjoyed you touching me."

Sian's eyes flew open with a gasp, wakefulness crashing down on her. The realization that Diego was no longer unconscious across the room on the couch but was now pressed against her, every hard inch of his body molded to hers, was enough to start a minor earthquake in her limbs. "Diego! What are you doing?"

"What were *you* doing, wildcat?" he murmured, his tongue tracing the curve of her ear. His hand slid down her arm and back up again.

If it was possible, her cheeks grew hotter as she realized he knew what she'd done. "You were unconscious," she said, her voice trembling as much as her body. How could he know? Had he been faking that deep sleep? She would have sworn it'd been genuine. "I—I was worried, I thought you were hurt or something. I was looking for injuries!"

"Were you, now?" His deep chuckle was a seduction all by itself. "And a very thorough search it was, *querida*. Did you find anything that interested you?"

The memory of pulling aside the sheet and seeing him in all his glory burst through her mind and Sian almost moaned again. She brought herself back to reality with an effort and tried to find the comforter to pull it back over her. "It wasn't like that!" she protested.

He chuckled again and kept nibbling and nuzzling at her ear. That minor earthquake was rapidly shooting off the Richter scale. "If it was all completely innocent, surely you won't mind me doing the same thing to you," he murmured in a voice like molten chocolate. "After all, I didn't examine you for injuries last night after the fight with the Outcasts. Are you hiding any wounds from me?"

His hand trailed down her ribs and Sian quivered from head to toe. "I'm fine, thanks," she squeaked in panic. "No wounds. I promise!"

He nipped her earlobe and a moan escaped despite her efforts to stifle it. Diego pulled her closer, his thigh sliding over hers. "I should have told you how a vampire sleeps," he whispered in her ear as his hand trailed back up her ribs and over her collarbone. "I sleep deeply, *querida*, and I don't wake during the day unless I feel danger. But I promise you, I am always aware of what is going on around me while I sleep." His fingertips traced a scalding line down the valley between her breasts and over her stomach. "Very aware," he breathed.

His hand was recreating the same path hers had taken over his body. Sian's breath caught in anticipation. "I didn't know," she whispered, remembering everything she'd done to him. "If I'd known I wouldn't have—"

He left her ear and brushed his mouth against hers, the imitation of the ghost-kiss she'd given him silencing her completely. "Then I'm very glad you didn't know," he said, his lips caressing hers with feather-light touches with every word. Every nerve seemed to be focused on the movement of his hand as it slid slowly up her abdomen and over her ribs. When he traced a fingertip around her nipple it was already stiff and aching and he let out a shuddering breath. "Were you as turned on as I am right now?" he breathed against her lips. "Did you like touching me, wildcat? Looking at me? Did you ache to taste me as I ache to taste you?" His thumb brushed her nipple, shooting hot desire through her entire body.

Sian didn't have the breath to answer. She didn't know how turned on he was, but she was in serious danger of spontaneous combustion. His hand went back to her waist, trailed down her thigh, and she knew he felt her muscles quiver beneath his palm. She didn't dare let herself move. If she put her hands out and felt bare skin, it would all be over. No way could she trust herself to push him away instead of pulling him closer. He paused there for a moment, his body pressed against hers, his mouth not quite touching hers, his hand very high on her thigh, and Sian was on the verge of begging him to do *something* when he spoke again.

"You looked," he said, and her cheeks went so hot she thought they must be glowing. His mouth moved to her throat, skimming down to rest over her pulse. "But you didn't touch. I wanted you to touch me, Sian. Didn't you want to?"

"I—" It was all she could get out. She seemed to have forgotten the English language.

Well, every word but *yes*, and she had just enough sense of self-preservation left to know she absolutely could not say that to him.

"I want to look at you," he whispered, pulling away from her throat to bury his face in her hair. "But if I look, I *will* touch, and if I touch you again I won't stop until I'm inside you." She shuddered at the vivid image his words painted. His lips brushed hers once more before he spoke again. "You can't touch me like that in my sleep again unless you want me as much as I want you. There's only so much any man can stand. Do you understand, *querida*?"

His low voice only stoked the fires burning her to the core and all Sian could do was close her eyes and nod. The thought of Diego inside her was enough to sear away every last shred of her reason. She knew if he kissed her now or touched her again, if he so much as breathed across her lips, she would throw herself at him. The strength of her desire shocked her.

And suddenly he was gone. She opened her eyes in time to see the bathroom door close. She sat up, shaking from head to toe, but only when she heard the shower start did she regain the ability to think again.

She hoped Diego got more out of his cold shower than she had out of hers.

Chapter Ten

Sian pulled her robe back on with trembling hands and tested the bedroom door again, praying Diego had unlocked it before he'd slipped into her bed. She really, really needed to get out of here before she gave in to the temptation to join him in the shower. When the door opened, she bolted for the stairs, not stopping until she found herself in the kitchen where she leaned against the sink, breathless and shaken. What insanity had made her touch him? What madness had possessed her to let him touch her back?

She closed her eyes, gripping the counter tightly and fighting to get herself back under control. The impact of his touch still reverberated through her. If he could do this to her without even kissing her, what would it be like if he—

"Feeling all right?"

Sian yelped in surprise and spun around at the deep voice, clutching her robe closed as she faced the intruder. Her gaze collided with the most intimidating man she'd ever seen in her life and her heart skipped a beat.

Well over six and a half feet tall with white-blond hair and midnight eyes, the man leaning in the doorway was like no one she'd ever encountered before. He reminded her of a raptor, elegant and gorgeous to a terrifying degree, but the coldness in his eyes made her feel about as brave as a mouse cowering on the ground when the owl's shadow fell over it. There was something about him that screamed power and danger. Intimidating as Diego was, this man made him look like a Boy Scout.

"You're a vampire, aren't you?" Sian asked, forgetting she didn't believe in vampires and blurting the first thing that came to mind.

He smiled at her, a gorgeous sexy grin that in no way softened his dangerous face. "Of course," he agreed. He straightened and walked toward her. "Eli, at your service."

Sian gaped at him, trying to back away only to find the sink at her back. She knew that name. She remembered Diego saying Eli's will had overrode both theirs when it came to this bonding thing, remembered him blaming Eli for this mess they were both in. "You—you're the one who—"

He laughed at her stuttering. "I'm the one who," he agreed. "How's it working out, by the way?"

His cavalier attitude toward the trouble he'd caused made her blood boil and she embraced the anger. It was so much better than fear. She took a breath to scream at him, but she could find no words vile enough to describe him.

"How dare you?" she finally spluttered, outraged.

"Hmm." One eyebrow rose, but apart from that he might not have noticed her anger at all from all the note he took of it. "Not good, I take it."

"How would you like it if someone did this to you? No, you bastard, it's not good. Take this thing off my arm right now!" She knew it wasn't a rational demand, but she wasn't feeling particularly rational. Besides, this man looked more than capable of doing the impossible.

He laughed again. "There's no undoing a bonding, little mortal, and I wouldn't if I could," he said calmly, further infuriating her. As she drew in a breath to yell at him again, he held up a hand. "Here," he said, and a bottle of wine materialized in his open palm. "A peace offering. Share it with Diego and talk things out. It might look better come morning."

She snatched the wine from him, intending to smash the bottle over his meddling head, but he was too fast for her and was out of reach before she could even lift the bottle in preparation of her strike. His laughter echoed around the room as he vanished through the kitchen door.

Sian set the bottle down on the counter hard, shaking with rage. Well, at least Eli's visit had accomplished one thing—fear and fury had a way of killing even the most potent desire. She found herself going through drawers as she fumed, searching for a corkscrew.

So what if she'd only woken up a few minutes ago. The clock on the stove said it was after eight in the evening, and right now a glass of wine sounded like exactly what she needed to soothe her shattered nerves.

She'd just found a corkscrew when Diego burst into the kitchen. "Who's here?" he demanded, scanning the kitchen. Not finding anyone but Sian, he turned those piercing green eyes on her. "I heard a voice. Who's here?"

Her own voice had deserted her. Diego had apparently come straight from his shower when he'd heard the intruder and hadn't bothered to get dressed. Water dripped down his chest from his wet hair and apart from a towel around his waist, he was completely nude. Her heart kicked hard and she wondered if he heard it.

He finished searching the kitchen and came back to rest on her with an intensity she felt like a touch. She turned back to the counter, refusing to look at him standing there wearing only that entirely inadequate towel, and started attacking the foil around the neck of the bottle with the corkscrew. It just wasn't fair for him to be this sexy. No man should be this divine.

"Your friend, Eli, was here," she said, managing to keep the aggravation out of her voice, "but he left."

Diego growled. The vicious sound sent a chill down her spine. Sian managed to peel the foil away at last and jabbed the corkscrew down. How in the world had she enjoyed touching someone who could make such a wolfish, untamed noise?

How could she be standing here wanting to touch him again?

She wrenched the cork out and dropped it, still attached to the corkscrew, on the counter before searching for a glass.

"What are you doing?" Diego asked, and she jumped at the sound of his voice coming from right behind her shoulder. The man could move as silently as a cat when he chose and it never failed to unnerve her.

"Having a drink of this lovely wine your buddy brought," she said, scooting away from him at top speed. Maybe distance would help her kill the persistent voice urging her to throw herself back into his arms. "Want some?"

His hand covered the top of her glass. "Shouldn't you eat something first?"

He'd followed her, negating her retreat. The concern in his voice warmed her but the heat coming off his bare body behind hers made her burn. Sian fought the desire to lean back against him and snatched the glass from under his hand instead. "Probably," she agreed, pouring a little wine anyway before turning to him, bottle in hand. "Now do you want some or not?"

It was a mistake. He stood much too close to her, bare-chested and wet and more tempting than homemade sin, and Sian backed up again. Diego gently took the bottle from her and set it on the counter. "Let me fix you something to eat first," he murmured, reaching for the half-full glass.

Sian didn't release it. Why did he have to be so determined to take care of her? It stole her anger and she needed it right now to help her ignore the other feelings racing through her. She'd never known a man like him, fierce and forbidding yet so soft beneath his tough exterior that he melted her. No one had ever taken care of her. No one had ever been concerned enough about her to try.

"I don't want anything to eat," she told him, but this time there was no edge to her voice. "Don't worry about me, Diego."

He released the glass reluctantly. "Comes with the territory," he said softly, and she couldn't stop her eyes going to the dark band on the skin of his forearm.

Territory. She shook herself back to reality. He was getting to her with this "bonding" thing he kept talking about. He almost had her believing it too. She had to get out of here before he completely brainwashed her. "I'm not your territory," she said, raising the glass to her lips.

Diego watched the glass touch her lips, watched them part and let the wine slide in, saw her throat quiver as she swallowed, and cursed the need that still pounded through him. Cold showers were good for nothing. He should know that after a hundred years of them, but he hadn't been thinking clearly when he'd left Sian on the bed.

Clearly? He hadn't been thinking at all or he would never have left. She hadn't said the word he'd ached to hear, but her body had been screaming it with every delicious shiver and it had been all over her mind. Yes. To everything.

She took another sip of wine and a ruby droplet clung to her lip. When the tip of her tongue flicked out to capture it, he bit back a groan. *Dios*, he wanted her so badly he thought he might shatter if he moved. She caught him watching and her cheeks flushed. He knew his desire was written in his eyes but he didn't care. She was his mate, whether she believed it or not, and he wanted her to know how he badly he needed her.

She shivered, her cheeks going from pink to crimson, and even from across the kitchen he heard her breath catch. He cursed his hypersensitive vampire senses for picking up these tiny clues to her desire because it made certain things stir under the towel that he really wished would behave.

But that particular part wasn't interested in behaving around Sian. When it came to her, it clearly had a one-track mind.

Sian started to take another sip of wine but she swayed before the glass touched her lips. Diego was at her side in a heartbeat, steadying her with a hand on her arm and frowning down at her in concern. "Are you all right?"

She pressed a hand to her forehead. "I don't know," she said. "I feel... strange."

Diego took the glass from her and set it aside. "Strange how?"

Her skin was flushed and she dropped her robe to the floor. "I feel..."

Sian's voice trailed off and Diego tightened his grip on her arm. She sucked in a breath and he instantly loosened his hands, afraid he'd hurt her, but when she met his gaze there was no trace of pain in her eyes. What was there was enough to make his own breath catch and he suddenly wished he'd stayed on the other side of the room.

She reached up and traced his mouth with a fingertip. "I want to eat you alive," she murmured in a husky tone he'd never heard from her before. His cock throbbed painfully in response. Her lips curved in a sensual smile when she felt it against her hip and when she looked back at him, those blue eyes were molten pools of desire. "Can I try?"

He had no chance to answer before her arms were around him, dragging his mouth down to hers. He didn't even bother resisting. Yes, she was acting strangely, but the scent of her lust filled the air and he didn't care what had caused her change of heart—

As soon as he tasted her, he wrenched away and cursed Eli with everything in him. "It's the wine," he gasped, hardly able to think when Sian's hands found his chest. "Sian, stop. He put an aphrodisiac in the wine!"

Sian wasn't listening. Diego grabbed her hands and tried to step away, but one step brought his back against the kitchen counter and she refused to allow him to push her away. She leaned close and caught a drop of water from his shoulder with the tip of her tongue. His shudder sent another droplet rolling down his chest and she chased it, catching it at his nipple and taking her time licking it away. He moaned, releasing one hand to cup her chin and make her stop before he lost his mind, but her newly-freed hand went straight down to the towel and started to peel it off him.

He caught it just in time and held on for dear life. "*Querida*, you have to stop now. This isn't what you want, it's a drug!" he said, but Sian only laughed.

"Touching you is definitely a drug," she murmured, her hot mouth moving to his throat and nipping. "Tasting you is even better."

He groaned and Sian pressed against him, trying without success to pull his hand free from the towel. He held on grimly, viciously aroused and trying to keep from losing every shred of his honor by imagining ways of killing Eli for this final outrage.

Forcing him to bond with a stranger was bad enough. This crossed the line.

Her thigh slid against his, an intoxicating caress of skin against skin that scattered his thoughts. She tried to tug the hand he still held captive free and he didn't let her, dreading what she could do to him with both hands loose, but it didn't slow her down. She gave up trying to take his towel with her free hand and simply cupped him through it. Diego felt his fangs start to lengthen with the surge of hot pleasure and forced them away as he caught her hand again, but the towel had already been loosened and as soon as he let go it fell to the floor.

Sian glanced down and a slow, seductive smile came over her beautiful face. "I think you don't want me to stop as much as you say you do," she teased.

"*Dios*," Diego whispered. If she kept looking at him like that, he was going to go insane. She pressed her hips against his and his entire body shook at the caress of satin but he forced himself to keep trying to reason with her. "Sian, stop this, you've been drugged! This isn't what you want—"

She cut him off by simply going to her knees in front of him and putting her gorgeous mouth right where he most wanted it.

He cried out before he could stop it, losing his hold on her wrists to reach behind him and grip the edge of the counter for dear life. All thought evaporated in a red flash of pleasure. Her newly freed hands roamed over his thighs, urging his hips closer as her lips slid down over his aching cock. Her tongue curled over him, around him, down his shaft and back up again, and he couldn't stop his hips from thrusting against her mouth. She caressed his sac and he sucked in a gasping breath. Sweet heaven, nothing had ever felt as good as her mouth and hands sliding over him.

Diego finally forced himself to move, to release the counter and lift her from the floor before he came apart completely. He set her atop the counter and she wrapped her legs around him, drawing him close, the heat of her core against his hip only heightening his arousal.

"You're killing me," he breathed, keeping a tight grip on her hips to stop her from moving against him.

She moaned in frustration and dug her nails into his shoulders, trying to pull him closer. The sting of pain only aroused him more. "Diego, please, I need you now," she cried. "Don't you want me?"

Honor was looking less and less appealing with every passing second. "I want you so bad I can hardly think straight," Diego growled. "But you're not yourself, Sian, and I can't make love to you like this!"

Sian released him long enough to grab the hem of her gown and pull it over her head. Diego closed his eyes, afraid of what he would do if he saw her naked and wanting him, but she took advantage of that by pressing herself hard against him and kissing him. The surge of hot lust she created in him brought his fangs exploding out. He shook with the effort of not responding and her cry of frustration when she pulled away hurt like a blade.

"Diego, look at me."

Despite every single instinct he possessed screaming this was the first step down the road to disaster, Diego opened his eyes and looked at her. He knew his eyes had changed, the lust throbbing in his veins bringing his vampire side fully to life. He didn't want to frighten her, but maybe the sight of his eyes would bring her back to herself. He hardly dared to hope for it.

Sian met his cat-like eyes straight on, and despite the passion clouding her gaze, he saw her sincerity and determination. "I want this, honey," she told him, emphasizing every word. Her hands roamed over him, emphasizing her point. "I want you. No magic made me feel like this. I've been thinking of doing this with you since you left the bed. Please, don't tell me no." Before he could even start to think of a reply, she pulled his head down and kissed him again.

This wasn't like the mad passion of before. This kiss was long and slow and explosively hot. When he opened his lips to her, she met his tongue with hers, drawing him deeper into the kiss as her hands plunged into his hair to hold him there for her pleasure. Diego groaned, lust flooding his veins until he thought he might die of it and wishing he dared to believe what she'd told him.

She kissed him again and when her tongue found his fangs, he didn't pull away.

If she truly wanted him, let her know all of him.

But she didn't pull back or shy away from his fangs as he'd expected and his arms tightened around her. He didn't remember letting go of her hips and putting his arms around her but it didn't matter. The movement brought her bare skin against his at last and the glorious sensation erased all other concerns. Her tongue touched first one fang and then the other, exploring them as thoroughly as she'd explored the rest of his body while he'd slept. His fangs were one of his most powerful erogenous zones and it was the most erotic thing he'd ever experienced.

The dance of her tongue against his was making him drunk. Diego somehow found the strength to force himself to pull back before he lost track of all the reasons why this was wrong. She nipped at his lips in retaliation, sending shivers straight through him, before pressing her mouth hard against his again and inadvertently catching her lower lip on his fang.

She gasped and pulled back, her hand flying to her mouth and touching her lip gingerly. Everything vampire in him rose up and focused on that tiny spot she covered with a fingertip, and when he saw the crimson stain on her finger, it was a temptation Diego couldn't resist.

Sian's eyes fell closed and she moaned when he captured her finger and sucked it into his mouth. Her electric taste sent a wave of need through him and Diego bent and claimed her lip, his tongue caressing the tiny cut, capturing every drop of her essence and feeling the connection it brought sizzle into his soul. Her taste was incredible. Diego made himself pull away, but when she bit her own lip and offered him more, it was the last straw.

Damn his honor, there was only so much a man could take. "Don't you dare regret this," Diego said fiercely, catching her hips and driving inside her with one deep thrust. She was hot and tight, wet and so damn good, stars exploded behind his eyes.

She arched and cried out in pleasure as he took her mouth, suckling her wounded lip before healing the tiny cut. Her taste was intoxicating. He had to have more. His mouth burned a hot path down her throat, feeling her pulse under his lips and not even trying to resist the need to take more of what she'd offered. When he sank his fangs into her neck, Sian tightened her legs around him and climaxed calling his name.

Diego drew her essence into him, reveling in her taste and the knowledge that he could find her anywhere now, could touch her mind at any time. He took her pleasure and fed on it, thrusting deeper into her body and into her mind, taking her in every way and giving back ecstasy. Her second climax came right on the heels of the first and the sensation of her body tightening around his cock in waves was incredible. Diego growled against her throat and felt her nails dig into his hips, urging him on, and he gathered all his powers and pushed pleasure at her until she was wild with it. When she came for the third time, he buried himself deep and shuddered with the force of his own climax.

He stopped the bleeding from the two little wounds on her throat but didn't erase his mark from her skin. The sight of it sent a surge of possessive pleasure through him. Sian's face was pressed against his shoulder, her breath coming as fast as his, and Diego closed his eyes and shivered as he felt the aphrodisiac in her blood start to work on him.

Dios, he didn't know where Eli had gotten the aphrodisiac he'd put in the wine, but it was irresistible. Rational thought was rapidly becoming impossible. Diego's skin burned where it touched hers, ached where it didn't, and within moments all he could think about was having her again.

Sian lifted her head and he kissed her before she had a chance to speak. She moaned into his mouth and Diego devoured her, loving the passionate way she still responded despite the shattering pleasure they'd just shared. When he pulled away her eyes were wide and misty, deeply fulfilled and laced with a touch of confusion.

She touched his mouth, slipping her finger under his lip and running it over a fang. "Wow," she whispered, her eyes awed and her voice very serious.

"Very wow," Diego replied just as solemnly. His entire body was focused on the movement of that single finger on his fang.

She ran her finger over his lips again and when she pulled it away he saw a trace of red on it. "You bit me," she murmured, staring at the blood on her finger as if shocked.

He leaned forward and licked it from her skin, loving the way she gasped and already addicted to her taste. All he wanted was more. No one had ever tasted so sweet.

"Yes," he agreed when her finger was clean. "You invited me to, *querida.*"

Her cheeks were flushed and he saw the spark of desire hot in her eyes, but the confusion was growing and threatening to extinguish it. "What—what just happened to me?" Sian asked hesitantly, not pulling away from him but clearly no longer under the influence of the drug. "Did I really—"

His gut tightened at her tone. After the wild passion they'd shared, while he stood here in her arms, still buried intimately inside her with the echoes of ecstasy still rocking him to the bone, Diego didn't think he could handle *hesitant* from her now.

He glimpsed the half-full wine glass on the counter and reached for it before he could think better of his actions. "Drink this," he commanded as he pressed it to her lips. She did, too surprised to resist, and only when she'd taken several swallows did Diego pull the glass away.

Suddenly Sian gasped, remembering. "Wait a second—I thought you said the wine was drugged with an aphrodisiac!"

Diego drained what was left in the glass and set it aside before lifting her from the counter. "It is."

"But why—"

He stopped her mouth with a long, deep, and intensely hot kiss. "Hate me later," he murmured against her lips, turning to carry her back to his bed. "But love me now."

☾ ☾ ☾

Sian awoke and stretched luxuriously, savoring the utter contentment of her body and the soreness in unaccustomed places. There was no confusion to find Diego's warm body wrapped around hers, no moment of wondering where her gown had gone. She remembered everything they'd done last night.

In exquisite detail.

Just remembering was enough to heat her blood. Whatever else he might be, Diego was a fantastic lover. After their first wild romp in the kitchen, he'd taken his sweet time with her, exploring every inch of her body at a leisurely pace that had made her insane with need. When he'd finally succumbed to her pleas and taken her, she'd been so incredibly drunk on passion she hadn't even resisted when he'd bitten her again.

Sian shivered at the memory as she touched the little mark he'd left on the swell of her left breast. Who would have ever thought a vampire's bite could be that erotic? If giving blood were like this all the time, she'd be at the local blood bank every single day!

She rolled in Diego's arms until she faced him. He was still sleeping, the same incredibly deep sleep that had frightened her yesterday. She touched his face gently, remembering how boldly she'd touched him. Would she have had the nerve to act so wantonly had she known he truly was a vampire, just as he'd claimed?

That thought still blew her mind. She was lying here next to an honest-to-God vampire. She'd spent the night before making love endlessly with a real vampire! He'd taken her blood the first two times but not afterward, and she'd actually been disappointed. She shook her head, smiling. She'd happily be his chew toy if he kept giving her such incredible pleasure when he did it.

Sian leaned forward and kissed him softly before rolling out of bed. As wonderful as the sex had been, it didn't change her determination to get out of here. If anything, it strengthened it. She hated the thought of Diego getting caught up in Santonyo's revenge. The least she could do for him after the incredible night he'd given her was to ensure his safety.

Her heart sank at the thought of fleeing again and she sighed as she stepped into the shower. She'd just never thought it would be this hard to leave him.

She started to reach for the shower gel and stopped, a warm glow banishing her gloomy thoughts and a goofy grin on her face. Beside Diego's sandalwood scented things were three new bottles, all jasmine scented—shampoo, conditioner, and shower gel.

Sian laughed silently at herself for being touched at the gesture. It spoke to his arrogance and assurance that she would inevitably wind up here in his room again more than anything else, but still, she wondered how he'd known her favorite scent.

A warm hand suddenly slid down her back, jolting her from her thoughts, and Sian spun around with a gasp.

Diego caught her around the waist when she slipped on the wet tiles and pulled her against his bare body. "Scare you?" he asked, grinning.

She punched his shoulder. "You know you did, and I think you did it on purpose," she accused, but from the twinkle in his eyes she knew he heard the laughter in her voice despite her efforts to repress it. "Five minutes ago, you were sleeping like the dead!"

He bent and nuzzled her ear before pressing a hot, open-mouthed kiss to the bite-mark on her throat. "I woke up the instant you left the bed, *querida*," he murmured against her skin.

Sian laughed despite the shivers his mouth sent down her spine. "You looked pretty dead to the world to me."

"Well, the sun set, too," he admitted, pulling back. His eyes grew serious and his smile faded. "Are you regretting it yet, Sian?"

Sian bit her lip at the concern in his eyes and reached up to touch his face. "No," she said, almost surprised to find out it was the truth. "I don't regret last night, Diego. It wasn't only the wine. I wanted what happened."

"Thank God for that," he murmured fervently before claiming her lips in a searing kiss.

Sian laughed into his mouth and he tightened his arms around her, bringing her body fully against his. Her laugh turned into a moan and Sian wrapped her arms around his neck. His taste was more intoxicating than last night's wine. She ran her fingers through his hair and explored his mouth just as avidly as he did hers, their tongues dancing and caressing as the warm water trickled over them. Sian slid her leg around his and ran the tip of her tongue over his teeth.

His fangs sharpened under her tongue.

Sian pulled back with a gasp and Diego froze, his hands pausing in their exploration of her back. "Don't be afraid of me," he whispered, looking at her with those cat-like eyes. "I would rather die than hurt you."

His words sent a shiver down her spine. Those odd instincts she couldn't help relying on told her he didn't lie. "It surprised me, that's all. I'm not afraid," Sian replied, and that was the truth too. She looked at him as the steam from the shower surrounded them, her gaze caressing his sharpened features, those incredible eyes and the slightest hint of a fang pressing against his lower lip. The impression of the wolf had never been stronger. She drew in a shaky breath and traced the edge of his goatee with a fingertip. "You know, Diego, you are one seriously sexy vampire."

The tension left his eyes as a slow and unbelievably sexy grin spread over his face. "You're pretty damn hot yourself, *querida*," he murmured in a tone that sent shivers down her spine.

Sian couldn't tear her eyes away from the fangs his smile revealed. Who would have thought fangs could look so sexy on a man? "Are you going to bite me again?" The question was out before she could censor it.

He touched the mark on her neck softly before running his finger down to trace the one on the swell of her breast. "Do you want me to?"

Sian felt her cheeks heat. Both bites tingled at his touch, the memory of the pleasure of his bite washing over her. She did want it but it felt almost shameful to admit it. "Actually, I think I do," she whispered.

His eyes flared with desire as he traced the mark on her breast again. "You have no idea how glad I am to hear you say that," he said softly. "If you'd said no I would have respected that, but I think it would've killed me to never taste you again."

She thought back to the shattering pleasure that had flooded her both times he'd bitten her last night and suddenly realized a vampire would have to eat regularly just like anyone else. The thought of him holding another woman close, drinking from her throat as she shuddered with ecstasy in his arms, bothered her more than she wanted to admit even to herself. "Do you do that to everyone you bite?"

Diego shook his head at once. "Not even a little," he assured her, stroking her hair as if he heard her unspoken jealousy. "I merely keep them calm and unknowing." He bent and nuzzled her throat again. "The pleasure I save for you, *querida.*"

A wave of heat and pure feminine possessiveness washed over her at those words. She didn't dare look at that possessiveness too closely. He wasn't hers. She needed to remember that. Sian closed her eyes, wanting to lose herself in the sensations Diego was evoking at her neck and forget about what she would soon have to do, but now that her curiosity was aroused she found she couldn't stop the questions. "What do I taste like?"

He chuckled low against her skin. "You taste incredible," he said, his low voice rumbling along her nerve endings. "You taste like the heat of summer and endless steamy nights spiced with ecstasy. You taste like you're mine to pleasure until the end of time, and when I look at you, I can't wait to get started."

She shivered again. Who would've guessed her forbidding vampire had the soul of a poet? Then she frowned as another thought struck her. "Do you have a soul?" she asked hesitantly, afraid of the answer.

Chapter Eleven

This time Diego's laugh was surprised. "Of course I have a soul, my curious little cat. I was born a vampire, Sian. We aren't evil, just different."

Sian drew in a breath to ask another question but Diego stopped her mouth with a kiss that wiped every thought from her mind. Sweet heaven, his kiss was a lethal weapon!

"Can't your questions wait a bit?" he murmured against her lips several long, hot minutes later. "I will tell you anything you want to know, but it's very hard for me to concentrate on playing twenty-questions while you're naked in my arms."

Sian abruptly remembered his passion last night and leaned fully against him, wanting to feel it one more time before she left. "Persuade me to wait," she whispered. Diego closed his eyes and drew in a shaking breath before claiming her lips again. It wasn't a gentle kiss. It was searing, devastating. It was a brand marking her as his.

And she reveled in it.

Sian moaned in protest when he pulled away, but he refused to allow her to pull his mouth back to hers. He reached behind her and picked up the shampoo. "Let me wash you," he murmured.

His voice was a temptation she didn't even try to resist. Diego worked the shampoo through her hair, his strong fingers massaging her scalp in rhythmic strokes. She leaned her head back into the spray at his urging and gasped when his mouth slid down her arching throat. She made a little sound of protest when he pulled away all too soon. "Diego," she whispered, aching for him.

"Patience," he murmured. He ran his hands through her hair, rinsing it until the water ran clear, before doing the same thing with the conditioner. She'd never imagined a man's hands in her hair could be this sensual.

Sian stopped him before he reached for the shower gel and took the washcloth from his hand. She couldn't bear to stand here looking at that gorgeous body for one more second without touching him. She squeezed a little of the sandalwood soap onto the cloth and worked it into a lather before reaching out and sliding it up his ribs.

Diego braced his hands on the wall behind her as she bit her lip and smoothed suds over his chest. "I thought I was washing you," he teased as his breath quickened.

Sian gave him a sultry look from beneath her lashes. "I'm not letting you have all the fun." She stroked the cloth around his nipples, watching them harden at the caress, before turning her attention to his broad shoulders. It was intoxicating to touch him this way. "You know, you have a gorgeous chest," she murmured as she smoothed soap over his muscles.

She gasped when his slick palms slid around her and found her breasts. "I was just thinking the very same thing about you," he said, rubbing the jasmine scented soap over her. He must have squeezed some into his hands when he'd reached behind her, Sian thought, but his thumbs brushed her nipples and she stopped thinking altogether.

He bent and kissed her as their slick hands caressed and explored. She dropped the washcloth and ran her hands down his arms, delighting in the way his biceps jumped at her touch, before sliding them to his back and down his spine. She reveled in the sheer size of him, the breadth of his shoulders and the ridged muscles of his back. She felt fragile in his arms, a rare thing for a woman of five foot ten. Even more strangely, she felt safe for the first time in three years when he held her. He kissed her again, slowly and tenderly as though her taste was something he treasured, and she lost herself in the pleasure of exploring this gorgeous man.

He let out a shuddering breath against her mouth. "I love the way your hands feel on me," he breathed as his own hands slid down her stomach. His strange eyes brightened with humor as he pulled back to look down at her. "It's even better when I'm awake."

Sian laughed and reached down to stroke a slow caress over his firm backside. "I'd have to agree with you there," she said. "There are parts of you I couldn't reach while you were sleeping on your back."

He chuckled and bent to nibble at her ear. "All you have to do is ask me to roll over, *querida*," he whispered. "I promise, I'm never sleeping too deeply to obey."

Sian let her head drop back, a thrill going through her at exposing her throat to his fangs. She'd never imagined such a thought would arouse her like this. Diego gave a low growl and nipped the side of her neck, and her breath hissed out in anticipation.

"Are you going to bite me now?" she whispered, wrapping a leg around his and feeling like she would burst into flames if she didn't have him inside her soon.

He groaned and kissed her vulnerable throat again. "You truly want me to?"

Sian slid her hands up his back and leaned forward to give a nip of her own to his shoulder, surprised at her own boldness. He sucked in a sharp breath as she swirled her tongue over the spot. "Do you like it when I do it to you?" she whispered, running her teeth gently over his skin.

He pulled her hips firmly against his and let her feel the answer for herself. "*Like* is far too mild a word," he growled in her ear. "It makes me so hot I can hardly stand it. You could say I definitely have a biting fetish."

She laughed, a sultry sound she hadn't even known she was capable of making. "And don't forget your foot fetish."

His passionate gaze took her breath away. "I have a *you* fetish, *querida*," he said, and she knew the feeling. She was beginning to think she had a fetish for him right back. She even liked his nicknames for her. She held him tight as he kissed her again, but he pulled away all too soon. He suddenly reached up and pulled down the hand-held showerhead before giving her a wicked grin. "Lie down," he said, his deep voice making it sound like the most carnal of propositions.

She hesitated only a moment before obeying and lying down with her shoulders propped against the edge of the oversized tub. Diego knelt at her feet and aimed the spray at her legs, rinsing the suds from her skin.

"Diego, what are you doing?" she asked, mesmerized at the sight of him in such an intimate position.

He put the showerhead aside and lifted her ankle to his lips. "Something I promise you'll like," he murmured. "Close your eyes, wildcat."

Her eyes were already closing with pleasure at what his mouth was doing to her ankle. She'd never thought of it as a particularly erogenous zone before but when Diego touched her, her entire body seemed to be an erogenous zone. She moaned as he licked his way up the back of her calf.

Keeping her eyes closed heightened all her other senses. The scent of jasmine and sandalwood permeated every breath she took, reminding her of the hot summer nights he'd spoken of, and the clean flavor of the steam surrounding them teased her tongue as her lips parted with pleasure. The hiss of the running water didn't quite cover her soft gasps as his mouth moved over her. His goatee scraped gently over her skin, its roughness a delicious contrast to the softness of his tongue and his smooth teeth when he nipped her again. She was drowning in erotic sensation. Heat stabbed her to the core.

"Diego, I need you," she moaned as his mouth moved up her inner thigh.

"And you'll have me." The hot spray of the shower suddenly bathed her calf, following the path his mouth had taken up her leg. "I promise you that."

Her entire body tightened as the massaging spray moved higher. She thought she would die with the anticipation of feeling it bathe her where she ached most, but the spray jumped from her thighs to her belly. "Diego!"

He laughed. "Is there a problem?" he asked in an innocent tone completely at odds to his wicked laugh. She couldn't speak. His free hand smoothed over her skin as he rinsed the soap from her abdomen and ribs. She moaned out loud when he aimed the spray at her breasts. Her hands found him and she threaded her fingers through his hair, trying to urge him to kiss her.

He laughed again and bent to her breasts instead. Sian arched and cried out as his tongue swirled over her. She felt the sharp points of his fangs against her tender flesh and tightened her fingers in his hair, hoping he was going to bite her at last. She was starting to wonder if vampire bites were addictive, she craved it so badly.

He didn't. The spray traveled down her body and this time he didn't tease her. When he came to the juncture of her thighs he aimed the spray low, making slow circles that aroused her to the point of madness as he slid a finger inside her. It was more than she could take and she cried out his name as she climaxed.

The spray disappeared at once but before she could protest its loss, his mouth replaced it. The sudden change in sensation was enough to send her over the edge for the second time. He groaned and slid another finger inside. She writhed, wanting more, when he suddenly turned his head and sank his fangs deep very high on her inner thigh.

The brief pain was forgotten in an instant as a tidal wave of pleasure crashed over her. The spray returned, dancing over her flesh, his fingers sliding in and out as his mouth sucked strongly at her thigh. She held on for dear life as wave after wave of ecstasy swamped her, erasing everything but Diego and the unbelievable pleasure he gave her.

She had no idea how much time passed before she heard the showerhead hit the tub as Diego threw it aside. She barely had time to protest its loss before his mouth was on hers. The salty, coppery taste of his lips only aroused her more. She wrapped her legs around him and welcomed him as he thrust deep inside her.

She moaned into his mouth and he growled in return, taking her with deep, fast strokes she felt all the way to her soul. He pulled away from their fevered kiss and pressed his lips to her neck as Sian's fingernails dug deep into his shoulder. He felt incredible inside her, so very right, and before she knew she intended to speak she heard herself whisper, "I wish you could feel this like I do."

"I can, now that you've invited me," he murmured against her skin. Almost at once she felt the strange invading presence in her mind, the same sensation she'd had in the alley when he'd read what the clerk had done, but this time the intimacy was glorious instead of disconcerting. She felt the bite of her nails in his shoulder and gasped, running her fingers over his muscles to make sure she wasn't dreaming.

She felt the same caress feather over her own shoulders.

She didn't know how he'd done it but somehow she felt everything he felt, both his rigid heat deep inside her and her velvet tightness around him. Diego thrust deep and she arched her back, the combined feeling of intimate friction beyond her wildest dreams. She wished he would bite her again and before she could even take a breath to request it, his fangs found her throat and sank deep.

The sudden intoxicating rapture overwhelmed her, and it was a moment before she felt the sharp pain on her shoulder. She ignored it, tightening her hands on his shoulders, but it only made the sting worse. It took her a moment to figure out her nails had pierced his skin.

Need rose up in her and she forced her eyes open to see a ruby droplet of his blood clinging to his skin. Obeying an instinct she didn't even know she had, she leaned up and caught it on her tongue.

A lightning shock of ecstasy burst through her and she felt it take Diego as well through the mental connection he still held. She bit his shoulder around the little scratch and laved it with her tongue, needing to prolong the extraordinary sensation as long as possible, but the wild passion overwhelmed her. They reached the peak together and the shared climax was the most incredible thing she'd ever felt in her life.

She felt Diego pull away from her throat and licked the cut on his shoulder again, wanting one last taste of him. Never would she have believed something as simple as a few drops of blood could create such glorious bliss.

Diego heard the thought in her mind and tore himself from her embrace, his hand flying to the cut on his shoulder. Sian smiled up at him, the faintest trace of red on her lower lip, and ice shot down his spine when he saw a matching smear on his palm.

"No, don't!" he cried as the tip of her tongue flicked out to catch the trace of his blood. His hand darted out and wiped it away before she could lick her lip clean. Dread filled his heart. "You didn't drink my blood, Sian," he whispered urgently, praying it was true. "Tell me you didn't." He gathered her close and held her tight.

She snuggled against him, completely unaware of his distress. "Just a taste," she murmured.

He swore softly in Spanish, squeezing his eyes shut as the warm afterglow of their lovemaking was extinguished by fear. This was a nightmare. He hadn't even thought to warn her about taking his blood. Why would he? He hadn't thought she would ever have the opportunity. He sent his powers searching through her, questing for any evidence of the Change starting in her body and cursing himself for not realizing what she'd done until it was too late.

He should've known the instant her mouth had touched his skin and that unimaginable ecstasy had taken him. The melding of body and mind and the exchange of blood between bondmates was rumored to be the most erotic thing a vampire could hope to experience, and what he'd just shared with Sian had certainly been that. Even now, despite his fear, his body still tingled with the power of it.

And now he might never feel it again.

Sian pulled back a little when he swore again. She rubbed a fingertip between his eyebrows. "You're frowning," she said softly. "What is it, Diego? Did I do something wrong?"

He shook his head at once. This was Eli's fault first and his second. Sian was innocent of everything in this. "No, *querida*, you did nothing wrong."

"Then why are you looking at me like that?"

He rested his forehead against hers for a moment before forcing himself to move. He lifted her from the tub, turning off the water with a thought, and carried her back into the bedroom without bothering with a towel. "Sian, not all vampires are born," he said softly, not knowing quite how to begin.

Her eyes widened as she caught his meaning at once. "You mean all that stuff in movies about people being bitten by vampires and turning into them—it's all true? Am I a vampire now since you bit me? Is that why I wanted to taste you?"

He shook his head and put her gently on the bed. He didn't feel any hint of the Change starting in her yet, but sometimes it took a little time to begin. He didn't dare relax his vigilance in monitoring her. "It's not the bite, Sian." He met her eyes even though he feared what he would see there. "It's the blood. To become a vampire, you drink a vampire's blood."

Her mouth opened in a silent "oh" and she gazed up at him for a long moment before confusion clouded her eyes. "Don't get me wrong, but you're all hung up on this eternal mate thing and you don't want me to be a vampire? That doesn't make much sense."

Diego pulled her into his arms and held her tight. "No, I want that more than anything in this world," he whispered. "But I can't be your sire, Sian. A sire has power over his fledgling—he has to, to teach everything they must know to survive. But for this reason it is forbidden for a sire and his fledgling to be bondmates. It's—it's like rape, incest. Abomination. If I make you a vampire I must be like a parent to you, never your lover."

She gasped in alarm and a part of him was actually relieved that the thought of never making love with him again was distressing to her. He shoved it away angrily. There was nothing to be relieved about in this.

Sian pulled away a little and he made himself let her even though every instinct he possessed protested. "I don't want to be a vampire any more than you want to be my sire. There has to be a way out of this," she said, pushing a hand through her hair. "I mean, surely some other vampire has been in this situation before. Someone has to know what to do about it!"

He shook his head. "No other vampire has ever had a mortal bondmate before, *querida*. We're in uncharted territory here."

She stared at him for a moment, clearly shocked. He knew the feeling. "What we just did—the sharing of mind, body, and blood—is how a bond is created, Sian. Three such exchanges bind two vampires forever. Until this happened to us, I would have bet my life it was impossible for a mortal and a vampire to bond." He cupped her cheek in his hand and closed his eyes. "I don't know if I could stand being your sire after this, wildcat," he whispered, aching.

If he had to have a bondmate, he wanted it to be Sian and no other.

Suddenly she looked up at him. "Eli," she said.

He frowned, not liking another male's name on her lips so soon after they'd made love, but Sian took his hand and squeezed it excitedly. "Call Eli! He's the one who did this thing you say is impossible. Surely he's got another trick or two up his sleeve. Call him and make him fix it!"

A fiercely protective instinct rose up and protested violently at the thought of sharing something this private with another male vampire. Diego ground his teeth and forced himself to reach for the phone anyway. The surge of jealous emotion surprised him.

It shouldn't have. He knew the legends. Along with the overwhelming bliss it brought, the blood exchange was supposed to heighten every single territorial, possessive instinct a male vampire had. Diego was finding out the tales of legend paled beside the real thing.

He shoved aside his reluctance and dialed, obligingly bending his head low so Sian could hear. Eli answered his cell phone on the first ring. "What?"

Diego's eyebrows rose at his irritated tone. "What's your problem?"

"Other than the complaint you filed with the Council that has the rest of them up in arms and trying to force me out, everything's fine. Why do you ask?"

Diego winced. He'd almost forgotten sending the furious email. So much had happened in the last few nights it had completely slipped his mind. "Um, sorry about that, Eli, but I was a little angry with you at the time," he said. It was the understatement of the year. "Listen," he rushed on, hoping his rash complaint hadn't wrecked his chances of getting Eli's help now, "we have a problem."

"You have several, Diego, in case you haven't noticed. Which one are you calling me to solve?"

He ignored that barb with an effort. Arguing with Eli was always pointless and would be beyond stupid right now. "Sian drank my blood, Eli."

Eli actually laughed. "You enjoyed the wine, I take it?"

Diego choked back a growl with difficulty. He hated the very thought of another male knowing anything about what he and Sian had done. His instincts stopped clamoring for privacy and started demanding blood and he was astonished at how strong they were. Why hadn't he felt this fierce protectiveness from the moment Eli had put the marks on them?

He forced his mind back to the conversation. "Damn it, this is serious! You know I can't be both her mate and her sire."

"Diego, breathe," Eli said, his tone still infuriatingly amused. "Is she going through the Change now?"

Diego paused for a moment, listening to what his senses were telling him. Sian watched him nervously, waiting for his answer. "No," he said at last, and she sighed with relief.

"Well, why are you worrying then? If she Changes, call me. Until then I would strongly advise you to pay attention to other things. Trust me, Diego, Sian drinking a few drops of your blood is the very least of your worries."

"And what is that supposed to mean?" Diego demanded, but the line was dead. Eli had already hung up. "I hate it when he does that," he growled, putting the phone back in its cradle with far more force than necessary.

Sian looked at him. "Does this mean I'm not going to turn into a vampire?" she asked.

"I don't know," he admitted. He thought over Eli's cryptic comments, trying to decipher some meaning from them. "He didn't exactly say you weren't, but if you were, it would certainly be something for me to worry about. It would be my chief concern, no matter what else was going on." He paused, listening to his senses again before shaking his head. "I don't know, Sian. I don't feel any sign of the Change starting and believe me, you'd know if it was. It hurts like hell when it happens. Maybe you didn't take enough or something, I just don't know."

She bit her lip, clearly less than reassured with this answer. "And Eli, he would know if that was the case even though he's not here? He's able to do that?"

Diego sighed in frustration. "No one really knows what Eli's capable of, Sian. He might know or he might not, and even if he did, it might amuse him not to tell us. The only thing that makes me feel the slightest bit better is that he pushed so hard for us to bond that I can't imagine he'd let something like this stand in the way. He wants this for some reason, and he's damn sure not telling me what it is."

Sian closed her eyes with a sigh. "Well, I guess we'll have to wait and see," she said. "No need to worry about what we can't change, and I'm too tired to think about it any more."

Diego let her slip out of his arms to lie down and started to stretch out beside her when he heard a car skid to a stop in the driveway. "Sounds like

James is back," he said, bending down to brush a gentle kiss over her lips. "Stay here, *querida*, and call if you start to feel strange. I'll be right back."

She nodded, lying back on the pillows and yawning. Diego glimpsed the bites he'd left on her as he drew the comforter over her—one on her thigh, one on the swell of her breast, and the pair on her throat. The sight of them made his chest tighten with fierce pride. Sian would certainly accuse him of being a caveman again if he let her know it, but he loved seeing his marks on her.

He pulled on a pair of jeans and slipped from the room just as the front door slammed.

"Diego!" James shouted, his footsteps thundering downstairs as he shoved open doors, banging them against the walls. "Diego, where the hell are you?"

"Quiet down!" Diego called back as he put on a burst of speed and raced downstairs. "Sian's sleeping. What's wrong?"

James stood at the foot of the stairs, his arms crossed over his chest as he glared at Diego. "What's wrong? What's *wrong?*" he repeated furiously. "I've been trying to call you for the past twenty hours and you want to know what's *wrong?* I'm stuck in Spain with a pack of lawyers trying to get hold of you and you can't even be bothered to answer your phone! I expected to come back and find you dead on the floor or something!"

Diego grinned a little sheepishly. The phone might have rang last night, he wasn't sure, but even if he'd been aware of it he certainly wouldn't have answered it. He'd been far too busy making up for a century of celibacy by enjoying Sian in every way a man could possibly enjoy a woman. It was no wonder she was exhausted. "Sorry," he said, even though he wasn't. Nothing could make him regret last night.

"Yeah, whatever," James snapped, turning on his heel and stomping angrily into the kitchen. "I took a supersonic flight to get here, I haven't eaten in hours, and all you can say is sorry—and you don't even sound like you mean it. Why do I put up with you again?"

"Because I pay you a king's ransom, you like living in a mansion, and the health plan is phenomenal," Diego shot back. "Now tell me what the lawyers said. What's the deal with this case? Did they get it dismissed yet?"

James pulled a package of hot dogs out of the fridge and started eating them cold. "If you'd answered your phone, you'd know this case isn't going to get dismissed," he said. His eye fell on the bottle of wine still open on the counter and he reached for it, clearly intending to add it to his snack.

Diego had crossed the kitchen and snatched it away before James's hand had moved more than an inch. James jumped at his unnatural speed. "I hate it when you do that, Diego," he complained. "And do you have to bogart the whole bottle?"

"If you want a drink I'm sure you can find something else," Diego said, carrying the bottle to the sink. "Trust me, you don't want this."

But he hesitated as he started to pour the wine down the drain, remembering the incredible feeling it had evoked. The image of Sian all but attacking him in this very spot brought a smile to his face, and the memory of their wild, totally uninhibited lovemaking when they'd both been under its influence sent heat spiraling through him. It seemed a shame to waste something so very powerful. Instead of pouring it out, Diego found the cork and stuck it back in before turning to James. "Consider this extremely off-limits," he said sternly as he put it in the refrigerator.

James raised an eyebrow at him. "Oh, yeah? What is it?"

Diego knew that tone. It was his *I-wonder-what-would-happen-if-I-did-it-anyway* tone and it had gotten him into trouble more times than Diego cared to recall.

"It's bloodwine," he lied, closing the door firmly. "A vampire delicacy. I don't think you'd appreciate it properly."

James made a face, his interest quelled instantly. "Eww, man, that's nasty." He shrugged and James suddenly frowned. "Hey, what are those scratches?" He blinked, staring harder. "And is that a bite-mark on your shoulder?"

An echo of the profound burst of ecstasy he'd shared with Sian shot through him and Diego unconsciously reached up and ran his hand over the spot, savoring the memory of Sian biting him there. Regardless of what happened now, that shower had been the most incredible experience of his life and he couldn't make himself regret it. "There was a lot of biting going on," he replied, unable to keep himself from grinning. He traced a scratch with a fingertip. "And my wildcat has claws."

James gaped at him for a moment before closing his mouth with a snap. Diego was stunned to see his unflappable Steward actually blush. "Okay, now I know why you didn't answer your phone, and for the record that is way more than I ever wanted to know about vampire sex," he said, turning away and popping the rest of his hot dogs into the microwave. "Please, Diego, swear you'll never go there again."

He laughed at his Steward's discomfort. All the times James had urged him to forget the Council and go get laid, and now he was blushing. "Well, you did ask," he pointed out, unable to resist needling him.

"And I have been more than adequately punished for it. I've seen the error of my ways and will never do it again."

Sian's laughter suddenly filled the room. "Okay, I'm dying to know what happened here."

Diego's gaze shot to the doorway to see her leaning against the doorframe, her lovely body wrapped in his thick black terry-cloth robe. Another surge of primitive, territorial emotion swamped him at the sight of her in his robe, the marks on her throat just visible beneath the collar. *Mine,* he thought fiercely. And God help anyone else who touched her.

As his gaze slid over her, he frowned. The dark color of the robe emphasized her unnatural pallor and the bruised-looking circles under her eyes. He swore, quickly going to her side. She hadn't looked that pale against the white porcelain tub. "I thought you were sleeping," he said as he put an arm around her waist. "You should be in bed."

"I'm too hungry to sleep," she told him, releasing the doorframe to lean against him instead. She smiled over at James. "Hi, James."

James glanced back at her and his eyebrows flew up. "Wow, Sian, you're white as a sheet," he said as the microwave beeped. "Damn, Diego, how many times did you bite her, anyway?"

The slight reproach in James's voice was all it took to bring Diego's fangs out. How dare James accuse him of harming his mate? He pushed the unexpected surge of anger aside, astonished at its ferocity. Something was definitely going on here. He'd felt responsible for her before, had been concerned for her safety, but nothing like this.

Sian answered before his silence became noticeable. "Four times, if I remember correctly," she said. She smiled up at Diego but her eyes were concerned and he knew she'd sensed his anger before he'd banished it.

"Which is probably three times more than I should have," he added. Much as he hated to admit it, James was right to be concerned. Her pallor proved he'd taken too much. He glanced back over his shoulder at James. "And I thought you'd decided to never ask about biting again."

"Yeah, well, somehow it's not disgusting to imagine nibbling on her neck," James replied as he retrieved his hot dogs from the microwave. "She is rather delicious looking, as I'm sure you've noticed." He jumped when he turned around and met Diego's eyes. "Whoa, Diego, what are you pissed about?"

He didn't need to be told his eyes had changed again. He felt his fangs pressing against his lower lip. "Watch your mouth, boy, or I'll watch it for you," he growled. How dare James look at her with lust on his mind?

James's eyes widened and he seemed at a loss for words for the first time since Diego had known him. "Hey, take it easy," he managed at last, his tone low and soothing as if he spoke to a wild animal. "Calm down, man. You think I would be stupid enough to ogle your woman while you're standing right there? I don't have a death wish. I was only joking around."

Diego nodded sharply, aware his arm around Sian had tightened possessively. She broke the tense silence a moment later. "You think I could have one of those hot dogs, James?" she asked, resting her palm against Diego's chest in an instinctive move to reassure him as she smiled at the Steward.

James shot one more glance at Diego before replying. "Naah, these aren't fit for human consumption. In fact I'm not sure there aren't humans in 'em." He checked the package. "Yep, they say it right in the ingredients— soylent green. I saw a couple of steaks in there, you want one?"

"Please," she said, leaving Diego's side to sit at the table.

Diego shook himself mentally, banishing the jealousy-fueled rage with difficulty. This was insane. He'd known James from the cradle and he knew to the depths of his soul James had meant no disrespect by his remarks. He walked to the refrigerator and poured a glass of orange juice for Sian, wondering what was wrong with him. Why was he losing his temper at every little thing now? Was this protectiveness how a sire felt for his fledgling? It was a worrying thought but one that made a strange kind of sense. He certainly hadn't felt like this when Eli had first put the marks on them. It wasn't like him. He'd always been calm, unshakable, even-tempered.

Now the thought of another man even looking at Sian made him want to break something. It was as though their bond was still tenuous and new instead of completed.

He had the uncomfortable feeling Eli had neglected to tell him something important and he didn't like it a bit.

When Sian's steak was done, which didn't take long since she requested it very rare, James set it beside her and turned to Diego. "This court thing looks bad," he said, clearly trying to steer conversation back onto safer ground. "It's definitely going to be a problem, Diego."

"What's the problem? That land has been in your family since I gave it to your however-many-times-great grandfather over three hundred years ago. How can they have a case against three hundred years of unbroken ownership?"

"It's not my right to the land they're challenging. It's yours."

Chapter Twelve

Diego frowned. "What are you talking about?"

James took a seat across the table from Sian and started cutting up his own steak. "You deeded the land to my family in 1688. It was all done perfectly legally, except for one little thing." He gestured with his fork for emphasis. "Diego Leonides signed it, and the last Diego Leonides who has any records to prove his existence was born in 992. Therefore, unless we can show that there was another Leonides of the same name alive in the 1600s, the transaction will probably be declared invalid and the land will revert to the government." He popped the bite of meat into his mouth. "And the government really wants this deal."

Diego pulled out a chair and sat down hard. This was worse than he'd thought. Sian glanced over at him and took his hand. "Didn't you will things to yourself or something?" she asked. "Move around and try to make it look like you were your own heir? Surely there's some piece of paper somewhere that says you—or your ancestor—were alive in 1688."

He shook his head, lacing his fingers through hers. "Where there are vampires, there are vampire hunters," he said. "When you're as old as I am, leaving any kind of paper trail isn't a good idea. That kind of thing only works in movies and books. No, that's why I took a Steward family. Technically, I have nothing and James is the one who owns everything."

Sian's mouth dropped open and James grinned at her. "Nice job, isn't it? I keep threatening to evict him but he pays no attention."

She couldn't laugh. She wasn't in the mood for humor, not when Diego looked so upset. "If there's no record that you existed in 1688, how are you going to prove the transaction was legal?"

Diego sighed and rubbed a hand over his face. "Surely we can plant a paper somewhere," he said. "Record-keeping wasn't exactly a fine science back then. We should be able to forge—what?"

James was shaking his head. "These people have been digging for records ever since the first lawsuit was filed," he said. "They've got sworn statements from every registry you can think of saying there's no evidence of any Diego Leonides in their records—Church records, bills of sale, government papers, and on and on. You were a prince, you were well documented as being born and living back around 1000 AD, and not a trace of you or any heirs can be found after that time. The demise of your family was equally well documented. If they forgot to check somewhere, I can't imagine where it'd be."

Diego fought the urge to growl with frustration. "Who the hell are these people?"

"The lawyers hadn't heard of them before. It's some kind of medieval name," James said with a shrug. "Apparently they set up these Renaissance things all over the place. The Templar Alliance or something like that."

Diego sat straight up at the name. James raised an eyebrow at him. "That name means something to you, doesn't it?"

"Damn right it means something." He released Sian's hand and jumped up to start pacing the kitchen, Eli's vague comments about Sian being the least of his problems finally making sense. "I had no idea those bastards were still around."

"Who are they?"

His face was thunderous. "The Knights Templar were vampire hunters, James. These people don't want the land. They want to find me."

"Wait, wait," Sian said, holding up a hand. "I've got a minor in history, Diego, and the Knights Templar were disbanded in the 1300s by King Philip of France. They were Crusaders, not—"

"With all due respect," James interrupted gently with a cautious glance at Diego, "I think Diego knows more about history than you possibly could, minor or not. He lived it."

She blushed and bit her lip. "Oh, yeah, forgot that for a second," she murmured, stabbing another bite of steak with her fork. She shot Diego a sheepish grin. "It's hard to remember you're a thousand years old when you look younger than me."

He smiled at her despite his tension. "I'll take that as a compliment." Unable to be still, he started pacing again. "The Templars might have started as Crusaders, but they became vampire hunters pretty quickly thereafter. What your history books don't tell you is that King Philip was also a vampire and his actions against the Templars were retribution for an attempt on his life."

"You're kidding!" Sian gasped. "The king of France was a *vampire?*"

"We tend to show up in royal families," he said with a shrug. "We're difficult to kill, a definite advantage for any monarch."

"You really are a prince? You weren't joking?" He nodded and Sian stared at him for a long moment as if trying to decide if he was teasing her. "All right, then how did they find out about you?" she finally asked. "I mean, it's not like this deed is news or anything. Why are they poking around back in three hundred-year old land transactions? You can't convince me researching deeds and filing lawsuits is the best way to flush out a vampire."

No, the best way to flush out a vampire was to find his mate. Could it possibly be coincidence that this had happened right after he'd taken a bondmate? Diego looked at Sian in sudden concern, wishing he hadn't thought of that and trying to think of an answer he dared to share with her.

James beat him to it. "I told you the website wasn't a good idea."

Diego shook his head at his own paranoia. Of course it was the website. The Templars might be good, but there was no way they could know about Sian. "There are tons of sites on the 'Net made by people claiming publicly to be vampires," he said, stopping behind Sian's chair and resting his hands on her shoulders. He needed to touch her right now. "I didn't think my little family tree would cause anyone to blink. I don't even mention the word vampire once anywhere on it."

Sian laughed. "Diego, come on," she said. "You put the dates of birth and death on there. I'm no vampire hunter but even I noticed everyone was several hundred years old when they died. Didn't you think it was a little conspicuous not to put a death date on there for yourself?"

"But I'm not dead," he said, strangely offended by the idea.

"And I'd like to keep you that way," James replied. He stood and took the plates to the sink. "Forget the land, Diego. I know all about your family and your pride, but don't fight this one battle. Time is on your side. Let whoever these people are have it and buy it back when they're dead and gone."

Diego scowled. "James, these people have been around almost as long as I have. They've survived every attempt to eliminate them and stubbornly refuse to die out. If I let them have this now, I'll never get it back."

☾ ☾ ☾

Sian tossed fitfully onto her side and sighed. Despite her exhaustion, sleep refused to come for her. Every time she closed her eyes images of fanged, cape-wearing kings warring with fanatical vampire hunters assaulted her mind. Her thoughts spun like a bad B movie and she forced herself to think of something else.

The vivid picture of Diego resplendent in shining armor astride a rearing stallion, his dark hair blowing in the wind and the moonlight kissing his features, arose to torment her next. Sian groaned out loud as the vision took hold. The stallion would be black as midnight, his mane matching his rider's. She saw Diego control the stamping, untamed beast with hardly an effort as he drew his huge sword—

Sian cut the thought off with a muttered expletive. She absolutely did not need to think about Diego's huge sword, not in any sense of the word. Her imagination was running away with her. She turned over again and tried yet again to go to sleep.

Twenty minutes later, she gave up. She was wound too tightly to sleep. She threw off the covers and dressed in the first things she touched when she opened the closet but action only made her more anxious. She sighed. She knew what this feeling meant.

Danger was coming again. She'd felt Santonyo's nearness too many times not to recognize it now.

And there was no way in hell she was going to lead him here. Diego had enough to deal with now with the Templars after him. The last thing he needed was a psychopathic murderer to worry about. She picked up her purse and reached inside, pulling out Diego's keys. It was time to go.

Something inside her cried out in protest as she slipped her shoes on and planned where she would run, but she pushed it ruthlessly aside. Okay, she could admit she'd felt safe here, had come to care for Diego and even James. She could even admit she would miss Diego desperately and wished she could stay here. That didn't mean she dared to forget that Santonyo would never stop chasing her. This had been a strange and wonderful reprieve from her real life, but as with all good things it couldn't last forever.

She would rather leave Diego with the memories of what they'd shared last night—memories she, too, would treasure—than see him hurt because of her. He might be an honest-to-God vampire and he might have taken out those three others in the alley, but she had no illusions what would happen to him if he got within range of one of Santonyo's snipers. Diego had said it was difficult to kill a vampire, he hadn't said it was *impossible*. Lightning reflexes and super strength only went so far. She didn't think his immortality could withstand a bullet to the head.

She left the rest of the clothes James had bought her hanging in the closet and went downstairs, dreading this. Diego wouldn't know it was goodbye unless she gave herself away and she had no intention of doing so. If he had any idea she was leaving, he would stop at nothing to prevent it, and he'd already proved how fast he could track her down if she didn't move quickly enough. Hopefully leaving her things here would keep him from knowing she'd fled long enough for her to make a clean getaway.

Her mind was an open book to him, though, and she knew she had to be extra careful. No amount of subterfuge or acting ability would save her if he plucked her plan from her thoughts. She drew on every shred of control she had and forced herself to think of going shopping, not running away, even as her heart was weeping.

She paused on the stairs, shaking her head in confusion at her rioting emotions. This just wasn't like her. She wasn't the mushy, sentimental type. Why should she be on the verge of tears at the thought of leaving a man she'd only known four days? She *never* cried.

Diego had gotten to her with this talk of eternal bonding more than she'd realized. It had to be that. Surely she'd get over it in a day or two once she was out of here.

But she wouldn't get out of here at all if he figured out her intentions, so she had to stop thinking about missing Diego. She pushed aside her sadness and pictured going to the huge twenty-four hour shopping club on the edge of the city instead. For good measure, she imagined picking out lingerie. Very, very sexy lingerie, something guaranteed to drive Diego wild, something even spicier than what James had brought home for her on his little shopping excursion.

Surely he wouldn't complain if he thought she was going out to buy *that.* "Diego?" she called when she reached the bottom of the stairs.

His voice floated out from the game room. "In here, wildcat."

Sian winced before she could help it. She wished he wouldn't call her that. The memories of what they'd shared were a complication she didn't want to think about yet. She couldn't bear to think about it or she really would start to cry, and she hated to cry more than anything in the world.

Diego was bent over the pool table when she entered the game room, his back to he as he lined up a shot. Her eyes caressed his tight ass and if she'd been a cat, she would've purred with pleasure at the view. Good God, every inch of him was magnificent. She couldn't quite stop the smile that spread over her face when her eyes traveled up over his muscular back and broad shoulders, loving that he wasn't wearing a shirt again and knowing he'd done it so she could admire him. The faint scratches on his shoulders were already almost healed and the sight of them brought a purely feminine surge of pleasure through her that surprised her. It was hard to believe she'd scratched him. She'd never marked a man in passion in her entire life before Diego. Damn, but he'd made her crazy.

"I'm very glad to know it. The feeling was entirely mutual," he chuckled and she jumped, glad she'd thought to concentrate on the shopping trip. It was just a little too eerie when he answered her unspoken thoughts and she wondered why she didn't dislike it more. He took his shot and the ripple of muscle down his back and across his shoulders was enough to make her mouth go dry. "I thought you were taking a nap, *querida*."

"I couldn't sleep." Another ache went through her at the endearment. He wasn't making this easy.

He put his stick down on the table before she'd even finished speaking and turned to face her. "What am I not making easy?" he asked, those green eyes searching hers sharply.

Shopping, think of shopping… She bit her lip at the sight of him leaning there against the pool table, holding her mind carefully in check. When she looked at him, it was easy to redirect her train of thought. He truly was a beautiful man. She smiled and crossed the room to run a fingertip down the center of his chest. Heat spread through her and she glanced up at him through her lashes, picturing what she would like to buy to model for him if she truly were going shopping for lingerie.

His skin was dark compared to her blonde fairness, and she had a sudden urge to wear ivory for him. She imagined his olive-skinned hand caressing her breast, a delicious contrast to the pale lace, and when his eyes darkened she knew he was reading the thought in her mind. By God, she would love to wear something like that for him.

"I was going to borrow a car and go shopping," she told him, trying to remember what she was supposed to be doing but unable to stop her finger taking a detour and circling his nipple, "but you are so very tempting I find I don't want to leave you."

And that was only the truth.

The tension left him and he grinned as he slid an arm around her waist. "Good," he murmured, bending and nuzzling her ear. "Because I just had a very interesting idea involving you and this pool table. Wanna hear it?"

She could just guess what it was. A shiver raced down her spine as his hands slid down to cup her bottom. "You are wicked," she whispered, leaning against him for a moment. *Let me have this,* her heart whispered. *Let me have one more moment with him before I go.*

"Mmm," he agreed as his lips moved down to her throat. "You seem to bring it out in me, *querida.*" He ran his tongue along her jaw and claimed her mouth.

Sian threaded her fingers through his hair and gave herself up to his kiss. She'd never met a man who could so utterly seduce with only a kiss, but she'd never kissed anyone else who'd had a thousand years of practice either. His fangs were out again and the feel of them sent a thrill down her spine, their strangeness exciting rather than frightening when she remembered all his bite had made her feel last night. Diego chuckled and she knew he was in her mind again, and yet she didn't resent the invasion of privacy. *I wish I could do that,* she thought as she stroked her tongue along his and felt him shiver. *What are you thinking?*

Suddenly a warm glow spread through her, a wave of sensations not her own. Sian's eyes flew open at the unexpected flood of emotion. She'd never felt anything like it. The intensity of them was staggering and she broke away with a gasp. "Is that—"

"What I feel for you," he murmured. His lips brushed hers and she felt the thrill that rushed through him at the soft touch. A wave of electric need seared her and she moaned. He chuckled. "To say you turn me on is an understatement, *querida.*"

"I can see that," she breathed. She tightened her fingers in his hair and pulled him back for a much more satisfying kiss. Hot desire swamped her and she wasn't sure whose it was, but it didn't matter. All that mattered was having more.

Diego growled deep in his throat and spun around until she was the one trapped against the pool table, the cool wood pressing against her hips and Diego's heat blanketing her from the front. Sian rubbed against him like a cat, loving the way his hard muscles felt against her and feeling the surge of desire that shot through him at the full-body caress.

Do that again and I swear I'll have you on this table, wildcat. You're far too tempting and I have no desire to control myself.

His deep voice murmuring in her mind made her gasp. Diego's mouth slid down the side of her throat, licking and nibbling until he reached the pair of bite-marks he'd left earlier. His tongue teased a circle around them and the memory of the pleasure his bite had brought her blended with his own possessive memory of biting her. It was the most erotic thing she'd ever felt, this merging of their thoughts. "This is incredible," she whispered. "Do you do this with all your girlfriends?"

She knew the question bothered him even before he growled again and nipped her skin hard enough to sting. *You're the first woman in my life for a century,* he thought back as he soothed the sting away with soft flicks of his tongue. *And I don't want to think about anyone but you. Do you honestly think I would let anyone else into my mind this way?*

A thrill shot through her at the confession and her heart ached at the thought of losing him. Sian forced her thoughts away from that, doing the one thing she knew would distract him from searching her mind for her plans. She kissed him with all the desire in her heart as she wrapped a leg around his waist and lay back on the table, pulling him with her. *Have I ever told you I've always wanted to have sex on a pool table?* she thought, trying to send the words to him as he had done to her.

Diego groaned and she sensed his intention to close the game room door an instant before she felt his power surge and heard the door slam. The use of his magic thrilled her. She was barely aware of the click of the lock as his hands found her breasts and cupped them through her shirt. *Fulfilling your fantasies is a rough job,* he murmured in her mind, *but I suppose I'll have to do it just this once.*

She laughed, her own hands going to the button of his jeans. *Just once? Don't tempt me, wildcat.*

Tempting him was exactly what Sian wanted to do. His desire and need filling her mind and his wickedly skillful kiss reducing her willpower to mush, all she could think of was having him inside her again. When he shuddered in her arms, she knew he'd picked up the thought and she stroked him through the denim, determined to make him as crazy as he was making her.

His hands left her breasts long enough to free himself from his jeans. Sian wrapped both legs around his hips as he slid inside her, blessing her lack of panties for once. Her moan mingled with his low hiss of pleasure as he sank deep. The shared sensations were enough to make her writhe with pleasure.

He thrust again and she arched against him. God, it was so good, so right with Diego, their joining an ecstasy like nothing she'd ever felt. Sian broke their fevered kiss to rain kisses all over his face and throat. If she dared to stay she'd do whatever it took to keep him, sleep all day and stay up all night to be with him, become a vampire if it was what it took to stay at his side. Surely she'd never find anything this perfect ever again.

His arms tightened and he buried his face in the curve of her shoulder, shivering with every caress of her hands over his back and hips. Her climax trembled just out of reach and he slowed, prolonging the moment, keeping her there on the edge of paradise. She dug her nails into his shoulders and whimpered with pleasure, beyond all words in her need. Diego growled and nibbled her shoulder. She felt him tremble an instant before fire swept through every vein.

Sian cried out, but the fire that consumed her wasn't painful after the first moment. It surged with every slow thrust of Diego's hips, heightening her ecstasy while still keeping her climax out of reach.

"Diego, please!" she cried, feeling her nails reopen one of the wounds on his shoulder. The sharp scent of blood intensified the burning and Sian finally realized the fire was consuming Diego, not her. "What—what is this?"

"This is the bloodlust," he grated in a voice unlike anything she'd ever heard him use. Dark and rough, his voice conjured images of black nights and mortal peril, yet she had never heard anything sexier in her life. *Take your pleasure, love. I won't climax without blood this time and I don't dare bite you again.* His thrusts quickened, driving her closer to the edge. *Let me feel you come instead. Share it with me.*

She fought the spell of his sexy voice and the mounting pleasure of each deep thrust. No way in hell did Sian intend to take her pleasure without giving Diego his own. Their mental bond gave him no way to hide his need, his painful arousal and his frustration warring with his guilt at having taken too much of her blood last night. *Come for me,* querida, he urged in his black velvet voice, and despite his temptation Sian refused to be that selfish.

Her body trembled with the effort of resisting her climax. He needed blood and wouldn't take it, but joined like this they shared everything. "Not without you," she whispered, finding the reopened scratch and tracing it with her tongue again.

The burning surged and Diego cried out, his fingers diving into her hair as if to pull her away. Sian clamped her teeth around the little cut and held on. *Not without you,* she thought fiercely even as her climax started to overtake her. *Come with me, Diego. I want you with me!*

An instant later, Diego's fangs pierced her throat. Pleasure overcame them both, a white-hot explosion that wiped every thought from her mind but the joy of the moment. Sian threw her head back and cried his name as the climax broke over her, wave after wave until she thought she might pass out from it.

The last crest had barely passed before Diego tore his mouth and his mind away, his hand flying up to his shoulder and coming away tinged with blood. The faintest red trace came away on his finger and he looked at it in horror.

"Not again," he groaned, dropping his head down on her shoulder and holding her tight. "*Dios, querida,* this is one scare I really did not want to repeat. I'm so sorry, Sian."

She smiled at his concern and threaded her fingers through his hair. She wasn't a bit sorry. Having felt the bloodlust with him, she couldn't imagine leaving him to endure it when she could do something to relieve his suffering. "It was my idea, and surely if what happened before wasn't enough to do anything this wasn't either," she pointed out.

He said something low and fierce in Spanish and she closed her eyes, savoring his voice. "I love it when you speak Spanish to me," she added, wishing she knew another language so she could whisper sweet nothings to him in it.

"That wasn't a very sexy phrase, actually," Diego replied, his forehead still on her shoulder and their bodies joined intimately. "And don't ask me to translate it because I won't."

She laughed. "Say something else, then."

He chuckled low and lifted his head to trace the shell of her ear with the tip of his tongue. "*Tú es muy hermosa,*" he murmured in her ear, his voice a deep, velvet seduction as he moved away from her enough to straighten her skirt and settle her feet back on the floor. "*No sé cómo viví sin tú. Te amo, mi gatita, y yo siempre voluntad.*"

His voice sent a thrill through her entire body and she pressed against him, loving the feel of his hands exploring her back in those long, slow strokes. He certainly knew how to touch her. "Now tell me what you said," she said breathlessly. Whatever it had been, it'd been too sexy for any woman to stand and when combined with the unbearable passion they shared, her knees felt like Jell-O.

Diego nipped her earlobe and his hand slipped beneath her shirt to rest against the small of her back. "I said you're very beautiful," he replied softly. "I said I don't know how I lived without you. I love you, my little cat, and I always will."

Those words, which should have reduced her to putty in his hands, had the effect of a bucket of ice water being thrown in her face. Sian gasped, pulling out of his arms and staring at him in shock. "You can't love me," she protested. "You've only known me for four days and you didn't even want me here!"

Diego didn't try to stop her retreat even though she felt his desire to. Sian didn't stop backing away until she felt the door at her back and she reached behind her for the handle, gripping it as though it was a lifeline.

"You don't love me," she repeated firmly, and she had no doubts which one of them she was trying to convince. "We had sex and it was great, but it isn't love, Diego!"

He smiled at her, still leaning against the pool table. The temptation to run back into his arms was strong but she resisted. "Yes, I've known you four days," he said, his voice utterly calm in the face of her panic. "And you're right, I didn't want this when it first happened." His emerald gaze held her when she would have run. "I didn't expect to love you, Sian. I didn't plan it, but it happened and I'm glad. I wasn't having sex with you last night, *querida*. This—" he gestured at the pool table, "wasn't *sex*. I was making love with you."

She closed her eyes, her heart pounding painfully in her tight chest. How could he love her? It had to be an illusion! "I have to go," she whispered, giving in to cowardice and bolting.

Diego sighed as he heard an engine start in the garage a few moments later. It had been a gamble, telling her he loved her. He'd known it was when he'd said it. And like all gambles, the chance to win was always tempered by the risk of losing.

No one needed to tell him which side of that line he'd fallen on this time.

He hadn't been able to help himself. She'd come to him like sex incarnate, wearing one of those short little skirts that tempted him viciously to let his hands disappear beneath it and thinking of some mind-blowingly sexy little scrap of a teddy she wanted to wear for him. All traces of rational thought had fled. Her unselfish passion rocked him to the core. When she'd begged him to speak to her in his native tongue the words had just tumbled out.

She didn't believe he meant it. He couldn't blame her. He hardly believed it himself. Sian was opinionated, stubborn, suspicious, and occasionally frustrating as hell, but she was also sexy, passionate, intelligent, and just about everything he was stunned to find out he wanted in a woman.

He'd always thought reaching the age of one thousand without ever feeling the sting of Cupid's arrow had meant he was immune to it. He shook his head, turning to resume his pool game in hope of making the time pass more quickly until their blood tie notified him that Sian was nearing home again. Some immunity. Four days with Sian and he was ready to start composing sonnets if that was what she wanted.

He actually found himself glad he'd been hit by her car that night, and if that wasn't proof he was in love, nothing was.

☪ ☪ ☪

Sian was almost to the gate before she even noticed what kind of car she'd taken. It was sleek and it was fast, which was all she'd cared about when she'd taken it.

Only when the gates opened in front of her did she finally let herself think about what she was doing. The Aston Martin purred as she sat there and hesitated, her heart warring with her reason. If she drove though those gates, it would be real. She couldn't take it back. She suddenly remembered her mother's twisted, broken wedding rings still sitting on the counter of Diego's bathroom and couldn't make herself care that she'd left them. She was leaving something far more important than any inanimate object, no matter how sentimentally valuable. Her hands shook on the wheel as Diego's face filled her mind and she closed her eyes, searching for the surety she was doing the right thing.

Her instincts told her to turn around and drive straight back, to tell Diego that Santonyo had found her and trust him to take care of her. They more than wanted it, they demanded it with a ferocity she'd never before experienced.

She didn't dare. "I love you, my little cat, and I always will." Diego's words echoed in her memory and she wiped her eyes furiously when the high iron gate blurred in front of her. If only he hadn't said those words to her.

"I love you, kitten, and I'll keep you safe."

Her father's voice this time, almost the last words he'd ever spoken to her. Sian choked back a sob and stomped down on the accelerator, tearing past the gate and all it symbolized and not caring if her recklessness earned her a ticket or a wreck.

She couldn't outrun the memory, though, not this time. Her father's voice echoed relentlessly in her ears, forcing her to replay the horrible scene. "Don't go into protection, Sian. I've been a cop for more years than you've been alive and I know how it works. They'll take you away from everything and everyone you've ever known, take your name, maybe even your face if you'll let them. They'll stick you in some backwater corner of nowhere and forget you."

Sian stared across the remains of her birthday cake, stunned at her father's vehement objections to her leaving. Frank Lazuro had never been demonstrative with his affections and had made no bones about the fact he would have given anything had she been born a boy. The Lazuros were dying out. Frank had been an only child of an only child, and Sian had always known she was the last of her line.

The loss of the Lazuro name had bothered Frank far more than it had ever bothered her. Besides, Sian had no intention of settling down and being someone's little housewife. It wasn't in her personality and those foundations certainly hadn't been laid in her childhood.

Frank had wanted a boy, and since all he had was Sian, he'd treated her like the son he'd hoped for. When other little girls were taking ballet, she was playing baseball. In high school, Sian wasn't a cheerleader on the sidelines, she was a kicker on the football team. In college, she'd joined the ROTC and majored in criminal justice, and after four years as a military policewoman she'd transitioned smoothly into the Savannah Police Department, following firmly in her father's footsteps.

She knew it was the loss of the Lazuro name that truly bothered her father, not the loss of a child who had always been a disappointment to him no matter how hard she'd tried. "I can't stay here and be a sitting duck just so I can turn out a litter of Lazuro heirs someday," she'd replied, demolishing her piece of cake with her fork and compulsively recounting the candles in a little pile beside it instead of meeting his eyes.

"Is that what you think this is about?"

The hurt surprise in his voice had drawn her gaze to his face and Sian was stunned to see tears in her father's eyes for the first time in her life. "Kitten, I don't care what your name is. You're all I have left. It's you I don't want to lose, not some damn name."

He reached across the table and took her hand, squeezing it tight. "Stay with me. I'll buy a house somewhere and we'll disappear. You don't need the Witness Protection Program, Sian. If you need a new name, we'll change our names. I love you, kitten, and I'll keep you safe."

Sian would never forget a single word her father had spoken to her that night. For twenty-eight years, she'd waited to hear him say he loved her, to show her he accepted her as she was, to say she'd won his approval even though she was a girl, and finally he'd done it. She'd risen from her chair, wanting to throw her arms around him. "Oh, Dad, I love you t—"

The movement had put her in line with the window. It had been such a beautiful night they'd left it open, and the closed curtains fluttered in the breeze. They were fluttering when Sian stood and took a step toward her father and the sniper Santonyo had sent took advantage of the opportunity.

The cake exploded as the bullet whizzed past Sian's shoulder and smashed into it. Frank vaulted over the table and tackled her to the floor just in time to catch the second one in the throat.

"Daddy!" Sian screamed, forgetting all the first aid she'd ever known and trying to clamp her hands over the pumping wound.

He shoved her away and pushed her toward the door with surprising strength for someone with a mortal wound. "Get out!" he croaked, drawing his service pistol and somehow struggling to his knees. "Car—go!"

And she'd gone, dialing 911 as she tore out of the drive to the sound of her father laying down cover fire through the kitchen window.

Sian wiped the tears from her face and tried to concentrate on the road—this road that led to San Francisco, not the one she'd driven, sobbing, to the Savannah Police Department three years ago. She'd run away that horrible night and she'd been running ever since.

And she was running now, running with Diego's declaration of love in her ears and the nightmare image of him bleeding from a mortal wound branded in her mind.

As she headed toward the city, she saw the first pink tendrils of dawn caress the eastern sky, but her heart ached too much to enjoy its beauty. *Never again,* she swore as she raced away from Diego and the safety she'd felt with him. *Never again will someone I love die to save me.* The admission didn't even make her pause. Yes, she loved Diego, loved him enough to leave him and save him, and despite all the reasons she knew it was right it still felt heart-wrenchingly wrong.

"Diego, I'm sorry," she whispered, not even bothering to wipe away the tears trickling down her cheeks.

☾ ☾ ☾

Two men watched the Aston Martin as it hesitated before the huge iron gates in the minutes before dawn. "Come on, girl," the driver muttered, his knuckles white as he gripped the steering wheel. "Come on, drive! Break the demon's hold, you can do it. Drive away!"

His passenger grimaced when the little car didn't move. "He's too strong," he said, reaching into his jacket and sliding his hand along the grip of his gun. "He'll never let her go. She's probably even one of them by now."

"No, it's too close to dawn," the driver said. "She wouldn't leave now if she was one of them."

"She's bewitched, I say!" the second man snapped. He pulled out the pistol. "We should finish her now before she breeds more of those monst—"

At that moment, the sports car surged forward, its tires kicking up a spray of gravel before catching on the pavement with a loud squeal. The driver let out a relieved sigh and crossed himself. "Our Lord be praised," he murmured, closing his eyes in prayer. "Another soul is saved from the fires of hell."

The passenger also crossed himself, but his face reflected anything but reverence. "Time to take the demon down." He pulled out his cell phone and dialed. "Bait the trap," he growled into it.

Chapter Thirteen

Diego paced anxiously, ignoring James's concerned stare. Dawn was almost here. Where the hell was Sian?

He tried her cell phone again, and again there was no answer. He threw the phone down with a snarl, running both hands through his hair. She knew to be back before dawn. Damn it, she knew there were vampire hunters out there! All right, perhaps he hadn't told her specifically to be extra careful, but she wasn't stupid. She *couldn't* be foolish enough to stay out alone when she knew he couldn't come to her aid should the Templars find her.

Not to mention the Outcasts. He groaned and clenched his fists. Those wicked beasts were able to walk in the daylight, unlike the vampires like him who did not harm their prey. Outcasts killed, devouring a human's life force and using it to endure the searing daylight. Sian didn't know that. He hadn't told her, hadn't properly educated his very mortal mate, had let her go out alone without the most basic education on the dangers of the vampire world. He'd let her run out of here in ignorance and now she was missing! Adrenaline surged through him at the thought of what those monsters would do to the mate of a Slayer—what they'd tried to do to her before—and his jaws ached with the effort of keeping his fangs hidden.

"Where the hell is she?" he growled, spinning on his heel and pacing some more.

James perched on the arm of the couch and watched his restlessness nervously. "I'm sure she's fine, Diego," he repeated for the umpteenth time. "You'd know if she wasn't, wouldn't you?"

"Of course I'd know," he snarled at James and instantly regretted it. He didn't snap at his Stewards. They were his family, his friends. James was not here to absorb his temper. Diego took a deep breath and attempted to rein in his worry-driven anger. "I'm sorry, James," he said, making an effort to speak normally.

He shrugged and gave Diego a ghost of a smile. "Hey, no problem. All those fighting lessons had to be good for—"

Diego, I'm sorry.

Diego's breath slammed out of his lungs and his palms flew to his temples, sending every ounce of concentration he possessed shooting along the brief mental conduit to his mate. *Sian, what's wrong? Where are you?* he demanded, but she was gone.

His heart froze as the truth struck him.

Sian was gone.

She had never planned to go shopping and she had never planned to be back before dawn. She was leaving for good.

Diego roared in anguish and bolted for the door, every sane and rational thought evaporating and every cell of his body screaming two primal instincts. His mate couldn't leave him. He had to stop her!

James blocked him before he could rip the door open. Diego shoved at him, reaching for the door, but he wouldn't be moved no matter how Diego clawed or fought. James pushed back with surprising strength and kept him from the door. Enraged, Diego snarled and redoubled his efforts.

"Diego, stop it! You'll kill yourself if you run out there now. Damn it, the sun's coming up! Do you want to get roasted alive? You're no good to her dead!"

Some vague part of Diego's brain recognized James's voice and understood the truth of his words. Something rational sparked to life again and Diego forced himself to stop fighting. The red haze of panic faded enough for him to scent blood in the air for the first time. Its sharp, coppery scent only fueled his animal side, all his instincts awake and demanding the hunt. He stumbled back and rubbed his hands over his face, trying to push away the fury burning inside him.

"Are you done or do I brace for round two?"

Diego opened his eyes at James's words and stared in horror at what he'd done. James didn't move from his station in front of the door despite the scratches marking his face and arms. Shame washed over him, killing the remainder of the irrational madness that had overcome him. Never in his life, *never* had he struck a Steward. He could have killed him.

"*Dios,* James, forgive me," Diego said, reaching out with his powers to heal his friend. The scratches were deep but the bleeding stopped at once. "You saved my life."

"Yeah, and I hope you plan on giving me combat pay for that." Despite his sarcastic reply, James's eyes were deeply concerned. He crossed his arms over his chest, still breathing hard from his struggle with the enraged vampire. "Tell me what you saw, felt, whatever the hell just happened. Tell me where she is and who's got her. I'll get her back for you."

Diego sat heavily on the floor as the daytime weakness started to overcome him. James's assumption that only an attacker could keep Sian from returning was agony. Without the numbness of rage, the pain was so great he felt like the slightest movement would shatter him, but he forced himself to answer James.

"No one has her," he said hoarsely, dropping his head to his palms to hide the moisture in his eyes. "She left, James. All on her own."

James swore viciously. A moment later, he reached down and tugged Diego to his feet. "You need to be in bed," he said shortly, pulling him toward the stairs. "I'll go look for her while you rest, but only if you swear to me you won't try another stupid stunt like running out of here again. I don't want to come back and find a bucket of extra-crispy vampire on the lawn."

Diego nodded and straightened, letting James help him up the stairs. "She was heading north," he said, weariness already slurring his words. *Dios,* how he hated the day-sickness. For all his great power and strength, he paid this price. Never had it seemed too high until now.

"North, got it. I'm all over it. Don't worry."

James pushed open his bedroom door and dumped Diego on the bed. When he started to turn away Diego grabbed his wrist. "Be careful," he said, fighting off sleep by sheer stubbornness. He'd failed to warn Sian. It was a mistake he wouldn't make twice. "We're being hunted."

"Gotcha." James nodded at the bedside phone. "Call me at sunset. Sweet dreams, and *don't worry*. I'll find her."

Diego grimaced as the door closed. Sweet dreams. His were likely to be nightmares. *Sian, come back to me,* he called, searching for her mind even as sleep claimed him. *Come home, wildcat.*

☾ ☾ ☾

North. It wasn't much to go on.

James pointed the Corvette in that direction and put down the accelerator. At least Sian had taken a distinctive car. Even in California, there weren't many sky-blue Aston Martins.

Still, he wished he had Diego's sixth sense for this. Without it, he was reduced to simply driving north and hoping he saw Sian's car. James made a face. There were a lot of highways pointing north, and he didn't even know if she was on the highway. Besides, she'd been going north at dawn. He had no way of knowing if she'd turned off since then.

Finally he sighed and pulled out his cell phone. Diego would hate it and Sian would probably try to deck him again for it, but James didn't see where he had a choice. He needed more eyes searching if he was going to have any chance of success.

A voice answered and James forced himself to speak calmly. "I'm calling to report a stolen vehicle." The police weren't infallible, but the more people he had searching the roads, the better the chances he'd have good news to give Diego at sunset. He described the car and gave the license plate as he drove, scanning the road and wondering how much of a head start Sian had on him. The Aston Martin could move at roughly the speed of sound, but his 'Vette was no slouch either and it wasn't completely beyond the realm of possibility that he'd catch up.

The dispatcher was asking if he'd seen the thief and James chose his words with care. Diego would probably understand his involving the police if it helped to find Sian, but if James got his mate in trouble with the law he was sure Diego wouldn't be nearly so understanding.

Fighting Diego once was more than enough for him.

"I didn't see who took it," James said. "And to tell you the truth, I'm a lot more worried about the woman who I lent it to than about the car itself. My friend borrowed it and I'm afraid she might have been kidnapped."

"Kidnapped?" the dispatcher echoed. "Are you certain your friend wouldn't have simply decided to keep the car a little longer than you agreed on? I'm not saying she stole it, but misunderstandings happen—"

"No, she called," James lied. Well, maybe it wasn't really a lie—Diego had certainly gotten some kind of message from her. "She said she was a few minutes away from my house around 3am, and she never got there." He hoped the time he'd made up wasn't too far off.

"Sir, we can't file a missing persons report until the person has been gone for more than twenty-four hours," the dispatcher said.

"Which is why I'm reporting a stolen car," James replied, keeping himself from snapping by sheer effort of will. "Look, that Aston Martin cost more than a house. Does it have to be missing for more than twenty-four hours, too? It'll be stripped bare in a chop shop in Tijuana by then!"

"All right, sir," the dispatcher said soothingly. "I'll put out an APB on your car. What number may we reach you at if we find anything?"

James gave his cell number and added Diego's at the last minute, telling her it wouldn't be answered until late evening. He hung up feeling no better than he had before he'd called. The dispatcher hadn't sounded overly concerned about his car, probably thinking his "friend" had stolen it despite his protests. Besides, this was California. They had murders, assaults, domestic violence, drug deals and gangs—all of which were of much greater importance than a missing rich-boy's toy.

The Corvette's police scanner squawked a minute later and James breathed a silent sigh of relief when he heard the description of the Aston Martin come over it. Whatever the dispatcher had thought of his story, she'd acted on it rapidly. Now all he could do was hope someone, somewhere, would see Sian before the sun went down. He didn't doubt Diego would be able to find her once it did, but he also was fairly certain Diego wouldn't be happy when he tracked her down. It would undoubtedly be better to tell Diego that Sian was safe and give him time to cool down before he actually saw her again.

It would be a long time before James forgot the look on Diego's face when he'd realized Sian had left him.

It was almost noon when James came upon the wreck. A sky-blue car had careened off the road and smashed against a concrete pillar, twisting it beyond recognition. He couldn't tell if it was an Aston Martin or not and the plates weren't visible, but the color was right. His heart froze with dread as he skidded to a stop on the shoulder and prayed.

No one could have survived that.

James jumped out of the 'Vette and ran over, his throat almost too tight to breathe through. It was hard to tell where the driver's door would have been in the wreckage but he guessed and ran over, dreading what he would see but knowing he had to look.

The seat was empty.

He registered the vacant seat as a footstep crunched on the gravel behind him. James whirled around, every nerve stretched taut with sudden foreboding. There was something going on here, something that had nothing to do with a car wreck.

Three men stood behind him, all three at least as tall and muscular as James. He saw a fourth go to his 'Vette and pull open the driver's door.

"Hey, asshole, get away from my car!" James shouted. The man paid no attention as he got in and slammed the door behind him. Ignoring James's outrage, he took off down the highway without a backward glance.

One of the other three smiled. "Brother Geoff has always wanted a Corvette," he said with a nod at the mangled wreck. "He thanks you for replacing his lost vehicle."

James clenched his fists. "Brother Geoff can kiss my ass. You think I'm just going to stand here and let him take my car?"

The man shrugged again and uncrossed his arms. As he did the collar of his shirt moved and James saw a red tattoo right at the base of his throat.

A cross.

James suddenly knew exactly who he was dealing with here. After Diego's words about the Templars he'd done his homework, and that red cross was the same as the ones that had graced the shields of the Knights

Templar during the Crusades. A glance confirmed the other two sported the same tattoo on their throats.

None of this had been an accident.

Still, he knew better than to let on that he'd figured them out. "Isn't this a lot of trouble to go to, just to steal a 'Vette?" he asked, waving a hand at the shattered debris. "You guys must suck at math because smashing one car to gain another one doesn't make much sense."

The leader smiled. "You assume the car is what we were after, James."

He raised an eyebrow, pretending to be surprised they knew his name. Where was the traffic? This was a highway, for cripe's sake—where was everyone? "If you wanted to talk to me, whoever you are, there are easier ways to find me than grand theft auto."

The leader laughed at James's heavy sarcasm. "Forget the car. We know it's not yours anyway, and taking from a demon isn't stealing."

Okay, this was getting old. James rolled his shoulders, readying himself for action. "Yeah, that's convenient reasoning. Works for me. Now, if you gents don't mind, I have places to go and things to do." He reached into his pocket for his cell, hitting the speed dial for Diego's and pushing "send" before he even drew it out of his pocket. He was smart enough to know what they planned and he couldn't let Diego fall into a trap if there was anything he could do to prevent it.

James wouldn't be the first Steward to die for his vampire, and he didn't regret it for an instant. He knew what Diego did for mortals. He was far too important a protector to lose.

As he'd anticipated, they jumped for him before he got the phone out of his pocket, but he'd learned to fight from a thousand–year-old warrior and if they thought he was going down easy they were in for a surprise. James caught the first man in mid-punch, grabbing his wrist as he swung and twisting it up behind his back until something inside snapped. The second man's punch ended up hitting his partner in the jaw and he slumped to the ground, unconscious.

James let him drop and grinned even as he ducked the third man's tackle, hoping Diego's voice mail had picked up. "And you call yourselves vampire hunters. You guys should be in ballet," he laughed, his voice a little over-loud to be sure his words were recognizable. "But I'd recommend working on your choreography first."

He heard a car in the distance and pushed down the surge of relief. Even if the driver didn't stop—and he hoped they wouldn't—surely they'd call the cops at the sight of a wrecked car and a brawl on the side of the road.

He didn't have time to look at the car, much less signal the driver. The leader was coming back at him and James feinted to the side, avoiding a punch that might well have taken his head off had it connected, while simultaneously hooking his foot behind the leader's knee and knocking him off his feet. Before James could deliver a kick to the head, which would've knocked him out, the second one attacked, wrapping him in a bear-hug from behind and squeezing tight enough to make James's breath hiss out. He had to do something before the Templar snapped his ribs.

James snapped his head sharply back, ignoring the burst of pain that shot through his skull when he smashed the man's nose. The grip around him loosened enough for James to take a breath and he kicked back, taking out his attacker's knee.

They fell hard and James managed to scramble to his feet, breathing hard but still ready to take out the leader. He heard the squeal of tires and groaned silently. He didn't want anyone else mixed up in this. He had his hands full enough without having to worry about an innocent bystander.

"Stay in your car!" he shouted without taking his eyes off his last adversary as he got to his feet.

The leader laughed at James's warning and stepped back. James barely had time to wonder why when a "pop" sounded behind him an instant before a sharp sting pierced the side of his neck.

He whirled, his hand flying up to yank the dart out of his skin as he finally saw the car that had stopped. His own Corvette.

Brother Geoff was leaning out the window with a tranquilizer gun still in his hand.

"Cheaters," James said thickly, and everything went black.

☪ ☪ ☪

Diego woke as the sun left the sky, the shrill ring of the phone harsh in his ear. He grabbed it. "James?"

The laugh that answered him was definitely not his Steward. "Lose something, demon?"

Diego literally saw red. At that moment, he didn't care how the hell the Templars had gotten his cell number. "Where is she, you bastard?" he demanded.

There was the briefest pause. "Well, well, well, how very interesting that you should ask where *she* is, instead of enquiring after your slave. And to think we actually let the woman go. Perhaps we grabbed the wrong prize."

Diego closed his eyes in horror. They didn't have Sian. They had James, and he'd just given them far too much information. In his fear for Sian, he'd inadvertently put her in far more danger and made his Steward much more disposable. He could have cheerfully bitten out his tongue. "Talk," he snarled into the phone.

"Testy, aren't we? Wake up on the wrong side of the coffin, demon?"

He wasn't in the mood for this. "Do you want something or are you merely calling to annoy me?"

"You know what we want," the Templar replied softly. "A stake through your heart, your head cut off, your body burned and the ashes thrown into swift water. We learned how to kill your evil long ago, demon."

He couldn't believe the lengths these people went to to kill his kind. In reality, it didn't take anything that drastic—destruction of the brain or heart would suffice—but he'd rather go through the whole process alive than give them that little tidbit of information.

"Well, gee, can you hold while I go do that?" Diego replied sarcastically. "Any particular wood you recommend for the stake? Oh, and you might want to send someone over with a dustpan for the ashes. I might have a bit of a problem dumping my charred ass in the closest river when I'm done."

When the Templar spoke again he sounded considerably less smug. "I'll make sure to tell your thrall you were making jokes as we cut off his fingers."

"If you harm him, I'll tear you to pieces and keep you alive to enjoy it," Diego snarled.

"The Lord God protects his servants, demon. You cannot touch us."

"Are you certain? Why don't you tell me where to find you and let's put it to the test."

The Templar laughed. "All right, demon. Come to us, it'll save us time." He gave an address and hung up.

Diego was on the balcony and already calling the form of a hawk when he paused. He couldn't run out like this. James needed him, yes, and he had no intention of leaving his friend in those fanatics' hands, but he had to think of Sian too.

The Templars would be looking for her now that he'd inadvertently let them know she was his mate. He tried to reach her, to send her a warning, but she was blocking him now as she'd been doing last night. He didn't dare use their blood-bond to scan for her location. He knew he'd go to her instead of James—instinct would demand no less—but James was in the most danger right now.

Instead he pulled out his phone and dialed. As angry as he was at Eli for getting him into this mess, he couldn't afford to hold a grudge. "I need your help," Diego said as soon as Eli picked up the phone.

"Yes, you do," Eli replied, and Diego ground his teeth to hold back his own scathing reply. "I've already called Ronin. You won't see him, but when you go after James, you'll have backup."

Diego closed his eyes in relief at the mention of the third Slayer in the city and didn't ask how Eli knew where to send Ronin. Eli just knew things, and Ronin's help was more than welcome. The Templars had been hunting vampires for almost a thousand years and Diego hadn't been relishing the thought of taking them down alone. "And you?" he asked.

"I'll be lounging around the house, feeding my addiction to reality TV," Eli drawled. "I'm going to look for your runaway bride, of course. What did you think?"

"You'll forgive me if I don't share your sense of humor about this," Diego growled.

"If you want to live as long as I have, Diego, you're going to have to learn to take things much less seriously," Eli replied in a gentle tone Diego had never heard him use before. "Don't worry about your mate. You can't afford the distraction when you go after James. If your mind isn't totally focused when you go in there someone's going to end up dead—probably you, and definitely your Steward. Let me worry about Sian."

Diego forced his anger and worry aside with difficulty. He really hated it when Eli was right. "You're telling me you know she'll be all right."

"I'm telling you no such thing," Eli replied. "The future is malleable, Diego. No one can read it, though many make a nice living by saying they can. Now unless you'd like to chat a little more, I'd recommend you get a move on. The Templars aren't fond of mortals who help the enemy and they're notoriously impatient."

Diego hung up and called the hawk's form again. He didn't want to think about Eli's last comment, but as he flew he found it hard to think of anything else.

☪ ☪ ☪

Sian had to stop only a couple of hours after dawn. She didn't know what Diego had done to her but there was no way she could keep on like this.

Her skin had reddened after only an hour in the sunlight, even through the car's tinted windows. An hour later, she was developing blisters. The daylight stabbed her vision, the brightness unbearable. Her eyes ached despite the dark sunglasses she'd found in the glove compartment and tears streamed down her cheeks constantly. The saltiness stung her burning skin. What in the world was wrong with her?

Even if she hadn't been roasting alive, she was utterly exhausted. After the third time she'd caught herself falling asleep at the wheel she knew she had to find a place to rest. She hadn't had much sleep since meeting Diego and her blood loss hadn't helped a bit.

Just after nine a.m., she stopped at a hotel on the outskirts of San Francisco, unable to force herself to endure the light any longer. The clerk looked at her strangely as Sian checked in, but she didn't offer any explanation for her burns and the clerk was too polite to ask.

When she accepted the key the clerk spoke hesitantly. "I can send someone to the drugstore for you, if you like," he offered. "There's one not far from here."

Sian nodded gratefully. "If someone would get me some aloe and some sunblock, I'd be eternally grateful."

She groaned at her own phrasing as she walked to her room. *Eternal* was the last thing she wanted to think about after spending the last several days with a vampire and suddenly developing such an extreme sensitivity to the sun. She was starting to think Diego and Eli had both been mistaken when they'd reassured her the tiny amount of Diego's blood she'd taken hadn't been enough to Change her.

Had she been foolish to tempt fate by doing it again in the game room?

If she had, it had been the most glorious mistake of her life. Strangely, the thought of becoming a vampire was almost comforting. At least if she was immortal, she could outlive Santonyo and come back to Diego someday, and no matter how she told herself she'd done the right thing, she ached to return to him.

She forced her thoughts from him, glad of the pain of the sunburn for the distraction it provided. While she waited for the aloe to arrive she filled the ice bucket, dunked all the hand towels and washcloths in it to cool, and pulled out the room service menu. Despite the pain of her blisters, she was starving.

And thirsty. She'd already drunk two bottles of water in the car and it hadn't touched her thirst. Maybe her body was trying to make up for the blood loss or something, she wasn't sure, but she felt like she'd been stranded in the desert for a year and all she wanted was to drink everything in sight.

Her food and the things from the drugstore arrived simultaneously. Sian tipped generously and bolted the door before devouring her meal—a rare steak, baked potato with everything, and big pitcher of orange juice to wash it all down. The red juices running from the meat didn't revolt her as they used to and she didn't want to think about that too closely, either. She paused every few bites to change out the hand towels she'd put in the ice bucket to drape over her arms and chest, cooling the painful sunburn. Only when the tray was empty did Sian breathe a sigh of relief.

The bed looked so inviting she didn't even try to resist it. Forgetting all about the aloe, she stripped off her clothes and crawled between the cool sheets.

She was asleep moments later.

Her dreams were incredibly vivid. She saw Diego pacing angrily as he waited for her to come home and guilt washed over her. She hadn't even left him a note or thanked him for helping to throw Santonyo off her trail.

She tried to go to him, to put her arms around him and comfort him, but her hands passed right through him. She spoke but he gave no indication he'd heard her. Her eyes filled with tears and she turned away. It hurt too much to look at him knowing she would never see him again.

At least in a dream, she dared admit the truth to herself. She loved him, and he would never know it. *Diego, I'm sorry,* she thought again, and from the startled, anguished look that suddenly crossed his face she knew on some level he'd heard her. He bolted for the door and she tried to stop him from running out into the sunlight, but everything went black before she reached him.

The dream changed and she suddenly found herself outside, standing on the side of a wide highway. She forgot she was dreaming and winced in anticipation of pain, seeing the bright sun in the clear sky, but nothing happened. Only then did she see four men she didn't recognize standing around a little blue car. "You're sure the demon will look for her?" one of the men asked, his hand on the roof of the car. "I will gladly sacrifice my car if we could be sure it wouldn't be in vain."

The taller man clasped his shoulder. "Your sacrifice will be returned tenfold in heaven, Brother," he said. "And the demon has already sent his human servant after her."

"We'll take him and save her," another man chimed in. "We cannot allow her to fall back into the demon's hands."

"Then do it," the first man said, stepping away from the car.

Sian watched in horror as they wedged a block of wood against the accelerator and aimed the car at the concrete support of an overpass. They released the brake and jumped back as the car leapt forward. Sian winced as it smashed against the concrete. It boggled the mind, the lengths they'd gone to to set a trap for James. She could hardly believe Diego had sent James after her!

No, wait. She had no trouble believing that at all. Of course he would've sent James for her, not knowing if she was in trouble or hurt when she hadn't come home this morning. She hadn't told him she was leaving for good. Diego would've come himself had it not been daylight—she'd seen him try to do exactly that and ached with worry, hoping he'd come to his senses before he'd rushed outside and burned alive.

But that meant James was driving into a trap.

The men surveyed the twisted wreck and nodded in satisfaction. Without another word, they moved away from the road and disappeared into the brushy area beyond the shoulder.

When James arrived and they ambushed him Sian tried to shout out a warning, but as with Diego she couldn't make herself be heard. Watching her fists pass straight through the four attackers reminded her this was a dream and she tried to wake up, but she was trapped. She was powerless, able only to watch the nightmare unfold.

James fought well, amazingly well, and she was almost positive he would win before the fourth man came back and pulled out the dart gun. Sian screamed and cursed her own helplessness when they shot James anyway. She burned with anger as she watched them bind his hands and feet tight enough to cut off circulation as a black van pulled up. James was tossed roughly into the back before the others picked up their fallen comrade and put him much more gently inside. Sian tried to get in too, wanting to see where they took James, but the sunlit highway swirled and faded despite her struggle to reach him.

Sian fought her way back to consciousness, struggling to the surface and panting with the effort when she finally opened her eyes. A glance at the wall clock told her it was late afternoon and she threw off her covers, wondering if the light was dim enough outside not to aggravate her burn. The unopened bag from the drug store was still on the dresser and Sian reached for it, intending to slather every inch of herself with aloe and sunscreen.

She froze when she caught a glimpse of herself in the mirror. Her face was raw and peeling but no longer bright red and blistered. She turned on the light, unable to believe her eyes. There was no way such a severe burn would've improved this much in only a few hours even if she hadn't forgotten to put on the aloe before falling asleep. She remembered the bullet graze Diego had gotten vanishing in hours and shuddered. It wasn't really possible for her to be becoming a vampire, was it? She'd been out in the sun for hours this morning, and while she'd gotten the mother of all sunburns she hadn't burst into flames or anything. She'd eaten regular food, something Diego claimed he didn't do, and she hadn't gotten sick.

Finally she shoved her whirling confusion away, deciding it would be best not to question her good fortune. Sian pulled her clothes back on and picked up her purse as the sense of urgency and danger built inside her again. Comfortable as this room was, she didn't dare stay here any longer. It was too close to San Francisco and therefore too close to Santonyo.

And Diego. She closed her eyes against a wave of regret. She hated Santonyo even more for forcing her to leave Diego behind without even saying goodbye.

Anger sparked through her, killing her sorrow with a rush of heat. Enrique Santonyo had taken everything from her—her badge, her home, her name, her father. How much more was she going to let him take? She reached into her purse for the keys and found herself clutching her gun instead.

She loved Diego. Was she really running away and surrendering him without a fight?

No. Everything in her rebelled at the very idea. Sian shoved the gun back into her purse and strode resolutely from the room. She checked out, ignoring the clerk's surprise to see her leaving so soon, and raced to the Aston Martin.

She'd been running long enough and now she had a new place to call home and allies to help her in her fight. Would she ever have a better chance of beating Santonyo than here and now with an immortal warrior at her side? Diego had promised to protect her, to do whatever it took to keep her safe, and she'd rejected his offer out of hand while silently promising to do the same for him. She thought she'd accomplished it by fleeing again but all her instincts, stronger now than they had ever been before, screamed the opposite. Diego needed her and she'd run away.

No more. Sian pulled out of the hotel's parking lot and shot onto the highway, pushing the Aston Martin hard. It was time to make a stand, and she would do it beside the man she loved.

She only hoped he could forgive her for leaving him in the first place.

It took Sian only about half the time to get back to San Francisco than it had to get to the hotel where she'd spent the bulk of the day. The pounding urgency gripped her and the need to hurry screamed in her brain, growing stronger with every mile she drove. When night fell, it intensified to the point that her hair stood on end.

She'd lived with this sixth sense, intuition, whatever she wanted to call it, all her life, but never had it been this strong or clear. Something was badly wrong. There was no longer any point in trying to tell herself those vivid dreams had been merely the imaginings of her guilty conscience. Every time she thought of James, the sense of pain and danger that swamped her made her feel physically ill.

Thinking of Diego was even worse. His desperation, his worry, his guilt beat at her. Sian finally had to turn on the radio loud enough to drown out her thoughts so she could concentrate on her driving.

She turned off the highway and drove as fast as humanly possible through San Francisco, aching to see the iron gate and serpentine gravel drive leading home. She didn't even pause at the word. After three long years, she finally felt like she had a home again.

And damned if she was going to give this one to Santonyo too.

She passed a police car and a feeling of foreboding swamped her. They were looking for her, she was sure of it, but she didn't know why. She couldn't imagine Diego calling the police about her disappearance—it was too soon for an official report in any case—and he'd told her she was welcome to anything he owned, cars included, and she didn't think he'd have reported a stolen car. The memory of the informant who had given her location away time and time again in the Witness Protection Program tickled her mind and she couldn't help wondering if Santonyo had dirty cops in his pocket in San Francisco too.

It would've been too easy to have someone follow James when he'd brought her Mini back to Diego's house the night she'd struck him, tracking her down, and she hated herself for not thinking of it before.

"Don't see me," she whispered as she kept an eye on the police car. "Don't see me until I do what I have to do. Don't see me." She kept repeating the mantra even as she readied herself to run for it.

She'd been hell on wheels in her poor deceased Mini. The cop didn't have a chance of catching her in the Aston Martin.

Chapter Fourteen

Diego flew toward the pier where the Templars had directed him and circled once before landing several blocks away and shimmering back into his normal form. There was no way he was going to walk into this blind, no matter how worried he was about James. He'd do no good to anyone if he rushed in and found himself at the wrong end of a stake.

Doubtless that was exactly what the Templars hoped he'd do.

Diego closed his eyes and was about to send his senses scanning over the area when his phone buzzed silently in his pocket. He snatched it out and flipped it open. "What?" he snapped.

"You're taking your time getting here, demon. Changed your mind?"

It was the same voice that had taunted him before. Diego made a silent vow that when he found the owner of that voice, he'd hear it begging for mercy.

"It occurred to me that I have no proof whatsoever James is with you," he said, stalling for time. He didn't know if Ronin had arrived yet. "Give me a reason to come to you."

The Templar laughed. "If it's proof you need, we're happy to provide it." There was a brief pause and Diego heard footsteps echoing faintly in the background. "Here's your thrall," the Templar said.

There was another pause. "James?" Diego said. "Talk to me if you're there."

There was no reply. He heard the sound of a slap and barely bit back a growl of rage. "Answer him!" he heard the Templar demand.

James didn't say anything. This time the sound was of a fist striking flesh and he heard the faint hiss of breath but nothing else. "James, say something if you're there!" Diego said again, his knuckles white on the phone as he imagined what they were doing to his friend.

There was still no answer and the silence was all the proof Diego needed that they truly had James. He'd taken an oath when he had taken over as Steward from his father and a part of that oath was to never put his vampire in danger.

"James," Diego said quietly, "I'm coming whether you talk or not, so there's no need to let them hurt you. Now say something!"

There was another long pause and finally he heard James take a deep and ragged breath. "Ten men with crossbows," he said all in a rush.

The Templar roared with outrage and Diego's anger rose to dangerous heights at the sound of him beating James. "Two on the roof!" James shouted between grunts of pain.

Diego almost shouted for the Templar to stop but caught himself in time. He wasn't far away from the address they'd given and he didn't want to give away his location. Stifling his shout was one of the most difficult things he had ever been forced to do and he swore vengeance for every blow that fell.

The phone went dead a moment later without the Templar saying another word.

Diego forced himself to dial Ronin's cell instead of charging in right that moment. The line clicked open and he heard Ronin tap once but he didn't speak. Diego kept his own voice quiet as he relayed what James had told him. Wherever Ronin was hiding, Diego didn't want to give him away.

"Roof's clear," Ronin breathed back before disconnecting.

It was exactly what he'd been hoping to hear. Diego turned and slipped down the alley, one more shade in a world of dark shadows, and made his silent way to the warehouse where his Steward was being held.

It was time to make these bastards sorry they'd ever heard of Diego Leonides.

☾ ☾ ☾

Sian didn't relax until she came within sight of Diego's gate. Relief filled her when the police car didn't follow her—she'd been positive they'd been looking for her, and even now she didn't doubt it. No, for some reason, despite the distinctive car she'd taken, they hadn't seen her. Her mantra, desperate as it had been, seemed to have worked despite all the rational reasons it shouldn't have.

Of course, *rational* had had little to do with her world lately.

She'd wondered how she was going to get through the gate since she hadn't found an opener anywhere in the car, but when she pulled up to the gate she was surprised to find it already open. She frowned for a moment before driving through. It didn't seem like something Diego would do, leaving his gate open like that when he knew full well there were vampire hunters after him.

With that thought her heart froze. Was the gate open because the hunters had found him?

Sian forgot caution and raced down the twisting drive like the hounds of hell were on her heels, not daring to slow even when she skidded on the loose gravel around a curve and almost lost control of the car. She remembered the nightmare image of Diego lying on the floor in pool of blood that had tormented her as she'd driven away and prayed it hadn't been a premonition.

Just before she came within sight of the house she made herself stop. If the Templars were inside, she'd be signing her own death warrant—or worse—to run in blindly like this. If these people knew anything about vampires, she'd bet her bottom dollar they'd recognize the mark on her arm and know she was Diego's bondmate. She killed the engine and took a deep breath, trying to quiet her racing thoughts and think like the cop she'd once been.

Finally she got out of the car and silently closed the door behind her, her gun hidden but easily accessible and her cell phone set to dial 911 at the touch of the send button. She crept through the trees, thankful that Diego had let most of his property run wild since it gave her such excellent cover. She made herself take her time and move silently even as everything in her urged her to hurry. This was too important to mess up with impatience.

Finally she parted the branches and saw the house in front of her. At first glance nothing looked amiss. The front door was closed and a few lights shone through the windows. There were no cars in the driveway or anything to indicate any intruders were there.

She wasn't fooled. Her instincts were screaming. Someone was in the house, an invading presence in her home. A stranger waited with violence on his mind.

Sian inched forward until she was pressed up against the house right under the study window. Slowly, cautiously, she leaned up, needing to glance inside and see who was in there. She only hoped she'd be able to see the intruders and formulate a plan of attack.

An arm suddenly snaked around her neck and a hand clapped over her mouth before she caught a glimpse of the room. Sian fought like the wildcat Diego called her and cursed herself for letting her guard down for even an instant.

She bit the hand over her mouth hard enough to draw blood and a surge of new strength rocked her as the salty taste filled her mouth. Some wild, animalistic side of her she'd never even known she possessed reared up and took control, and she didn't try to fight it. She snarled and clamped her fingers around the strangling arm and squeezed with all her might. There was a loud *crack* as the bone shattered under her hands. Her attacker screamed with pain. Sian took advantage at once, slamming both elbows into his chest. She planted her foot against the wall and kicked back, driving her body hard against his.

They fell together and Sian jumped to her feet, stumbling a little when her body responded to her thought with a speed she'd never before imagined. Her attacker reached out and grabbed for her ankle but she was out of his reach before his hand moved more than an inch. He started to get up but her fist shot out and caught him hard on the temple. He dropped like a stone.

Sian stared down at her attacker for a moment, stunned. He was enormous, a walking mountain of muscle lying unconscious on the ground— and somehow she'd put him there. She'd always been a fighter but there was no way she should have been able to take out a man this size, especially when he'd caught her by surprise.

She wasn't even out of breath! Where had that burst of strength come from?

Sian didn't dare question it. She didn't have time to figure it out right now. Her attacker's shout when she'd broken his arm would surely have alerted someone in the house and she couldn't afford to be caught again. The strange strength still surged through her but she didn't know when it would wear off. Adrenaline didn't last forever. She darted around the house and did the last thing she thought they would expect her to do.

She walked straight in the front door.

Once inside she didn't linger, though. She darted into the first door she came to, hiding in Diego's dark study, and pressed her back against the wall as she listened.

Whatever had happened with her strength and reflexes had apparently also affected her ears because she now heard everything. The refrigerator kicked on in the kitchen. A tree branch tapped the roof. Somewhere upstairs two men were chatting about a woman they were planning to have in ways that made her nauseous.

A man exhaled not two feet from her.

Sian whirled, her gun in her hand at the speed of thought. She had no trouble seeing in the darkness—another strange new development she didn't dare think about too closely—and the face staring back at her was sickeningly easy to recognize. It had been branded on her brain for all time.

"Decided to join us, have you?" he said, smiling.

Sian was too stunned for words. Enrique Santonyo was the very last person she'd expected to see here. She'd been so worried about Diego and James, she had completely forgotten the danger she was in. His hand moved toward his jacket and she cocked her gun, pulling her thoughts back and focusing every ounce of her attention on the murderer who had made her life a living hell for the last three years.

"Give me any reason to shoot you," she growled. "Please, I'm begging you."

He snorted derisively but Sian noticed he pulled his hand back. "You don't have the nerve," he said. "You never fired a shot the entire time you were a cop."

Sian curled her lip. "That's only because I never had a gun when I was around you," she snapped back.

Santonyo shrugged. "You've got one now and you haven't shot me yet. Put down the gun, little girl, before you shoot yourself in the foot. You don't have the guts to kill me."

Sian knew he was stalling in hopes that one of his goons would come in and take her out. She pulled her cell phone out of her pocket. "I think I'd rather see you serve your jail term than earn one for myself," she said coldly. "I hear it's going to be a nice, long one."

Santonyo snarled as she hit "send" and waited for the dispatcher to answer. Sian didn't take her eyes off him for a second, not even to blink, and her gun stayed rock-steady. She didn't have to be told he would jump her at the first opportunity and she hoped her expression told him she wouldn't hesitate to put a bullet in him if he gave her reason. Apparently it did because he didn't move.

Disappointing.

Sian sensed the man outside the door before she heard him, the strong aura of anger and recent violence reaching through the walls and engulfing her. Sian spun, dropping the phone, and fired as the door swung open.

Eli grunted as the bullet splintered the door before ripping through his shoulder. He shot her a look of such astonishment she could almost have laughed had she not been so horrified at what she'd done. She'd never stopped to think that whoever was coming through the door might be on her side!

"Oh God, Eli, I didn't mean—"

He raised an eyebrow and glanced at Santonyo. Sian jerked the gun back to him, catching him as he reached into his jacket again. Santonyo froze instantly but his eyes jumped from Sian to Eli and back again.

It didn't take a genius to know what he was thinking.

"Don't bother trying to get your gun again. I'm not going to go help him," she told Santonyo without looking at Eli. "I don't even like him. He can bleed to death for all I care."

Eli chuckled and Sian started to have serious doubts about his sanity. She'd just shot the man and he was laughing about it? "You think it's funny?"

His chuckle burst into a full-fledged laugh. "You're something else, Sian," Eli said a moment later, wiping tears of mirth from his eyes. "Here I take care of all his thugs for you and you shoot me instead of him. This is the thanks I get?"

She shrugged, not taking her eyes off Santonyo. "You shouldn't have snuck up on me," she said, too tense to really register what he was saying. Eli unnerved the hell out of her and having him standing out of sight was the opposite of comforting.

Eli stepped forward, putting himself in her line of sight as though reading her thought. "You're the first person to wound me in several thousand years. You should be impressed with yourself. I take it you called the police for your friend here?" He glanced down at her phone, which had broken when it hit the hardwood floor. "Or maybe not. Actually it works out better for me that you haven't called them."

Sian fought not to gape at him in disbelief at his blasé attitude. Santonyo took advantage of her brief inattention and his hand darted into his jacket again. Eli sighed and before she could blink, Eli punched Santonyo hard enough to send him flying back several feet. He'd moved with such speed, she hadn't even seen a blur. Santonyo slid down the wall in a heap, unconscious.

"You're much too nice," Eli told her when she gaped at him. "You should've just shot him and been done with it. Besides, we don't have time to waste waiting for the police to arrive if you want to help Diego."

All her fears for him came rushing back and Sian closed her eyes, struggling to push past them and think clearly. The force of her longing to see him, to run her hands over him and make sure he was unharmed, staggered her. "Where is he?" she asked, hardly recognizing the strangled sound of her own voice. "Is he all right?"

Eli had whipped the curtain tie down and was trussing Santonyo up like a Thanksgiving turkey. "He's fine," he said. "For now."

Her heart skipped a beat. For now? What the hell did *for now* mean? She shoved the gun into her waistband and rushed over to Eli. "Tell me where he is," she begged hoarsely, all thoughts of Santonyo and her unexpected victory over him forgotten. Her fear for Diego was a living, breathing monster inside her, a panicked beast destroying rational thought. "I'm sorry I shot you. I'll make it up to you somehow, just please tell me where he is!"

Eli finished with his knot and turned to her. Those eerie black eyes were compassionate as he gazed at her. "Breathe, Sian," he told her gently. "I have every intention of taking you to Diego. Don't worry, the things you're feeling are natural. It's the bond."

Sian didn't know about that. She'd never felt such an overwhelming desire to see someone in her life and didn't really think it was either natural or normal, and she sought for something else to say. She didn't want to discuss what was between her and Diego, whatever it was, with this man.

Whatever *he* was.

She shook her head. Eli was her ally, regardless of her fear of him. "You need to let me tend your wound before we go," she forced herself to say. She dreaded touching him and she hated the delay in getting to Diego, but she knew she owed Eli this much for taking care of the men Santonyo had brought with him. She remembered the conversation she'd overheard of the two men discussing raping a woman, and knew now they'd planned those things for her. "I didn't mean what I said to Santonyo about not liking you and not caring if you bled to death."

"No need," Eli said. He smiled and unbuttoned the first two buttons of his shirt. He pushed the material aside to expose his undamaged skin. She shivered again, reminded of how her sunburn had faded to almost nothing as she'd slept today and how Diego's wound had healed. Still, neither of them had anything on Eli. Not even a pucker marked the place where the bullet had pierced his skin.

"And there's no need to try to protect my feelings," Eli added when she didn't reply. "I appreciate your effort, but I got rid of those long ago—they're far more trouble than they're worth." She couldn't think of any reply to that. "Ready to go?" he asked, pretending not to notice her gaping at him.

Sian nodded at once. The certainty of seeing Diego soon was the only thing keeping her together right now. Eli stood and walked to the window. "I know you've never flown before so you're going to have to let me do this," he said as he pushed the window open.

"Do what?" she asked, and then the rest of his words sank in. "Did you say *flown?*"

She had her answer a moment later as Eli transformed into an enormous owl. She barely had time to gasp before a strange shimmering feeling engulfed her body. She screamed as the floor rushed up to meet her and put her hands out to try to protect herself.

Instead of her hands, she saw two tiny paws. "What the hell!" she tried to shout but only a squeak came out.

The owl swooped down and she squeaked again in terror as it snatched her up in its talons. *Relax, little mouse,* Eli's amused voice echoed in her head as the owl shot through the window and into the night sky, and Sian was forcefully reminded of her first impression of him. *Enjoy the ride. I probably won't eat you before we get to Diego.*

☪ ☪ ☪

Diego stopped in the shadows and surveyed the building he'd been directed to with a critical eye. It was little more than a crumbling shell, a beaten down warehouse on the docks, but he was certain the Templars had chosen it for a reason. He didn't dare burst in until he had a sense of the layout of the place.

He didn't see a sign of Ronin, not that he expected to. Ronin was less than half Diego's age but he was a consummate hunter. Rumor had it that he'd been trained in by a true samurai during his mortal life despite his clear European heritage, and everything Diego had ever seen of him backed up the legend. The man was incredible with swords and unstoppable hand-to-hand, and he could hide in plain sight like no one Diego had ever seen. Diego knew he wouldn't see the warrior unless Ronin wanted to be seen.

Diego slowly circled the building, noting the padlocked loading docks along the sides and the one unlocked door at the front. Every entrance but the front door was blocked, either by chains and bolts or simply welded closed. One way in, one way out. Diego narrowed his eyes, disliking the layout intensely. All advantage to his enemies, and none to him but his natural abilities.

Finally Diego sighed and stepped out of the shadows, walking in plain sight up to the door and bracing for attack. It wasn't how he wanted to do it, but he had no choice. There wasn't any other way and he couldn't transform into anything small enough to get through any of the little breaks in the wall. He was truly grateful for Ronin for clearing the roof because he had no doubt if Ronin hadn't, he'd have a crossbow bolt in his chest right now. He pushed open the door and stepped inside, ready to duck or shape-shift at the first hint of movement.

Besides, if they knew he was here, maybe they'd stop hurting James.

A splash of cold water doused him as soon as he stepped through the door. Diego blinked, taken off-guard. "Thanks for the bath, but I already had one this morning," he called into the darkness.

"That was holy water, demon, blessed by Pope Alexander IV," snarled a voice in reply. The warehouse echoed too badly for Diego to pin down its source.

He made the sign of the cross, knowing it would infuriate any who were watching him. Anger made people foolish. "Well, I certainly thank you," he replied. "Such a blessing, five hundred year old holy water from one of the most corrupt popes in history. Maybe it'll grant me long life, eh?"

He heard the click of a crossbow and rolled to the side as the bolt flew. It was relatively easy to trace its path back to the source and his thrown dagger was in flight before the bolt clattered to the floor. The wet gurgle which followed a moment later was highly satisfying.

"Well, then again maybe not," he added. "It certainly didn't help that guy."

He was already twenty feet away by the time the crossbow bolts flew through the spot where he'd been. He rolled his eyes even as he rushed silently along the wall. How the hell had these morons hunted vampires for eight hundred years without learning how fast a vampire could move when he wanted to?

They hadn't.

Diego dropped down behind a crate as floodlights pierced the darkness, illuminating every inch of the warehouse and temporarily blinding him. They knew damn well he'd be on the move, and a moving target was easy to spot. He'd almost fallen for it.

He couldn't afford to underestimate his enemy again.

The lights swiveled inward when they failed to reveal his position and Diego sucked in a silent breath at the sight of James tied to a chair in the bare center of the room. He literally saw red at the evidence of what they'd done to his friend.

James's face was battered and bloody, every inch of exposed skin purple with bruises. One eye was completely swollen shut. His ankles and hands were bound to the chair legs. The ropes around his wrists were tight enough to cut off his circulation. There was a puddle of blood under his right hand and Diego barely restrained himself from rushing straight to James to aid him. This he couldn't heal.

In the center of the blood lay a finger.

"Your power must be great, vampire," the voice taunted again. "Your thrall didn't make a sound as we punished him for his little trick on the phone, not even when we extracted the required flesh sacrifice from him to free him from your bondage. Don't you feel any remorse for using a living being so cruelly?"

The hypocrisy was almost more than Diego could bear in silence, but he didn't make a sound or move a muscle. He knew they were doing just what he'd tried to do to them only moments earlier, make him angry enough to make a foolish mistake. Instead of giving in to his fury, he concentrated on James. He just made out the rise and fall of his Steward's chest and relief flooded him. They'd beaten him severely—and oh, they would pay for it—but they hadn't killed him.

They'd tied him too well for Diego to rush out and grab him, though, and he saw they'd sunk the chair legs deep into the concrete to prevent him from dragging his friend away, chair and all. He ground his teeth and searched the shadows for targets but the bright lights were playing hell with his vision. Closing his eyes, forcing all the distractions of his anger at what they'd done to James and his worry about where Sian was to the back of his mind, Diego sent his senses winging through the cavernous building again, searching for prey.

☾ ☾ ☾

Sian had never been happier to get anywhere in her life as she was when Eli landed on the roof of a cruddy warehouse and released her from his talons. A moment later, she found herself sprawled on the metal roof in her own body again as Eli shimmered back to his own imposing form. "Don't you ever do that again," she hissed at him.

Eli just smiled. "You asked to come to Diego," he said nonchalantly. "You're here, it was fast, and you didn't specify how I was to transport you. Don't complain."

If this wasn't payback for shooting him, she'd eat a toad. She drew in a breath to really let him have it when his eyes sharpened and he held up a hand. He looked like a lion on the scent of prey and she froze, not daring to breathe lest she break his awesome concentration.

He abruptly knelt beside her and pulled her gun out of her waistband before she could react to his sudden nearness. He pulled a silencer from his pocket and screwed it onto the barrel before handing it back to her.

"I'm always prepared," he told her softly when she looked at him in shock that he happened to have the right silencer for her gun. "Be ready to use it, and for heaven's sake keep your head down in there. Diego would be really ticked if you got hurt and I don't want to have to find him yet another mate."

"Well, I'll be really ticked if he's hurt," she whispered back, deciding she wasn't going to comment on the rest of his remark. "Let's go."

Eli led her across the roof silently as a cat. Sian followed, trying to mimic his stealthy movement. She didn't think anyone would hear her unless they were listening hard, but she couldn't imitate Eli's complete silence no matter how hard she tried. He might have been floating an inch above the roof for all the noise he made.

He led her to a broken skylight and jumped straight down without hesitation. Sian looked over the edge carefully, hesitant to trust Eli that much, but he reached up, grabbed her wrist, and yanked her down. She barely bit back a yelp of surprise and fell soundlessly, but it was an effort.

It was a greater effort to keep from screaming when she found herself suspended in midair sixty feet above the ground, supported by nothing more than Eli's hand on her wrist as they floated just below the skylight. "Shh," he breathed. "They're close. You see?"

After a moment she did. Three men hid on a catwalk running the perimeter of the building ten feet below them. Not trusting herself to open her mouth without a terrified squeak coming out, Sian just nodded stiffly.

"Good girl," Eli murmured in the same barely-there voice. "We're going to get rid of them, understand?"

If she didn't he made sure she got the point by dropping slowly down until their feet touched the catwalk less than five feet from the nearest man. She raised her gun but Eli stopped her with a gesture. He walked silently up behind the man and grabbed him around his throat, lifting him with one-armed ease as he simultaneously crushed his vocal cords and kept him from pounding on the metal catwalk and attracting attention. Sian watched him strangle the Templar in silent horror, unable to move or look away until Eli laid the still body silently back on the deck. He glanced back at her and raised an eyebrow. He pointed to her gun, then his ear, and she understood.

Even silenced, a gun made noise. If she'd fired, someone definitely would've heard and come to investigate. While she didn't think anyone was going to get past Eli—something about the man was too spooky for words, yet he inspired utter confidence—she didn't want to distract Diego from his rescue of James, wherever he was.

Sian caught sight of the second man and nodded in his direction, wanting to get Eli looking somewhere else. She didn't much care for being the focus of his attention. Eli turned and crept toward the second man, taking him out just as he'd done with the first man. Sian managed to keep from staring at it this time. She'd been a cop, she'd seen dead bodies, but the only killing she'd seen before this night had been the unfortunate woman Santonyo had shot. Watching Eli so casually subdue these men with nothing more than his enormous hands sent shudders down her spine. Logically she knew this was war, a definite us-or-them situation, but her skin still crawled at how easily Eli had taken a life just moments before.

A movement caught her eye and she saw the third man on the catwalk suddenly jerk toward Eli. His crossbow was ready to fire and he swung it around silently. Sian forgot all about secrecy and silence, reacting instinctually to save the only ally she had. She raised her gun and fired all in one motion as she'd been trained to do an eternal time ago.

There was a click and a sharp *whuff* of air as the gun bucked in her hands. The Templar jerked and spun with the force of the bullet piercing his leg and the bolt he fired at Eli went wild. He shouted in pain and anger before his momentum carried him back over the railing. His scream echoed in the cavernous space as he plummeted to the floor many feet below. A second later, he went silent with a sickening *smack*.

Sian hadn't even had time to lower her gun when Eli grabbed her, taking her straight over the other rail and down to the floor in a split second. It was only the paralysis of shock that kept her from shooting him a second time out of sheer fury that he'd push her over the edge like this. An instant later, a spotlight illuminated the very spot she'd been standing and she understood why Eli had done it.

Sian barely noticed the impact of their silent landing. Her eyes were glued to the man she'd shot who now lay twisted and still on the concrete floor. Her stomach clenched. She'd done that. She hadn't meant to make him fall, only distract him from taking a shot at Eli, but there was no doubt it was her fault he was lying there dead—

"Shoot to kill, damn it," Eli hissed in her ear. "If he'd lived, he'd have gleefully peeled your flesh from your bones. He'd have used you for bait and burned Diego alive. Your soft heart is commendable, but now is not the time for it!"

Sian pushed angrily at him, ignoring the way he'd put his own body between hers and the rest of the room and had very likely just saved her life. In her mind, that made them even. She glared at him and gripped her gun tighter. "I'd think you'd be glad I don't shoot to kill," she breathed back, aching to yell at him and wishing they didn't have to be silent.

Eli shook his head at her. "I don't die from bullets," he told her. "Or crossbow bolts either, for that matter. Now hush and stay put. I have work to do and I don't want to have to move you again."

She didn't want him to do it again either. Okay, so he'd brought her to Diego, and he'd been a good sport about getting shot. It didn't mean she particularly wanted to get close to him again. He terrified the hell out of her, to put it mildly, and the further he was from her the better she'd like it.

He was already gone before she could gather her thoughts and tell him off, and she bit her lip, suddenly alone in the dark and surrounded by God only knew how many Templars. She scanned the darkness for them even as she hoped she would see Diego instead. Every flickering shadow made her heart jump and she couldn't stop shaking.

It made no sense, this trembling, and it made her angry with herself. All right, all she had to do was glance at James to know what would be her fate should the Templars catch her, but she was well hidden, she had no intention of giving away her position, and she'd been in dangerous situations before. She'd trained for this, damn it. She'd been in the military and she'd been a damn fine cop. Why was she sitting here freaking out in a situation she'd spent a decade honing her skills to handle?

She caught a glimpse of a black shadow across the huge room, saw it take down a Templar she hadn't seen before that moment, and the sudden pounding of her heart both identified the shadow and answered her question. *Diego*, her heart cried, but she remembered how he could read her mind. Instead, she locked down her thoughts to prevent herself from calling out and distracting him. She had no problem putting herself in danger, but she hated seeing Diego do the same.

She really hoped she didn't have to shoot again, because right now she was shaking so hard there was no telling what she'd hit.

Chapter Fifteen

Diego worked the perimeter of the warehouse, honing in on each bright life-force he sensed and not moving away until he'd snuffed it. Normally he would rather cut off his own arm than injure a mortal—he'd taken a vow to protect them and he'd meant every word—but this was most definitely an exceptional case.

If only the Templars would get a clue and hunt Outcasts they'd actually be doing the League a favor, but no, they didn't care to see the difference between the evil killers and normal, law-abiding vampires. If it had fangs, it should be dead, seemed to be their motto.

Well, better men than these had tried to kill Diego and failed.

Diego was closing in on his third Templar—he was keeping count, wondering if James had meant ten total or ten in the warehouse with two extras on the roof—when someone suddenly got there first. Diego rushed forward when the Templar dropped his crossbow, catching it as it fell—no need to let the thing hit the concrete floor and give them away with its clatter—and glanced up at Ronin.

Except it wasn't Ronin.

"Enjoying yourself?" Eli asked in a ghost of a voice only another vampire could hear, returning the now-still Templar to the ground and grinning.

Diego couldn't even reply for a moment. When he finally did, it was an effort to keep from shouting. "You're not supposed to be here!" he breathed furiously. Damn, but it was hard to get anger across when he had to be quiet, but Diego was certain Eli got the message from his glare even if he couldn't get it from his voice. "Did you forget you're supposed to be finding Sian before the Templars do?"

Eli shook his head as though disappointed in Diego's lack of faith. "Your mate is perfectly fine," he replied, standing completely at ease as though that bright white hair of his didn't make him a walking target, as though they weren't in the middle of a battle here. "Or at least she will be, if she stays where I put her."

Diego's mouth dropped open but he didn't dare allow himself to reply. He really did not want to know what that little comment meant. Besides, he was fairly certain anything that came out of his mouth right now would be considerably louder than they could afford and contain more profanity than his daily limit.

Eli smiled as though reading his mind. "Go get your Steward," he told him. "He needs some attention and we don't have much time left." And he was gone before Diego could trust himself enough to reply.

Sometimes there was only one thing to do with Eli's cryptic comments—forget them and finish the task at hand. Diego turned toward the brightly lit center of the room and tried to plan how he was going to accomplish this without getting James or himself killed. He didn't know how many Templars Eli had taken out and Eli's little comment of Sian being safe only if she stayed still utterly wrecked his concentration. He was no longer able to summon the concentration to find the hidden Templars, if any remained.

There was no help for it. Diego rushed into the light, slashing through James's bonds with elongated talons and tensing with the expectation of an attack at any moment. Nothing happened, though, and he lifted James over his shoulders in a fireman's carry. James groaned and Diego sent a quick spell through him to ease his pain. "Had all the fun you can stand yet?" James whispered in a cracked and hoarse voice.

"Not as much fun as you've had," Diego replied, hiding his anger behind their customary sarcastic teasing. "What have I told you about these wild parties?"

A sudden movement across the dark warehouse caught Diego's eye and he froze, the lights glinting off the barrel of a gun pointed straight at him while leaving the shooter's face in shadow. He didn't even have time to duck before the gun went off and every muscle tightened in anticipation of impact.

A breeze tickled his temple and Diego's first thought was gratitude that the shot missed him before he heard the heavy thud of a body hitting the floor behind him. He whirled, provoking another groan from James, and saw a man lying on the ground not five feet behind him with a wooden stake still clutched in his hand. It took him a moment to find the bullet wound.

Finally he saw it. The Templar had been bulls-eyed right through the red cross tattoo at the base of his throat.

Diego turned back around, intending to thank Ronin for his incredible shot since he knew Eli's disdain for guns, but Diego didn't know where the hell the other Slayer was because this definitely wasn't Ronin. Sian was running straight toward him with the gun still in her hand and her blue eyes deep and dark with emotion, and Diego's heart stopped in his chest.

He understood Eli's comment perfectly now and he could've killed him for it. He sprinted for Sian and managed to grab her while still holding onto James. He didn't stop until his momentum had carried them straight back into the shadows and out of the line of sight of any Templars who might remain.

"What the hell are you doing here?" he hissed furiously, not sure if he wanted to kiss her blind or shake her to pieces. "Damn it all, Sian, this is no place for you!"

The shimmering emotion in her eyes died in a wave of ice and she glared at him. "It looked an awful lot like I was saving your ass," she snapped back. "Or didn't you notice the guy with the stake about to turn you into a Diego-kabob?"

Her incredible feat finally penetrated his brain and he stared at her in shock for a moment. There'd been a reason he'd thought Ronin had fired that shot. The spotlight had been between her and the Templar who'd fallen just outside the edge of the bright circle of light—such contrast should have completely confounded her human vision. From that position, it should have been damn near impossible for her to find an angle that wouldn't put either himself or James in the bullet's path. Still, despite all this, she'd managed a shot that would make the most seasoned marksman drool in envy.

"Where did you learn to shoot like that?" Diego asked, staring at her as though he'd never seen her before.

"Can we resume this later, children?"

Eli's voice shook Diego from his paralysis and he turned furious eyes on the reason why his mate was in danger in the first place. "How dare you bring Sian here?"

"Well, I couldn't just leave her at your place with Santonyo no matter how well he's tied up," Eli said as he ushered them toward the door. "She's too damn softhearted for her own good and I'm not sure she'd shoot him if she needed to. Now I'd rather not be here when their reinforcements arrive, so if you could please get your butts in gear—"

Diego didn't need to be told twice. Shoving Sian in front of him, he balanced James on his shoulders and sprinted for the exit with Eli bringing up the rear. Sian glanced back at him once and he growled at her not to worry about him before he realized she was running faster than any mortal he'd ever seen.

What was going on with her?

She was faster than a mortal, but not as fast as a vampire. She'd taken that Templar out with a shot more accurate than any human could hope to manage, yet she'd clearly been in the sun today if her pink, sunburned cheeks were any indication. Confusion started to overwhelm him but he chalked it up on his list of things to figure out later—if they were allowed a later—and kept on running. Right now her strange new abilities were far too useful to question.

Eli passed them when they reached the street and Sian followed him without question. When they caught up to him two streets later, he was calmly standing by the open door of a taxi. "Your chariot," he said, gesturing at the empty back seat.

They didn't ask how he'd gotten a cab in the middle of the night in this seedy section of town. Sian got in first and cradled James's head on her lap when Diego eased him down beside her. James cracked open the one eye that wasn't swollen shut when she stroked his hair and managed a smile as he looked straight up at Sian's breasts. "Nice view," he mumbled.

Diego shook his head at him as he climbed into the front seat. Even knowing how badly injured his Steward was, even knowing Sian was only comforting him because she would comfort anyone in that much pain, even understanding that James didn't have any idea what he was saying, Diego found it hard to repress the instincts demanding he tear James away from his mate. His territorial possessiveness didn't seem to care that he was mad enough at Sian to strangle her either.

"Enjoy it while it lasts, because I guarantee it's a position you'll never be in again," he said, and he was pleased to hear the growl in his voice was at a bare minimum.

Sian rolled her eyes at him anyway as the cab began to move. "Hey, what about Eli?" she asked suddenly, turning to glance behind them.

Diego shrugged. "I'm sure he can make it home on his own."

"But the—" Sian cut her sentence off with a glance at the driver, but his blank eyes clearly said he'd remember none of this later. "He's not going to wait for them there, is he?"

"He'll be fine, Sian," Diego said, irrationally angry that she was worried about another man when he knew Eli had found her and saved her from God knew what tonight. "He always is."

"Not always," Sian muttered.

☾ ☾ ☾

Sian was stunned to see Eli lounging on the front porch when they got back to Diego's house, and she could tell Diego was as shocked as she was even though he hadn't spoken another word to her during the entire drive home. Diego stayed silent until the cab disappeared down the drive before turning to Eli. "Haven't you caused enough trouble for one night?" he asked acidly as he carried James inside.

Eli shrugged. "You have questions," he said. "I have answers. But I'd be just as happy to go on home and let you two figure it out on your own, if you prefer."

"No," Sian said quickly, not trusting what would come out of Diego's mouth if she didn't beat him to the punch. "Come in, Eli. We really want to hear what you have to say, don't we, Diego?"

He shot her a look that clearly said he didn't agree with her even a little bit but didn't argue as Eli followed Sian into the living room. She bit her lip. Clearly Diego was more than a little ticked at her for running off and hadn't forgotten it despite her saving his life in the warehouse. She couldn't blame him. If their roles had been reversed and he'd left her right after she'd told him she loved him, she wouldn't have been quick to forgive, either.

"Don't worry. He'll get over it," Eli said as she watched Diego disappear upstairs with James, his back to her as he surveyed the books on one of the bookshelves lining the walls. "Just don't do it again."

She fought the urge to throw something at him. Did he have to pick on her while she was already sick with nerves? "It's bad enough when Diego reads my mind," she said, crossing her arms over her chest with the uncomfortable feeling she'd been x-rayed, "and I would prefer if you didn't do it either."

He shrugged, moving to a different shelf and running a fingertip along the spines of the books. "James will be fine," he told her, and grinned before she could snap at him for reading her mind again. His black eyes glinted with humor. "I didn't read your mind for that one, it was a lucky guess."

She didn't know if she believed him, but she did know she was way out of her depth with this man. Relief filled her when Diego arrived and she turned to him anxiously, but the feeling quickly died when Diego refused to look at her and sat in an armchair across the room, as far from her as possible. She sank down on the couch, feeling completely rebuffed and not knowing how to bridge this gulf between them. *I'm sorry, Diego,* she thought, hoping he would hear her.

His face tightened until it looked carved from stone. *I don't want to hear those words in my head ever again, Sian,* he replied, the tone of his voice cool even in her mind. *And we'll talk about it later.*

Without even glancing in her direction Diego looked at Eli. "All right, you wanted to talk to us," he said. "So talk."

Eli grinned at his lack of manners and didn't seem to take the slightest offense, but instead of answering Diego, he leaned against the fireplace and nodded to Sian. "Tell us about your family," he invited.

She stared for a minute, wondering if Eli had lost his mind. "What does my family have to do with anything?"

"Tell us about them and we'll see."

Sian couldn't see what this would resolve but she didn't quite dare look to Diego for guidance, not now while his hurt and anger buffeted her in waves. "Well, there's none of them left now," she said, not knowing where to start. "I don't have any brothers or sisters. My dad raised me—he was a cop too. Is that the kind of stuff you want to know?"

Eli smiled. "And your father was a very good policeman, because he had the same kind of intuition you have," he said. "Isn't that right?"

She blinked in surprise. She'd never, never told anyone her family had shared the strange sixth sense she had, not even Diego. "How did you know that?"

Eli just kept that enigmatic smile and didn't bother answering. "You and your father weren't the only ones," he said. "It's stronger in some, weaker in others, through generations of your family. It's quite strong with you, isn't it, and it's been getting stronger every day."

"Yeah, and so what?" Sian snapped. She hated mind games and Eli seemed to specialize in it. "All right, pretty much everyone in my family has been a low-level psychic. You want to tell me how this relates to anything that's been going on?" She suddenly remembered Santonyo and leapt to her feet, glancing out the door at Diego's study. "And what are we going to do about—"

Eli waved a hand dismissively. "We'll get to that. Don't worry about him for now," he said. "Your family has quite a lot to do with everything that's been happening. Everything, in fact. Doesn't anyone in your family know why you all have this psychic power?"

Sian sat again, not wanting to forget about her longtime nemesis tied up in the other room but reluctantly going along with Eli. "Not that they're alive to talk about it with me," she said pointedly, "but no, I don't think anyone did. It's just one of those things—weird, unexplainable, but basically harmless. Some families have birthmarks, we get premonitions."

"It's actually quite common," Eli replied, still lounging at ease against the fireplace. "Among dhampyrs, that is."

Diego sat straight up as though he'd been zapped by a bolt of electricity but Sian frowned. "I'm not a vampire," she said. "I was out in the sun today and ate real food and everything." All right, maybe she had turned into a fairly crispy critter, and her lunch had been a steak so rare she'd almost expected it to moo when she'd cut into it, but still—

"Not *vampire*," Eli told her. "*Dhamypr*. It's an old term for a mortal descendant of a vampire."

"*Dios*," Diego breathed, finally looking at Sian again, but his gaze brought her no comfort. He wasn't looking at her like she was the woman he loved. He was looking at her like she was a particularly interesting exhibition in a freak show. "That explains—it explains everything."

"To you, maybe," Sian said impatiently, crossing her arms over her chest and glaring at him for looking at her like that before glancing back at Eli. "You're telling me I've got a vampire great-grandma or something? That's nuts!"

"It'd be a great-grandpa, if anything," Eli told her. "The Change is a violent thing, Sian. Dhampyr women are fertile since they are born into it, but vampire women can't have children, only the men—and not many of them. Diego's High-blood, and like you he's the last of his line. It only made sense to put you two together." He glanced over at Diego when Sian looked even more confused at the mention of the words "High-blood."

"You really didn't tell her any of this?"

Diego's eyes flashed as he returned the look. "It's been an intense few days, Eli, and it didn't exactly come up. How about cutting me some slack?"

"How about you two quit talking over my head and explain this dhampyr business to me, in small words, without referring to any obscure vampire High-blood stuff?" Sian suggested, not liking where Eli was going with this "last of Diego's line" business, especially when it was mentioned in conjunction with her fertility. She loved Diego, but she was no one's brood mare.

Eli laughed. Diego didn't look amused. She wondered if they were both reading her mind now and started humming "It's a Small World After All" in her head to chase them out. "High-blood is basically a fancy term for a vampire who was born instead of created," Eli told her. "You're one, too, or rather you will be once you finish what you started."

"And that would be?" Sian prompted, but in her heart she already knew. She remembered the rush of strength she'd felt when she'd bitten her attacker below the window, the way she now saw clearly in the dark and her sudden vicious hypersensitivity to the sun. "I'm not turning into a vampire," she said, the denial instinctive. "I'm not! I like the beach, I like regular food at picnics and painting outside in the sunshine—"

"You like something else more." Eli's voice cut across her protests with absolute surety, and though she saw his lips create the word *something* what she heard in his deep voice was *someone.* "This isn't something that was done to you, Sian. It's something all dhampyrs must choose, to embrace their mortal side or their vampire nature. No one forced you to pick the night."

And she had. Sian remembered the exact moment as she'd held Diego on the pool table. She'd have done anything to stay with him, including never seeing the sun again. "I really am becoming a vampire?"

"You really are," Eli said. "Which means you have a very long time in which to drive poor, love-struck Diego insane, so slow down and pace yourself."

Diego glared at the suggestion. "I can't wait to see the day you fall, Eli," he growled. "I hope the poor woman turns you upside down and inside out, and I'm going to enjoy every second of it."

Eli laughed. "Never happen. What fool would have me?" He stood, stretched, and smiled at the two of them. "And with that, I'm off. I've got a care package to leave on the steps of the police station. Have a nice night, you two."

"Wait!" Sian cried, overflowing with questions and not wanting to be left alone with Diego's wrath just yet. She was too late. Half a minute later, Eli was already out the door with Santonyo slung over his shoulder like Santa with a very strange bag of toys.

There was no more putting it off. She turned to face Diego, but he merely brushed past her and started up the stairs.

"Diego?" she said, wanting to follow him and wondering if he'd let her.

He stopped without looking back. "I have to take care of James," he said stiffly. "Be here when I get back, Sian. Don't make me chase you down again or this time I might very well handcuff you to something to keep you from leaving."

"I didn't mean to hurt you," Sian whispered to his retreating back, but he either didn't hear or pretended not to. She watched him until he disappeared at the top of the stairs and sighed miserably.

Finally, having nothing else to do to occupy her until he was done with James, Sian went into the study and turned on the computer to search for information on dhampyrs. It took her several tries to get the spelling right and even when she did there wasn't much information to be had. Most of it concerned the Spanish Inquisition, where people claiming to be dhampyrs had hunted vampires for money.

Descended of a vampire father and mortal mother, often a gypsy, dhampyrs were said to be exceedingly rare. Legend held that they were able to detect a vampire no matter how the vampire tried to hide, and could destroy them with a word. Sian rolled her eyes at that but something was niggling in her brain. She remembered how her intuition had always clamored when Diego had claimed to be a vampire, even before she'd seen his fangs and truly believed him. Some part of her had known.

The part about destroying vampires with a word, though, was ridiculous. She imagined some medieval vampire hunter battling an invisible vampire and saying some nonsense word, pretending to win the battle, collecting the village's gold and moving on. No one could destroy with a word.

"You're right. Sometimes the lack of words destroys far better."

Sian looked up and found Diego leaning in the doorway, his arms crossed over his chest, and her heart ached. She'd really hurt him. She opened her mouth but he cut her off sharply.

"If you say you're sorry one more time I won't be responsible for my actions," he growled. "I don't want apologies. I damn well want to know why I had to send James and Eli out to drag you home!"

She stood and went around the desk even though her knees felt like water. She'd never seen him look more imposing. "At the time I thought I had to do it, Diego," she told him softly. "I felt danger coming and I thought it was Santonyo closing in. I didn't want to lead him to you."

"Damn it, Sian, why didn't you just tell me?" he demanded, running a hand angrily through his hair. "I told you I would protect you from him!"

"And I was trying to do the same thing for you," she admitted. Now that she'd seen him in action it seemed a little silly, but it was the truth. She couldn't hold his angry stare any longer and looked down at her hands as they knotted themselves together in front of her. She knew Diego was about to take her to task again for not believing he would protect her and explained her fears the only way she knew how. She opened her mind and gave him the memory of her father dying to save her, ready to relive each painful word, every agonizing moment of it if it would help him understand why she'd been so terrified of him getting caught in the crossfire, too.

Diego was across the room in a second, pulling her into his arms and holding her tight. "Stop it, Sian, stop it, don't hurt yourself like this for me," he whispered fiercely in her hair. "You should have told me. You should've told me what you feared. Didn't I tell you I'm not that easy to kill?"

She put her arms around him and held on tight, but she knew things weren't right between them yet. Despite his physical closeness, he was still holding himself apart where it counted—his heart. He'd hardly ever used her name before and she missed him calling her *querida* or wildcat. He hadn't forgiven her yet.

"I know that now," she said softly, knowing she'd only relax when she heard him call her by one of his pet names for her again. "That's why I came back."

Diego froze for a long moment, his cheek still against her hair. "You came back?"

She nodded. "I came back," she repeated. "Eli didn't drag me anywhere, Diego. I was already here when he found me." He didn't speak and she rushed on, afraid to let the silence stretch out between them. "God, Diego, I was worried about you! When I came home and the gate was open, I thought—"

Suddenly his hands framed her face, tilting her chin up until she met his surprised gaze. "You called this home," Diego said, staring down at her in open shock.

Sian reached up and covered one of his hands with hers. "Home is where the heart is, or so they say," she said, hoping he'd understand what she was trying to tell him.

He closed his eyes and shuddered. Sian wanted him to kiss her, wished he would, but he didn't. Instead he whispered, "Say it, Sian. If you mean it, say it. Don't make me guess."

He was asking more than he knew. She hadn't said those words to anyone in more years than she wanted to remember, not since she'd said them to her father moments before he'd died. Saying them out loud made her commitment to Diego real in a way she couldn't explain. Her heart pounded and she felt like she was standing at the edge of an abyss, but surely something she wanted this much was worth the risk. She took a deep breath and jumped.

"I love you, Diego."

She hadn't even gotten out his entire name before his mouth covered hers and he kissed her as though he were trying to taste the words on her lips, to draw them out and memorize the shape of them. He urged her back until her hips hit the computer desk and Sian wrapped herself around him, her entire body sparking with the sudden surge of pleasure his kiss always brought her. There was so much more she'd wanted to tell him but right now she couldn't remember what it was. She could hardly remember to breathe. Sweet heaven, she'd never known a man who used his mouth so sensually, and she was more than willing to stop speaking altogether for the night and communicate with him on this much more enjoyable level.

But Diego pulled away several long, hot minutes later and refused to let her pull him back down. "You're going to have to say that to me several times a night for the next century or so to make up for scaring me to death today," he told her sternly as he cradled her against his chest. "Don't you ever leave me again, Sian. It totally wrecks my wicked, scary image to have you reduce me to a gibbering pile of nerves."

She laughed shakily against his chest and closed her eyes in relief at the warmth coming back into his voice. No *querida* yet, and he hadn't said those three scary words back to her either. She clearly still had some more explaining to do. "If I didn't love you, I never would have left you," she said.

He groaned. "I'm not even going to try to follow that logic. I think it would take considerably more than a thousand years for that to make any kind of sense, Sian."

"No, really," she said, raising her head and meeting those intense green eyes. "I didn't want Santonyo to come here because I was afraid you might get hurt—no, don't go looking all offended like that, I hadn't seen you fight before tonight," she added when he frowned at her. She'd *heard* him do it in the alley, but she hadn't seen a thing and those sounds might've been anything. "If I didn't care what happened to you, I'd have sat tight and let him come get you."

"Or you could have loved me enough to trust me," Diego countered. "You could have loved me enough to tell me what was going on and trusted me to keep you safe. Did that ever cross your mind when you were planning on running off without even telling me goodbye?"

She bit her lip, trying not to squirm. "I already apologized for that."

He gave her a look that said exactly how much he wanted to hear another apology and she decided not to say it again. He nodded once, clearly approving of her decision, before going on. "Would you like to explain the thing with Eli carrying Santonyo out of here over his shoulder now? I think I've waited very patiently but it's really starting to bother me."

"He must have had someone follow my Mini when James brought it over. I don't know how I got away without him seeing me and trying to catch me on the road, or how he got in here, but when I came back and the gates were wide open I knew something was wrong. I thought it was the Templars come for you until I got inside—"

Diego let loose a stream of Spanish that didn't sound anything like an endearment and spun away from her, running his hands through his hair again in agitation. "*Dios,* woman, you thought the *Templars* were in here and you just waltzed in anyway?" he practically shouted. "They are *vampire hunters,* Sian, and you're standing there with a vampire's bondmark on your arm. What the hell were you thinking?"

She stayed where she was on the edge of his desk. "I was thinking you might need my help," she answered honestly. "And you did need it in the warehouse. Which reminds me, you never said thank you for stopping that guy from staking you through the back."

Diego stared at her in utter disbelief and she smiled sweetly back. He was still mad enough to spit nails but his pain was fading. In that moment, she blessed her sixth sense for leveling the playing field a bit—Diego was able to read her mind, but she could read his feelings, and the knowledge helped immensely.

"You want me to *thank* you for putting yourself in danger?"

"No one had a stake at my back," she reminded him. When he looked ready to explode she sighed. "Diego, I didn't live my life wrapped in cotton wool before I met you and I won't do it now. All my life I've trained for exactly that kind of situation and even you have to admit I was pretty useful there."

"And all my life I've been trained to keep my bondmate *out* of that kind of situation, and I don't want to admit anything." Sian crossed her arms and waited. Finally he looked at her again and scowled. "All right, fine. Thank you for keeping me from becoming a Diego-kabob, as you so poetically put it. Now can we get to the part where you promise never to do anything like that ever again?"

She shook her head. "Nope," she said. "Now's the part where you tell me whatever Eli left out and we discuss my joining this League of yours where I can make myself useful."

He looked pained. "How about if we skip that part in favor of the part when you drag me upstairs and apologize properly?"

Sian laughed. "Not yet," she said, even though she would much rather fast-forward to some intense making-up. He still hadn't said what she needed to hear. "How about—"

He crossed the room with that insane speed of his and Sian found herself swept up in his arms and headed up the stairs before she could so much as blink.

"*Dios,* Sian, is that all you want from me?" he murmured as his bedroom door flew open when they reached it a moment later. "Is that really all you're waiting for?"

Sian drew a breath to reply—which was very difficult because the sudden nearness to his incredible chest had robbed her of it pretty completely—but Diego tossed her onto the bed and covered her body with his before she could get a word out. His mouth found the side of her throat, the roughness of his goatee a delicious tickle on her sensitive skin, and any breath she had left came out on a moan.

"*Te amo, querida, te amo,*" he murmured against her neck. Sian gasped, loving the sound of his voice speaking those sexy words almost as much as she loved what his talented mouth was doing to her throat. "That means I love you, in case you forgot," he added as his mouth moved up to her ear.

"I didn't forget," she whispered, threading her fingers through his hair as her heart sang.

He chuckled low and she shivered when his hand slowly slid up her thigh, reminding her vividly that she still hadn't managed to procure any panties. "Now's the part where you say it back," he prompted gently.

Sian's smile came from her very soul. She pushed him onto his back and straddled his waist, reveling in the surprised pleasure on his face. "Then pay attention," she said huskily, reaching down and tracing that wicked, delicious, totally sinful mouth of his with a fingertip. "Because I can think of quite a few ways to say it, and you're about to hear them all."

Chapter Sixteen

Sian delighted in the anticipation flaring in Diego's eyes as she let her gaze travel slowly over his body. His breathing quickened and she licked her lips. "You're way overdressed," she said, letting one fingertip trail along the collar of his shirt. "Shall I remedy that for you?"

His hands were sliding up her thighs again and she closed her eyes on a sigh when they disappeared under her skirt. *At last*, he whispered in her mind, his thought a rush of heat. *Do you know how long I've wanted to do this?* A moment later his palms cradled her bottom and his breath caught.

"You didn't manage to find any lingerie shops while you were gone, I see," he murmured in a very approving tone. "And yes, now that you mention it, these clothes are a little—" his hips shifted under hers, "—constricting."

Sian laughed and let her wandering fingertip trail down the center of his chest before twirling around one of the buttons. She was about to slip it free when she remembered how he'd reacted to her biting him in the shower and inspiration struck. "So, tell me," she said as casually as she could manage with what his hands were doing under her skirt, "would you prefer I use my hands for this, or my teeth?" She glanced through her lashes at him and ran the tip of her tongue over her teeth. "I have to be sure I give you an apology you'll accept, you know. You haven't seemed to like any of the ones I've offered before now."

Diego took a shuddering breath and his hands tightened on her hips. "*Dios*, wildcat, which do you think?"

She bent to his chest, hiding her smile as she nuzzled his throat and slowly made her way down to the top button. She didn't know if it was just being with Diego or if it was the vampire side of her nature coming out at last, but the thought of biting him was suddenly very tempting. She dared a glance up at him before she went to work on the button and a thrill shot through her at the look of bliss and anticipation on his face. Another inspiration struck and she pulled away and gave him a sensual smile. "It's a little warm in here, don't you think?"

He groaned. "You're playing with me now, aren't you?"

She wiggled a little atop him and he groaned again. "Not yet," she murmured. Diego closed his eyes and she clucked her tongue disapprovingly. "You'll want to look, I think," she told him.

He opened his eyes and a thrill shot through her at the sight of them, cat-like and passionate. How she loved knowing she brought out this wild side of him! She grasped the hem of her top and slowly pulled it up over her head, revealing a lot of skin covered by very little lace, and reveled in his sigh of appreciation. Diego's hands left her skirt and slid up her stomach to cup her breasts. She captured one before it found its goal and brought it to her lips, drawing his index finger into her mouth and sucking it lightly while she held his eyes with her own.

His breath caught and his hips shifted under hers, bringing the proof of his desire firmly against her. Sian closed her eyes on a moan and a shudder shook him. She was starting to get seriously distracted and made herself release his finger. He started to make a sound of disappointment but when she guided his hand down her throat and over to her breast it turned into a sigh of pleasure.

"*Querida,* please," he breathed, rocking his hips against hers again.

She smiled and opened her eyes. "I thought I was pleasing you," she teased, leaning forward and tracing the edge of his goatee with a fingertip. "Am I not?"

Before he could answer, she nipped his collarbone through his shirt. One arm went around her waist and he growled with pleasure. "Do that again and I'll bite you back."

She laughed softly. "That's not much of a deterrent." She moved lower, trying her best to ignore what his talented fingers were doing to her breast, and fastened her teeth around the first button. She felt him holding his breath and laughed softly. She wasn't really sure she'd be able to bite it off—after all, her teeth weren't exactly extra sharp like his—but she was pretty sure he'd appreciate the effort all the same. She pulled back slowly, glancing at him through her lashes and biting down on the thread that held the button in place, knowing by his rapt expression how much he was loving this.

When the thread parted with the lightest touch, she was so surprised she almost swallowed the button. Luckily she recovered her wits before she did something to spoil the mood and glanced around, trying to decide what to do with the button. Finally she turned her head delicately to the side and plucked it from between her lips, intending to drop it to the floor or something, but she was suddenly distracted when her fingertips met something she didn't expect.

She ran her finger over her teeth in shock, feeling their strange new sharpness. When she got to her incisors, she gasped.

Diego was watching her closely and Sian stared at him in shock, still touching the tooth that didn't feel remotely like her own. It wasn't anything like what Diego revealed when he smiled reassuringly at her, but it was definitely a fang.

"Diego?" she whispered, confused. What else had changed? What did she look like now? She was almost afraid to know.

He stroked her hair. "Your eyes have changed as well. Don't be afraid of it, *querida*," he murmured softly when she gasped again. "I've never seen anything sexier in my life. You're beautiful."

He pulled her forward and kissed her, gently at first and then with growing fire, and Sian forgot the strangeness of her new fangs and her curiosity about what her new eyes looked like and kissed him back. He groaned as she broke away.

"Don't let me keep you from what you were doing," he said, leaning back and giving her such a suggestive grin, she couldn't help but smile in return.

She traced a little pattern on the skin she'd revealed when she'd bitten off his top button. "Liked that, did you?"

His eyes darkened. "Hmm, can't remember," he said in a voice a full octave lower than his usual. "Why don't you remind me what it was like?"

Sian laughed and shook her head at him. "Subtle, aren't you?" she teased.

His thumb stroked her breast, surprising a moan from her. "Whatever works, *querida*. Whatever works."

She smiled and kissed a path down his throat to the second button. He sighed when she made short work of the button and ran her tongue over his skin.

"Feel free to bite anything else that strikes your fancy," he groaned when she nuzzled her way over to his nipple.

Sian laughed and went for the next button, a little afraid to actually bite him with her new fangs. He'd told her before how much he liked it, but that was when she'd had normal teeth. These things—she snapped off another button as easily as biting through butter—could do some real damage.

She felt him in her mind then, a warm wave of love and pleasure and amusement filling her senses. *You won't hurt me,* he reassured her. *I promise you. Didn't I tell you that to vampires, biting is foreplay?*

She remembered the first time he'd kissed her when she'd bitten his lip to get away and he'd told her that. At the time, she'd thought he was insane but after she'd experienced the earth-shattering pleasure his bite had brought her she completely understood. God, she'd love to give Diego such ecstasy, but she felt the sharp edge of her teeth against her lip and still hesitated. Could she really bring herself to sink those through his skin and—

He groaned, clearly still a ghost in her mind. "Will you stop thinking about it and do it before I burst into flames?"

Sian bit off the last button, holding his gaze the entire time and loving how he didn't try to hide how crazy she was making him. She ran her tongue in a circle around his navel and his muscles jumped. She laughed. "Ticklish?" she murmured against his skin.

"If you want me to be," he said, closing his eyes and breathing fast. Sian laughed at the raw desire in his voice and in his mind as she flicked her tongue on a delicious journey down to the waistband of his jeans. She tugged his belt loose before resting her cheek against his thigh and smiling up at him as she ran a fingertip around the button of his jeans.

"I don't think I can bite this one off," she told him, watching his eyes dilate as she played with the button. He started to say something and she reached up and pressed her finger against his lips. He caught it between his teeth and a bolt of heat pooled low in her belly.

"I'm going to need that back," she whispered, her pulse quickening as his tongue slid over her skin.

He took his sweet time releasing it. "Do you have any idea how sexy you look right now?" he murmured as she slid her hand slowly down his chest to the waistband of his jeans.

"If it's half as sexy as you look, we'll burn the house down," Sian said, loving the view from this vantage point. Diego was stretched out before her like a lush feast of pure sin and she was suddenly starving to death.

"I'm already burning," he told her hoarsely. "Are you going to put me out of my misery soon, wildcat?"

She laughed and unbuttoned his jeans. He drew in a shaky breath when she raised her head from his thigh and pressed a feather-soft kiss to the inch of sensitive skin she'd exposed. "I couldn't do the button with my teeth," she breathed against his skin, "but I think I can handle the zipper, don't you?"

He arched with a moan when she took the tab of the zipper between her teeth and slowly tugged it down. "You're killing me," he growled, both hands in her hair now.

"You say that like it's a bad thing," she said when she released the zipper. She glanced down at him and grinned up his body into those velvet green eyes. "Look, I'm not the only one not wearing underwear."

"You're a bad influence on me."

She laughed as she freed him from the denim and let her hair caress his skin. Diego moaned something in Spanish and she thought she'd never heard anything sexier in her life.

Something like that definitely deserved a reward. He cried out when she ran her tongue along his length, his fingers tightening in her hair and his body shaking. Sian smiled, reveling in this intimate power over him, before taking him fully into her mouth.

I love you, she murmured in his mind as she pleasured him with her mouth. *I love you, Diego.*

Te amo, he thought back, his thoughts in her head so hot she felt in serious danger of bursting into flame. *And I'm going to lose my mind if you keep doing that,* querida.

She chuckled around him and the deep vibration made him cry out with pleasure and need. *I like making you lose your mind,* she teased. *You're not complaining, are you?*

Dios, *no,* he groaned. *I'm not complaining, but I wish you'd hurry up and bite me. You have no idea how much I want that.*

Sian laughed out loud, pulling away from him and meeting his eyes. "You're awfully brave to say that while I was doing that. What if I'd taken you up on it right then?"

"I'd be a very happy man right now."

The next thing Sian knew she was on her back with Diego blocking her view of the room and pinning her beneath his very hard, very male, and very sexy body. "You don't understand what it feels like for a vampire, Sian. You've only felt it as a mortal. Let me show you what I want you to do to me," he murmured before bending to her breast and sinking his fangs deep.

The pleasure that flooded her mind and body was erotic, intense, wild and glorious. Sian almost climaxed from the incredible sensory onslaught. Apparently her hearing and vision weren't the only senses to be enhanced by whatever process seemed to be turning her into a vampire. Her sensitivity to pleasure had shot through the roof too. Diego drew lightly against the little wound and she arched on the bed, crying out with surprised ecstasy. Good Lord, had she thought this felt good last time he'd done it?

Diego chuckled against her skin and pulled away only a moment later to trail hot, open-mouthed kisses over her skin. "Nice, isn't it?" he murmured.

"Oh yes," she gasped, even though *nice* didn't even begin to cover such exquisite ecstasy. Every inch of her skin ached with the echoes of intense pleasure. "Very—very nice."

His fangs found the curve of her waist next and she did come that time, moaning his name as her head whipped back and forth on the pillow. He moved again, sliding down to her thigh and nuzzling at the hem of her little skirt.

"Do you have any idea," he growled as he pressed her thighs apart, "how crazy it makes me to know you're bare under these short little skirts? I may never let you wear anything else."

He didn't give her a chance to reply as he eased her skirt up and bit her on the calf. Sian moaned his name and he growled, his own pleasure at driving her wild filling her mind. "*Dios*, you taste so damn good," he whispered as he moved again, kissing his way higher still.

Her breath came short as she remembered his incredibly sensual bite on her inner thigh in the shower. She hadn't fully appreciated it then, even though it had been the most erotic thing she'd ever experienced. She ached for him to do it again now when she could enjoy it properly.

He pulled away though, kissing his way back up her body even as his clever hands made short work of her skirt and bra. She cried out with pleasure when he bit her on the throat, wrapping her arms around his shoulders and her leg around his waist as another incredible climax overcame her, wave after wave of pleasure she never wanted to stop.

But he did, rolling onto his back and taking her with him. "Your turn," he whispered, his voice a black velvet seduction she couldn't resist.

She could hardly breathe, let alone think, but the temptation wouldn't be denied. To give him the same pleasure would be truly intoxicating and she couldn't decide where to start first.

"You're still overdressed," she whispered, running a hand down his thigh and feeling denim between her and his hot skin. Diego had his buttonless shirt off in an instant and started to push the jeans off but she stopped him. "Let me finish what I started," she murmured, curling her fingers around the waistband and tugging them down.

She followed their path with kisses, part of her aching to give him the same incredible pleasure she'd just experienced, but another part still afraid. What if she did it wrong and hurt him?

"*Querida*, please," he groaned when she tossed the jeans aside and started kissing her way back up his body. "You can't hurt me, I swear it."

His longing, his obvious craving, finally made the decision for her. Sian lay over him, covering him like a blanket, and ran her tongue down the side of his throat. His pulse kicked beneath her lips, calling to her in a way she'd never felt before and couldn't resist now. "Here?" she whispered.

"Yes, there, anywhere, just do it," he moaned, his arms tightening around her waist. "Share this with me, *querida*. I promise you won't be sorry."

She couldn't refuse him anything. Pushing aside all her doubts, Sian took a deep breath and bit down over his throbbing pulse.

For a moment, everything disappeared in a white-hot flash of ecstasy, everything but Diego. She heard his cry of pleasure, felt his arms around her and his body hot beneath her, his taste perfect on her tongue and his joy and love deep in her mind. Something deep inside her cried out at the rightness of it, a firestorm binding Diego to her so tightly she knew she'd never be without him again, knew she had only to think of him to know where he was or touch his mind. It was the most incredible thing she'd ever felt in her life, so wonderful she felt no disgust at all at drawing his essence into her.

There's more, Diego whispered in her mind, even his thoughts breathless with ecstasy. *Do you want to make it better? The ultimate?*

Sian moaned against his skin at the very thought and started to pull away from his throat to ask what he meant, but his palm cupped the back of her head and kept her there. *Don't stop,* mi amor. *Trust me.*

He shifted her atop him until she was again straddling his hips with his erection pressing against her core. He didn't have to urge her to slide down over him, drawing him deep inside her. Sian quivered from head to toe, feeling him with every sense she possessed, and she thought she understood what he meant by the ultimate. Surely nothing on Earth was better than this.

That thought went flying out the window when he bit her shoulder.

Nothing could have prepared her for the incredible ecstasy which whipped through her mind and body. For that moment, there was no Diego and no Sian, only one being created of love and pleasure, giving and taking both and lost in it. She threaded her fingers in his hair and felt the caress against her own scalp, felt her skin beneath his hands as he grasped her hips and guided her in a rhythm that stoked the fire to a fever pitch. They reached the ultimate peak together, exploding in rapture.

Long minutes passed before Sian was aware of anything again, still feeling Diego so strongly she wondered how she'd ever felt whole without him before now. Finally she felt him pull away from her shoulder and she reluctantly released his throat.

"Wow," she whispered. It wasn't nearly adequate praise for what they'd shared, but it was all she could manage for now. Her brain hadn't started working again yet.

Diego chuckled and held her tight. "Wow just about covers it," he teased. His hands slid down to her hips in a slow, sweet caress. "Can we do it again?"

She laughed shakily and tried to find the strength to raise her head. "I don't think I've got the energy," she told him sadly. The mere thought of loving him like that again was enough to make her pulse race despite the utter satisfaction of her body. She smiled against his chest. "And to think, I was afraid I'd hurt you when I bit you."

She felt his grin even though she didn't see it. "Please, feel free to hurt me like that anytime the mood strikes you," he invited.

Sian snuggled closer. "Is it always like this for vampires?" she asked. Mortals were missing out. She'd certainly had no idea anything could feel so incredible. Maybe being a creature of the night wouldn't be so bad after all.

Diego shifted at her words, rolling with her until her head rested on the pillow, and cupped her cheek in his hand. "It's *never* been like this," he told her fiercely, his eyes so deep she wanted to drown in them. "That was like nothing I've ever felt in the thousand years of my life, wildcat. What we have, what we just did, you'll never find with anyone else."

Sian couldn't help but smile. How could he even think she'd consider doing that with anyone else, especially right now when she was still so replete with his lovemaking, every muscle was limp and trembling?

"Caveman," she said affectionately, twining her fingers in his hair. "Do you honestly think I would ever bite anyone but you?"

"You'd better not," he growled, scowling at her in mock ferocity. She giggled and he pulled her close and held her tight. "How do you feel?"

She pinched him for asking such an obvious question. "Like I've been loved to within an inch of my life," she murmured. "Blissful, boneless, never better."

"Mmm, I think I like that." He kissed her in reward, a long, slow kiss that was pure hot seduction. She moaned in protest when he pulled away. "But as delightful as your answer was, it's not what I meant."

She opened her eyes and finally saw the concern in his and understood. He was worried she'd have some kind of bad reaction to his blood or something, go through the Change he and Eli had said was so painful. "Didn't Eli say I'd already made my choice to be a vampire and that was all it took?" she asked. "I mean, I already had the fangs before I bit you, honey. How much more changing would I need to do to become like you?"

He smiled, the tension leaving him, and pressed his hips suggestively against hers. He was already ready to go again and she blinked at him, astonished. "I think you'll always be a bit different from me," he teased. "But tell me if you start to feel strange. I've never known a dhampyr before and I don't know what to expect any more than you do." He bent and nuzzled her ear. "But you can call me honey again if you want. I think I like it better than caveman."

She laughed and wound her arms around his neck, relatively certain he'd get called both from time to time. His heart kicked against her breast and she shook her head in wonder as she sensed his desire. "How can you want me again already?" she asked, unable to keep herself from wiggling against him for the sheer pleasure of hearing his breath catch.

He pretended to consider it. "You mean other than the fact that you're the sexiest thing I've ever seen and I love you more than life itself?" He brushed a kiss over her lips that left her wanting much, much more. "You're still a little weak from when I took too much blood from you," he pointed out. "Otherwise I'm sure you'd be jumping me again right now. You'll find vampires have incredible stamina for this sort of thing."

Sian rolled her eyes at him but his palm had found her breast and she was discovering she wasn't as tired as she'd thought. "Hmm, how do you suggest I make up for the blood loss?" she asked, glancing at him from beneath her lashes. "Too bad there's not someone around here I could bite."

He growled and nipped her lower lip, not breaking the skin but sending a thrill down her spine before he quite thoroughly kissed the sting away. "I wouldn't be a very good mate if I didn't make this sacrifice for you," he murmured between kisses. "I guess I'll just have to endure it for your sake."

Later—much, much later—Diego held Sian as she slept and basked in the sheer joy of having her in his arms. She was exhausted despite taking his blood again, but he didn't mind. She'd get stronger with time as she continued to embrace her vampire side. For now it was enough to hold her. Diego traced her beloved face, ran his fingers through her golden hair like spun sunlight, before tracing his fingertips over the random lines of the dark band on her arm that marked her as his.

It took a moment to notice something was different. Diego lifted her arm to get a closer look, careful not to wake her.

The strange runes that marked her skin, had changed. Simple, subtle changes that nonetheless altered it completely. Instead of a nonsense pattern, Diego was now able to read words written in a flowing, ancient script across her skin. They were words as familiar to him as his own name.

Honor and Love Eternal.

The same words had graced his family crest for generations before his birth.

The realization of what this meant came right on the heels of that and Diego closed his eyes, shaking his head. Eli hadn't bound them. He'd tricked them both into thinking it, but he hadn't done it.

And Diego should have known it the first time he'd looked at the "bondmarks" Eli had put there.

Bondmarks were special, unique to each couple. They were always something of deep meaning and for Diego, no symbol could mean more than seeing his family's motto on Sian's skin. Those words had followed every Leonides for centuries and, with the love of this woman, he knew they would follow his heirs instead of dying with him. No, Eli couldn't create a true bond, no matter how old and powerful he was.

He and Sian had bonded all on their own and he hadn't even known they were doing it. When she'd tasted the trace of his blood from the scratches Diego had been afraid it would Change her. He'd never expected it to start the bonding instead. How could he? As far as they'd known, the bond was already established the instant Eli had put those bogus marks on their skin.

He'd been terrified enough after their first exchange to call Eli in panic, and Eli had known. He'd known both that the bond was new and that Sian was a dhampyr, damn him, and hadn't said a single word. Tonight, Sian had used her fangs for the first time and completed the last step, the third exchange binding them together for eternity. No, Diego was foolish to have thought anyone could force such a thing on another, but he'd believed it and acted accordingly.

Still, with Sian lying soft and sated in his arms, Diego found it hard to summon up any anger about it. Had he known they weren't truly bonded that first night, there was no doubt in his mind Sian would've been long gone from his life and he wouldn't be lying here now feeling like he'd died and gone to heaven.

He felt the dawn coming and pulled Sian closer. She snuggled against him with a soft sigh and he closed his eyes, wrapping himself around her and loving how very right she felt in his arms. He'd never been happier to be tricked in his entire life.

Maybe Eli wasn't so bad after all.

Epilogue

"You did *what?*"

Sian reached out and took Diego's hand as she sat out of sight of the camera, fighting not to laugh at the shocked look on his face as he stared at Eli on the computer screen. They hadn't been awake for more than five minutes—just enough time for Diego to give her a really nice kiss to start off the night—when James had knocked on the door to tell Diego the Council wanted him for an urgent video conference.

It was maybe the only thing on Earth that could have gotten him to leave the bed, and he'd been in a rotten mood ever since they'd followed James downstairs and into the study. James was hardly limping at all now and Sian was immensely glad to see it. He claimed the most annoying part of his recovery was learning how to type again without his right little finger and while he'd laughed about it as they'd followed him downstairs, Sian hadn't needed to touch Diego's mind to feel his anger surge. The reminder of James's ordeal at the hands of the Templars had done nothing for Diego's mood. Eli's pronouncement had definitely been the last straw. Sian knew it wouldn't help matters if she laughed right now.

But she wanted to. Oh, how she wanted to, because Eli had done with one move something she'd spent the last week trying to persuade Diego to agree to.

She shifted on the edge of the desk and glanced at the monitor to see Eli in the corner of the screen, a rich tapestry behind him and the light flickering as though the room was lit by candles or a fireplace. Eli was smiling, an expression Sian knew far better than to trust, and she hoped Diego would hold onto his temper. The things racing through his mind right now were far better left unsaid.

The other people on the screen she didn't recognize but Diego had murmured their names in her mind when she'd first sneaked a glance at the screen. In the top corner by Eli's image was an imposing looking man named Talus, a dark-eyed warrior with three deep scars twisting one cheek. Below him a man and a woman sat side by side, Quaid and Maelisa Naomhan, bondmates from Ireland now living somewhere on the East Coast. The last corner was taken by a blond man in a motorcycle jacket named Gareth Ambrocio and it looked for all the world as though he were lounging in an internet café instead of a private study.

All of them looked not a day past thirty, and all of them with the exception of Quaid were older than Diego. Sian knew it wasn't the entire Council since Diego had told her there were twelve Council members in addition to their Head, but the five people held in that computer screen were still quite enough to make her feel like a child playing way out of her league.

And now Diego was one of them, if Eli was to be believed. She squeezed his hand again and touched his mind. *It's quite an honor, honey.*

He shot her a look. *It's a trick, if I know Eli,* he replied without hesitation. *Why in the world would he give me his place, Sian?*

"You filed the complaint," Eli said calmly on the screen, and if Sian didn't know better she would've sworn he was reading Diego's mind long-distance. "I've decided I've been the Council's Head for too long anyway. It's time for me to let some younger blood in, and who better than you?"

Diego glared at the screen. "How about any one of these other people who are trying to railroad me into this?" he shot back. "What about Talus? How about Quaid if you want young blood? He's younger than me and he actually wants to be on the Council. He's served on it for a hundred years. Why not offer it to him?"

Maelisa laughed and shook her head. "No one is trying to railroad you into anything, Diego," she said soothingly.

"And I don't wish to lead," Quaid added. "We simply want you to add your knowledge and experience to the Council. You've reached an age few achieve and with it comes a unique perspective."

Sian glanced at Quaid and Maelisa's hands entwined and felt Diego's thumb caress the band of her mother's now-repaired wedding rings on her left hand. She wondered if she and Diego would still be finishing each other's thoughts and snuggling like that in a few hundred years. She found it unbearably sweet.

Yes, they're very cute, but let's not lose sight of the fact they're trying to force me into something fairly big here, querida. "Is that the same kind of unique perspective which led you all to meddle endlessly in my life?"

Sian raised an eyebrow at him and drew her hand away to cross her arms over her chest. *And what, now you wish they hadn't meddled when I came along?* she asked pointedly. *Just think how much simpler everything would've been for you if you'd been allowed to heal me and send me on my way. Maybe you'd prefer they'd left you to pick your own mate and—*

Diego reached out and reclaimed her hand. *I'd have chosen you whether they'd meddled or not and the fact that I love you should prove that* simple *holds no appeal for me,* he told her with absolute assurance. She grinned, trying to figure out if that was a compliment or not. *It's merely an example of the kind of things they do with their power, Sian. They go too far on a regular basis.*

So why not get in there and put a stop to it? Sian asked, lacing her fingers through his again. *Eli's offering you the chance to be top dog. Why don't you go show them who's boss?*

Maybe because if I accept this it means you become a Slayer and put yourself in danger every night, you think? His voice dripped sarcasm even in her mind.

She made a face at him and sent him the memory of the Templar she'd shot during the battle at the warehouse. Brilliant debater that Diego was, even he hadn't found an adequate comeback for that yet.

I've been in law enforcement in some form or another for all of my adult life, hon. Think of this as simply another branch. Besides, isn't vampire hunting what a dhampyr is supposed to do? You know I'd be good at it—

Please don't start in on that again, he cut her off wearily. *I don't want you hunting Outcasts and that's final.*

You think so, do you? She had no intention of giving in until he agreed and she was positive Diego knew it. She'd never wanted to be a housewife in her mortal life and she didn't intend to become the vampire version of June

Cleaver. There wasn't anything wrong with it, it just wasn't her style. *Diego, I know you'll be good at this, and you can't keep me in bubble wrap for the rest of eternity—*

"Diego, are you still there?" Gareth asked as someone put a steaming cup in front of him. Sian couldn't help blinking in surprise. He really *was* in an internet café! She couldn't believe any vampire would conduct Council business in such an open place. Diego had even made James leave before starting the meeting. "Did he lose his connection?"

"He speaks to his bondmate, Gareth," Eli supplied before Diego even had a chance to reply. "He'd be wise to listen to her, too."

Sian gasped and Diego looked like he wanted to punch the screen. "Get out of my head, Eli," he growled.

Eli's face was pure innocence. It wasn't a look that suited him. "How could I be reading your mind, Diego? I'm nowhere near you," he said reasonably. "All I meant is that women are intelligent creatures."

Diego muttered something that was luckily unintelligible. Sian shot him a look and murmured in his mind, *It's very rude to mumble, honey,* and Diego took a breath to repeat himself more clearly.

"Your mate is with you now?" Talus asked, cutting through whatever Diego had been about to say to Eli—a good idea, in Sian's opinion. "Put her on and let's meet her, especially since Eli thinks she should join us."

Her approval of Talus's idea suddenly evaporated in a sizzle of nerves and Sian shook her head frantically at Diego. Eli had recommended to the Council that she take the League oath and help Diego with his Slayer duties since he'd have to dedicate most of his time to leading the Council. She'd known they would want to meet her at some point, but she hadn't anticipated it being right now. She was wearing nothing but one of Diego's T-shirts and while he looked perfectly comfortable facing the Council in jeans and a lot of bare skin, Sian had no desire to have these people meet her for the first time while she was less than half-dressed.

Oh, and you were all gung-ho for me to join up with them a second ago, Diego teased. *Now you don't even want to meet them?*

I want to get dressed first! she replied emphatically. He grinned and she knew that look. *Oh, no, Diego, you wouldn't dare—*

He dared. One tug and a tumble later, Sian found herself facing the camera and computer screen from Diego's lap, her cheeks burning and his arm tight around her waist to keep her from bolting.

I will get you for this, she threatened furiously as she smiled and tried her best to return the others' warm greetings. She wished she hadn't seen the amusement on their faces as she blushed hotter. *Just wait, Diego Leonides. You'll be begging for mercy by the time I'm done with you.*

Querida, *you can have me begging any time you want,* he replied as one of his hands found her knee and started to inch upward. *All you have to do is ask.*

If you don't stop that I'm really going to make you regret it, Diego.

I doubt anything could make me regret touching you. His fingers slid a bit further.

"I'm honored to accept your offer, Eli," Sian told the camera firmly. "Diego has been trying to persuade me to take the League oath for days now. I'll be proud to help you out so you can lead the Council, Diego," she added, gazing up at him with adoring eyes. "Don't hesitate because of me, hon. I know how you'd love to take the job."

Except that. "Of course," he agreed between gritted teeth, as she'd known he would. He would never embarrass her by publicly disagreeing with her though Sian was positive he would definitely have something to say about this later. *Did you* have *to do that?*

Yes, I did. Now stop letting your fingers do the walking or I'll do something else you'll like even less.

Diego's hand stilled on her thigh at once and Sian smiled. The video conference ended minutes later with Eli officially resigning from the position he'd held longer than anyone could remember. His last official Council duty was to oversee Diego being sworn in and Sian taking the League oath afterward. Sian tried to slip away when it was done, hideously aware of her mussed hair and Diego's shirt enveloping her and knowing she couldn't have advertised that she'd been bedded well and recently any more clearly had she tattooed it on her forehead, but he didn't let her go. *You got me into this,* he told her sternly. *You can sit there and enjoy every last second of it with me.*

Finally the others signed off and Sian flicked off the camera with relief before turning to Diego. His dark face was set and his mouth tight. He wasn't just mad, he was furious. Diego hated to be manipulated and she'd jumped ship to side with the Council, making him do yet another thing he hadn't wanted to. Oh, she was in trouble now.

But Sian knew how good he was going to be at this, even if he didn't, and luckily she knew how to get out of trouble.

"You look mad, honey. You're not really mad, are you? Maybe just a little mad?" she asked, biting her lip and looking up at him anxiously through her lashes. She held her absolute conviction that he would excel as the Head of the Council foremost in her mind. He was going to turn them on their ears and make them like it. He just had that way about him.

Besides, he was a prince. Who better to hold such a powerful position?

Diego groaned and rested his forehead against hers. "Dirty pool, *querida*," he complained. "You know I can't be mad at you when you give me that look and think such things about me."

She smiled and settled more comfortably in his lap before leaning up to nibble at his ear. "Why do you think I do it?"

☾ ☾ ☾

Eli turned off his camera and sat back in the chair. The silence pressed in around him and he hoped he'd done the right thing. He hadn't been lying when he'd told Diego he couldn't see the future, and right now he truly wished he could. Powerful as he was, that was an ability that had never been granted him.

Diego would be good for the Council, that much he was sure of. Eli knew he had a tendency to get carried away in trying to steer his vampires down the right path and Diego and Sian were living proof of it. Yes, their bonding had worked out fine, better than fine if Eli knew anything about how a well-loved woman looked, but it might very well have turned out horribly. Even Eli knew he'd gone too far when he'd tricked Diego into thinking the dhampyr was his bondmate.

It had been too perfect to resist, though, the way Sian had fallen into Diego's life. Diego needed a dhampyr if he was going to continue his line and grow his Clan, they weren't easy to find, and suddenly there'd been one in his bed. Eli hadn't believed much in the omens the others had sworn by until that moment—such things were too easy to interpret to mean whatever one wanted—but his disbelief hadn't stopped him from acting. He'd seen the chance to stop the extinction of two lines with one stroke and he'd done it. It hadn't been right and they were damn lucky it had ended well.

It was too easy to fall into that habit, even the way he kept thinking of them as "his" vampires. They weren't his. Well, they were, every last one of them, but it didn't mean he had the right to try to control their lives, even if he did usually know best.

Eli sighed and stood, stretching and taking pleasure in the way his back arched and his shoulders twinged after hours of sitting. Simple pleasures were the key to living this long. After a time everything got old, music and books and all the varied diversions of the flesh, but simple pleasures were always the same—comforting, easy, always there for the taking.

Diego would do a good job as the Council's Head. Eli knew he would, even if Diego didn't know it himself. Sian knew he would, too, and Eli knew she was going to be a great help to Diego despite her youth. The faith of a woman in love was a powerful thing. Yes, it was good to let go of the Council at last. Diego didn't share Eli's desire to run things to the nth degree and Diego certainly didn't have Eli's power. Too much power was not a good thing.

And he should know.

Why, then, did he suddenly feel so aimless?

Eli paced through the rooms of his home, his footsteps muffled by the thick Persian rugs he'd taken a fancy to hundreds of years ago, his gaze drifting over all the priceless treasures he'd amassed over his long, long life without seeing them. It was quiet here, no sounds of traffic or chatter of televisions and radios, though it was all only steps away—none of the modern annoyances that people these days thought of as conveniences and believed they couldn't live without. The quiet was familiar, comforting. A simple pleasure few appreciated anymore.

It wouldn't be quiet at Diego's, though. Eli would stake everything he owned on it. There wasn't much room for simple pleasures around that house. Diego had televisions and stereos, state of the art computers and fast cars and video games. He had a Steward to talk to and even his own website, for

Luna's sake. He'd fully embraced this new age as he had all the others that had come before it.

Diego had Sian now too, and if there was anything simple about women Eli hadn't found it yet. No, it wouldn't be quiet at Diego's.

"I can't wait to see the day you fall, Eli. I hope the poor woman turns you upside down and inside out, and I'm going to enjoy every second of it."

He closed his eyes at the memory of Diego's parting shot. He didn't need to see the future to know he'd spoken the truth when he'd assured Diego it wouldn't happen. Sian's terrified reaction to him only reinforced his certainty. No, he had no need to worry about his home being disrupted like that, thank the gods.

Not that they'd ever done anything to deserve his gratitude.

Eli spun to grab his jacket and jerked it on, suddenly desperate to leave the house, no longer comforted by his solitude or his thoughts, and hoping to leave both behind. Maybe when he'd rid the night of a few more Outcasts, maybe when he'd made the world a little safer for the mortals he'd wronged so long ago, he'd start to feel like his normal self again.

He only wished the thought held more appeal.

Amelia Elias

To learn more about Amelia, please visit. Send an email to AmeliaElias@gmail.com or join her Yahoo! group to join in the fun with other readers!

http://groups.yahoo.com/group/AmeliaEliasgroup

Samhain Publishing, Ltd.

It's all about the story...

Action/Adventure
Fantasy
Historical
Horror
Mainstream
Mystery/Suspense
Non-Fiction
Paranormal
Red Hots!
Romance
Science Fiction
Western
Young Adult

http://www.samhainpublishing.com